HUMAN REMAINS

The Hope Sze novels, in chronological order
Code Blues
Notorious D.O.C.
Terminally Ill
Stockholm Syndrome
Human Remains

Additional short Hope Sze works by Melissa Yi
No Air
Student Body
Blood Diamonds
Sin Eaters (forthcoming)

Additional titles by Melissa Yi
The Italian School for Assassins
The Goa Yoga School of Slayers
Reckless Homicide
Wolf Ice
High School Hit List
Dancing Through the Chaos
Mr. Chef & Ms. Librarian
The List

HUMAN REMAINS

MELISSA YI

For Bill, Lisa, and Marie-Pascale

Copyright © 2017 Melissa Yuan-Innes
First edition
Cover design by Design for Writers | www.designforwriters.com
Cover photo © 2015 Sutthaburawonk | Dreamstime.com

Printed and distributed in Canada by Olo Books
http://olobooks.com/
Distributed in the United States by Windtree Press
http://windtreepress.com/

Join Melissa's mailing list at www.melissayuaninnes.com

Library and Archives Canada Cataloguing in Publication
Yi, Melissa, author
Human remains / Melissa Yi.
(Hope Sze crime novel; 5)
Issued in print and electronic formats.
ISBN 978-1-927341-68-1 (softcover).
--ISBN 978-1-927341-69-8 (PDF)

I. Title.
PS8647.I12H852017   C813'.6   C2017-901661-X
                                                 C2017-901662-8

For typographical errors, please contact olobooks@gmail.com.

Intelligence plus character—that is the goal of true education.
Martin Luther King, Jr.

Kill one man, and you are a murderer. Kill millions of men, and
you are a conqueror. Kill them all, and you are a god.
Jean Rostand, *Thoughts of a Biologist*

CHAPTER 1

SUNDAY

Even if the terrorists don't win, they can make your life an icy hell.

My name is Hope Sze. Last month, I was one of two Montreal doctors taken hostage by a domestic terrorist/killer/idiot on an obstetrics ward, along with a woman in labour.

I survived "in body, although considerably rumpled up in spirit," as Anne of Green Gables put it. Unlike that spunky, fictional heroine, I felt paralyzed.

I couldn't even step out of my own car and into the mid-December darkness.

An ambulance siren wailed in the distance. I'd parked my Ford Focus a kilometre away from my destination, the Ottawa Health Science Centre's stem cell lab. The hospital's white on blue H lit up the inky sky.

Most houses had switched on their Christmas lights and activated their blown-up Homer Simpsons in Santa outfits, so I gazed at the deserted park to my right. I was more in the mood for empty swing sets covered in softly falling snow. Around the block, behind me, police had set up a stop to catch drunk drivers at the relatively ridiculous hour of 9:35 p.m.

I should have felt safe. I didn't, but I should have.

Fog built up on my windshield as I forced myself to inhale and exhale slowly, as per the instructions from my PTSD therapist.

Seeeeeeee the snowflakes dissolve as they hit my windshield. Feeeeeeeeel the cool air on my face. Heeeeeear my phone buzz with a new texxxxxxt.

Where are you?

Ryan Wu. One of the loves of my life.

My heart pounded in my throat. Only a few people in the world still made me feel something, and one of them was texting me right now.

I pulled off my mittens and picked up my iPhone. *Parked near the stem cell lab.*

He answered right away. *Are you on Lindsay Lane?*

No, first right around the park. RIDE program. Reducing Impaired Driving Everywhere was laudable, but I didn't need a Breathalyzer.

Wait for me. I'll walk with you.

I exhaled and shook my head. Security probably wouldn't let him inside the lab. Well, I couldn't blame him for playing bodyguard, although if I'd known he was coming, I would've worn my contact lenses instead of my glasses.

I flicked on my lights to make it easy for Ryan to find me. He's an engineer. Bankable and bangable. Once upon a time, Ryan and I had made out for hours in his parents' Honda, steaming up the windows like this. That was before we'd broken up and I'd fallen in love with another guy, Dr. John Tucker, in addition to Ryan. Because my life just wasn't complicated enough.

Breeeathe.

A car drew into a space on the opposite side of the road. Ryan's black Nissan Sentra? I couldn't tell. Too far away from the street lamp.

My breath hitched. I locked my doors.

The driver moved like Ryan, with a long and easy stride, but he was snapping a leash on a dog.

I scrunched down in my seat. Ryan doesn't have a dog. His parents, like a lot of Chinese immigrants, don't care for canines. Dogs bark, they pee, they poop, they make for expensive vet bills. My Taiwanese-born dad likes dogs, but my mom fits the stereotype better, so we've never had one, either.

Human Remains

The man shielded his eyes from my headlights, shadowing his face. Closer up, he looked even more like Ryan. Those hips. That runner's build, even hidden under a black parka.

Were there more than two guys in the world who could give me supraventricular tachycardia from ten feet away?

The man raised his hand in greeting.

I cracked my door open without turning off the headlights. The car screeched in protest. "Ryan?"

"Hope," he said. The dog pounced on Ryan's legs with its muddy front paws.

Ugh. I didn't like surprises any more. But closer up, the dog looked more like a puppy, with floppy ears and brown apostrophe-like markings around the eyes. I got out and locked my door. "Who's this monster?"

Ryan grinned. "Her name's Roxy. My friend Rachel got her as a foster dog."

Rachel. He never talked about a Rachel before. And wasn't that too cute for words—Ryan and Rachel and Roxy. They all matched.

I tried to swallow down the acid and breeeeeeathe. Ryan was here with meeeeeee.

Plus, it's harder to hiss when a puppy sneezes on you. I reached out to pet her head.

"You're supposed to let her sniff you and decide if she wants to let you touch her first," said Ryan.

I pulled off my mitten. Roxy licked the back of my hand. I laughed, and Ryan's teeth lit up the gloom as he grinned. "That's the first thing she did to me, too. I knew she'd cheer you up."

"How old is she?"

"A year next month. She's a Rottweiler shepherd mix."

"A Rottweiler?" I snatched my hand away.

Roxy woofed and wagged her long, black, elegantly-plumed tail at me.

"They were originally working and family dogs. Roxy's cool. I wouldn't have brought her otherwise."

I touched the silky fur on her ears. She nudged her head against my hand, searching for more rubs.

I laughed, and so did Ryan. He and I leaned together to pet her, our breath mingling in the cool air.

Then I raised my chin to look at him. We rapped heads, and I said "Ow!"

Ryan touched my forehead with his bare fingertips. "You okay?"

I nodded. "You?"

He smiled, and I blushed, which embarrassed me.

Our fingers entwined in the soft fur between Roxy's ears. Ryan's eyes turned serious, watching me as his head bent toward mine. He was going to kiss me.

I felt numb, and not only because my naked hand was starting to cool off between Roxy-licks.

Ryan kissed the tip of my nose, just once and lightly, like an exclamation point.

I laughed. My heart started beating again.

Ryan dropped back to pet Roxy, smiling a little.

I petted Roxy, too, before I reminded him, "I wanted to check the lab. I need to get the lay of the land tonight, so I don't mess up on my first day." I left nothing to chance anymore.

But first, I grabbed Ryan's face, one hand on each cheek, Hollywood-style, and kissed him hard, on his warm, full lips. If I died in the next five minutes, I wanted to go out knowing that I'd kissed one of the men I loved.

Ryan kissed me back so deep and so long that Roxy started trying to edge between us.

We both laughed. I said, against his chest, "How long are you keeping this dog?"

"Until Rachel picks her up tonight. But I kind of like her." Ryan patted Roxy's head, and I admitted, "I like her, too."

I pulled my mittens out of my pockets and aimed my body north, cutting through the park toward the Ottawa Health Science Centre's Central Campus.

Parks are creepy at night. The blue plastic slide could be hiding a marijuana stash, if not a guy with a knife. Ottawa has gangs and shootings and hate crimes now. So I was slightly relieved when Roxy barked and Ryan fell into place beside me, our boots crunching together in the icy grass and snow. He pointed east. "Don't you want to take the road?"

I shook my head. I avoided people as much as possible now. I'd rather walk past the empty climbing wall and kid-free jungle gym.

"This isn't a trail, Hope. They don't clear it in the winter."

"Okay. If I get stuck, I'll take the road."

Ryan sighed. "You can't cut through to Lindsay Lane. There's a ditch between the tree line and the sidewalk that won't be frozen yet. And did you hear about the Muslim woman in Vanier who got jumped from behind while picking up her kids from school?"

"No, and thanks for telling me. I've got back up." I pointed south east, through the sparse screen of trees, at the RIDE police cruiser.

Ryan shook his head, but he and Roxy followed me into the park.

Another siren whooped in the distance, setting my teeth on edge. As a medical student, I'd loved the sound of ambulances bringing me traumas and other fun cases to play with. That felt like forever ago, but had only been last year.

Roxy drifted from side to side, testing the limits of her leash, before she sniffed a lump of snow with great interest. I glanced at the houses along the west edge of the park. A TV screen's lights flickered behind some horizontal blinds.

My boots sank in the overgrown, dead grass and the few centimetres of snow before I paused at the foot of a barely-iced pond now blocking our path.

Municipal money didn't stretch to maintaining off-road paths in winter. I couldn't tromp around the lab with half-frozen, muddy feet.

When I turned to admit defeat to Ryan, Roxy broke away from him, jerking her leash out of his hand.

Ryan swore.

Roxy barrelled east, toward Lindsay Lane.

Towards traffic. And drivers who might not see a black dog at night.

We both ran toward her, screaming, "Roxy! Roxy!"

I skidded on the snow. My right ankle turned over. I wobbled, pain knifing through my lateral foot.

Ryan spun around to catch me, but I was already righting myself— obviously a sprain, not a break—and yelling, "Get Roxy!"

He broke into a sprint. Even as I hobbled after him, yelling at our borrowed dog, I marvelled at the way Ryan cut through the trees, never missing a step, despite the darkness and the uneven, slippery ground.

I stumbled after Ryan. Tree shadows fell on me, but so did the street lamps and a bit of moonlight, so I concentrated on tracking Ryan, who had almost caught up to Roxy.

She wagged her tail, picking her way into the ditch bordering Lindsay Lane.

Ryan scooped up her leash, but his back stiffened so abruptly, I rushed to his side, gasping, "What?" as cars whooshed on the road a few feet above us.

He pointed at Roxy.

She was sniffing something that looked awfully like a dead human body.

A body with a black bag over its head.

CHAPTER 2

The body wore a shiny, new, navy ski jacket. It lay crumpled on its left side, its black-jeaned legs slightly bent, and one arm rolled up underneath it, while the other arm hung forward, half-blocking the chest. Its skimpy black gloves and beat-up Converses didn't look like much protection against the snow.

But of course, the most shocking thing was the black bag over its head.

Ryan stood frozen. His breath spun into the air, making white clouds in the night.

Roxy bent her head, tipping her floppy ears forward. Her nostrils flared and glistened under the dim light of the street lamp.

"Let me check it while you call 911," I said to Ryan. Before I finished speaking, he pulled his phone out of his pocket. With the other hand, he reeled Roxy's leash in tight to his body. He yanked off his left glove so he could work the buttons while watching the body.

If this was a crime scene, I shouldn't touch anything, including the bag taped around its neck.

But I was a medical doctor.

Okay, a resident doctor. But still. My job was to make sure he was alive.

And if he wasn't, my job was to bring him back.

There's a saying in medicine, "They're not dead until they're warm and dead."

Snow meant zero degrees Celsius or lower. This man was definitely not warm and dead.

I swallowed hard.

I had to do my job.

If only I could do my job with gloves and a face mask.

I crouched low. "Hello?" I raised my voice to be heard above the traffic, including the stuttering roar of a helicopter. Normally, I'd shake him, or do a sternal rub, but I didn't want to touch the body.

More snowflakes landed on the jacket.

The bag didn't flutter with the man's breathing.

No airway. No breathing.

"Hope, he's—" Ryan didn't want to say it, but we both knew he was thinking the D word. Not Disability, but Death. "Don't touch it, Hope."

If only I had an ultrasound machine to do a sono pulse check, looking for a beating heart, instead of going skin to skin. "Just the radial artery," I said. I reached for the closest arm, the right arm, sheathed in the painfully new ski jacket.

The wind carried Ryan's words toward me as he spoke on the phone. "Ambulance. But maybe police. We found someone with a bag over his head. He's not moving. He looks … gone."

I touched the man's sleeve first, through my mitten. His arm felt firm, even with that light touch, and it belatedly occurred to me that I didn't have to check for a pulse if the man had rigor mortis.

The arm did move, but only a few centimetres before I'd have to apply greater pressure. Yet it didn't feel locked-in, like I imagined rigor mortis would.

Was I feeling rigor mortis, or one very cold person?

I didn't trust my numb hands to undo the black tape around his neck, and surely there might be fingerprints or hair trapped in the tape that constituted police evidence, if this was a homicide.

I yanked off my mittens and used my nails to lift a bit of the right sleeve and expose the skin. In the dim light, I couldn't detect bruising or obvious lacerations on his dark brown wrist.

Human Remains

Since I didn't have any open cuts or sores either, it was probably safe to touch him bare-skinned.

Ryan was giving directions. "We're near the corner of Lindsay and Bullock. Yes, south of the hospital. My girlfriend is a resident doctor in Montreal. She's checking for a pulse."

I slid my hand inside the radial styloid, pressing hard to compress the artery against the bone and maximize any pulse.

His skin felt slightly cooler than mine, but not icy. Faintly warm.

No pulse.

The radial pulse is the first to go. Unless you've got a blood pressure of at least 80 millimetres of mercury, the body shuts down circulation to the arms.

The blue lights of a police cruiser raced up Lindsay Lane toward us, its siren splitting the air.

"Ryan," I hollered, above the din, "there's no radial pulse."

Roxy barked twice and jumped onto her back legs. I sucked my breath in. Nice dog, but she was still a Rottweiler who wanted to snack on a dead body, as far as I was concerned.

"No radial pulse. That's right, no radial pulse," Ryan yelled into his phone while winding Roxy back into place beside him.

"I'll have to open that bag over his face!"

"What?" Ryan frowned at me, trying to triangulate between 911, Roxy's antics, and my voice.

I enunciated short, hard sentences. "The bag over his head. He can't breathe. Do they want me to rip it open?"

Ryan's eyes were so wide, I could see the whites glowing under the street light. "What? No, Hope, he's dead. I think they want you to leave it for the police!"

I was already reaching for the bag, bracing myself for whatever sick smell that would balloon out at me as I tore it. "Just ask them. He's still warm."

"Uh, my girlfriend, the doctor, she's worried about the bag over the head. Do you want her to take it off?" He shook his head. "Yeah, he looks dead, and he has no pulse, but he's still warm ... yes, I'll hold." He glared at me. "Hang on a second."

I nodded. In the ER, the staff and I could make the decision, but not in the field, at what could be a crime scene, with the police car screeching to a halt on the other side of the street.

I stood up, and my vision started to blacken at the edges. I hadn't eaten much today. Too busy packing and driving from Montreal through the snow. I blinked, waiting for my vision to come back. I'd never fainted in my life. I had no intention of doing so over a corpse.

"Hope, they said not to touch the bag. Hope? Are you okay?"

"Fine," I said, too loudly. My vision was starting to clear. "I'll do CPR."

I donned my mittens to nudge the body onto his back. He wanted to stay curled up. Ryan had to hold down the shoulder while I twisted the hips flat on the ground.

I dropped to my knees, stacked my hands on top of each other, and extended my arms to begin CPR. The new Advanced Cardiac Life Support algorithm is all about CPR. Get that blood pumping. Even if he's hypoxic with a bag over his head.

His ribs cracked under my first compression.

I've never broken anyone's ribs during CPR. It's one of the risks of resuscitation, but it's never happened to me.

I could be puncturing his lungs with the jagged ends of his own ribs, on every compression.

I swore.

"Over here!" Ryan's cry pierced the night air. Roxy barked ferociously as a police officer bolted across the road toward us.

Another siren whooped.

The first police officer yelled on his radio while I continued compressions, gritting my teeth.

Roxy barked and leapt in response. Ryan had to beat a retreat, holding her back.

A second officer sprinted to my side and took over CPR while I checked for a pulse in the wrist. It was strong, thanks to his efforts.

"Good compressions. Can I take off the bag?" I pointed at the garbage bag.

Sweat trickled down the side of the CPR officer's face as he pounded the man's chest. He shook his head and glanced at the officer on his radio, possibly for a second opinion, before turning back to his compressions.

Human Remains

Two more officers crunched through the snow toward us, already calling on their radios for more back up, but I was most relieved when an ambulance jerked to a halt on Lindsay Lane.

Paramedics hustled to the scene with a stretcher, a kit, and a monitor. One of them sliced open the head bag with scissors, reminding me that it's better to ask for forgiveness than permission.

The sour smell of vomit hit the air. I held my breath while the other paramedic cut open the jacket to apply electrodes to the man's chest. Yes, it did look like a man. No breasts.

The CPR officer was gasping, so I said, "Do you want to switch off?" He nodded, and I signalled another officer, who ran in, dropped to his knees, and started compressions so enthusiastic that the man's slim, dark brown-skinned chest indented with each one.

We paused for a second to check the rhythm: an occasional narrow QRS complex at 30 beats per minute. No pulse.

Hypothermia is one of the causes of pulseless electrical activity. So is hypoxia.

"Restart CPR! And I can get an airway in!" I called, moving to the head, but the airway guy was already on his stomach, shoving what I assumed was a laryngeal mask airway or a Combitube into the man's mouth. It was hard to see what was going on, in the dark, with everyone shouting on their radios, and Roxy still barking up a frenzy.

"Got it!" called the airway guy.

"Great. Let's get him warm and oxygenated. Can you get a sat?" I turned to stare at the yellow tracing on the monitor, which spiked with every compression. No oxygen saturation.

"It's not picking up, but the CO2 detector is yellow."

"Good job! Give him an amp of Epi!" I said. We had airway and we were providing primitive breathing and circulation. Epi is controversial in hypothermia, but you can give one dose.

"Let's load him up and protect his C-spine," said the second paramedic. I helped lift the legs on to the stretcher while they managed to get a cervical spine collar on him and some padding on either side of his head. A third officer took over CPR.

"I can take over compressions," I told the CPR police officer, even though I've never done them while jogging along beside a stretcher, but he shook his head.

The patient's belly looked distended. I opened my mouth to mention a nasogastric tube, when they had the chance, but a female police officer took my arm and said, "We have some questions for you. Could you come to the station with us?"

CHAPTER 3

"Where were you, before you found the body?" asked the female police officer.

I blinked before answering. I wasn't crazy about how they'd split me and Ryan up to question us at the police station.

But I was raised to answer police officers, and two of them sat in front of me, in this small, white-walled, table-free room.

It was hard to resist looking at the ceiling-mounted camera, after giving them permission to film me, but they'd instructed me to treat this as a normal conversation. I glanced at the male before turning back to the female officer. "I was driving to Ottawa from Montreal. That's where I'm living as a resident doctor." Should I explain that they used to call us interns? No, maybe not. "I'm staying with my parents in Orleans. It was snowing, so I didn't take any detours."

"What time did you leave Montreal?" said the woman. The bronze badge on the right side of her chest, gleaming against her black uniform, said E. Edwards.

E. Edwards seemed awfully interested in my whereabouts today. The hairs tingled on the back of my neck.

I stared at E. Edwards, then at the man. They both met my gaze, unblinking. The man smiled a little, as if to put me at ease. E. Edwards did not.

They were both white, probably in their thirties. The woman had wrapped her dark hair in a neat bun. The man, R. Antunes, had opted for a brown buzz cut. The metal police badge on the left side of their chests and the fabric Ottawa police badges on their arms were unstained. I noticed a billy club hanging on their hips, and I'm sure they had guns or Tasers, but they had so many things hanging on their belts, it was hard to identify each item without seeming to gawk at their crotches.

At a glance, they both looked pretty fit. No doughnut police jokes here. Neither of them needed glasses, so they continued to stare back at me, unfiltered. Her eyes were blue and his were brown.

"Do you think I had something to do with the body?" I asked. I crossed my arms in front of my chest. They wouldn't be able to see the goose bumps under my long-sleeved, cobalt blue shirt, although I suddenly wished I had a sweater.

"We're looking for information, Hope. That's all," said the man.

I didn't like the way he said my name. Maybe I should tell him to call me Dr. Sze.

"You understand why we need that information, right, Dr. Sze?" said the woman.

Somehow, she'd picked up on the fact that I didn't like them using my first name. That was both impressive and dangerous.

I licked my lips. They felt cracked under my tongue. My lips got dry in the winter, and I hadn't had any water since I'd left my car. "I understand that you need information, but I'm wondering if Ryan and I should have a lawyer present," I said.

I glanced around the room. No table, no carafe of water, only chairs and the omnipresent eye of the video camera. I couldn't stand hunger and thirst. Not since I'd been trapped in a foodless room with the possibility of a bullet through the brain. But I didn't want to request any favours from the police. Especially when I'd asked for a lawyer.

"That's your choice, of course, Dr. Sze. I can't give you legal advice," said the woman.

"We're only asking some questions, Hope," said the man. "Would you like some water?"

Human Remains

It was like they could read my mind, but of course they couldn't. My lips were flaking and peeling under their scrutiny. Plus, I know that I broadcast every thought across my face. I lie as well as a two-year-old. So even though I didn't answer, the man nodded and left the room.

Montreal police had saved my skin more times than I cared to count. But I was starting to recognize that I'd changed cities, and even changed provinces. These cops wore black uniforms instead of baby blue. They didn't know that I was the "detective doctor," unless they read the newspaper. They had no idea who I was.

The man returned with a plastic cup, and I sipped the tepid water, trying not to grimace. Both of them had placed their hands on the table, probably thinking that it made them look more open and showed that they didn't have any weapons, but really made me think, *What big hands you have, officers.*

"I want to know that Ryan's okay," I said.

"He's fine," said the man. It was possible he could've gotten an update through his radio. They wore little grey radios on their right shoulders.

"I'd like to see him myself."

"Dr. Sze," said E. Edwards, "if you answer our questions, which shouldn't take more than a few minutes, we'll bring you to Mr. Wu."

I glanced at the clock behind my head. It was 10:37 p.m.

"You can time us," said the woman, reading my thoughts again. "We'll be done here by eleven, if you answer the questions quickly."

"Okay." The boy and girl in blue (or black) were on my side. I was willing to give up my theoretical lawyer if that meant I could see Ryan faster. "I left Montreal before 6 p.m." I meant to leave in the wee hours of the morning, but of course, that didn't happen. Saying good-bye to John Tucker took a lot longer than that.

"And you drove straight to Ottawa?"

"Yes."

"To your parents' house?"

"I had to stop for gas." I'd stopped once I crossed the Ontario border. "I have the receipt, if you want it."

"That would be helpful," said the man, which gave me an excuse to dig through the purple leather wallet my mom had bought me for my birthday. Of course I had ten million receipts in there—more receipts than cash, which was a measly $20 bill—but I passed the correct stub across the table, thankful that the ink hadn't already worn off the receipt. "I took the 40 and then the 417 to Orleans."

"Where do your parents live?"

I drained the cup. "Are you going to harass them?"

They exchanged a quick look. The man said, "We don't harass people. We're the police. We may have to ask questions, but only when necessary."

I didn't like it. I glanced at the neighbouring wall, where Ryan should be, and I told them, "They live on 288 Silver Lane. My brother—I don't want you to bother my brother. He's only eight. My family has nothing to do with this."

The woman nodded acknowledgement while the man took notes. "What time did you leave your parents' house tonight?" said the woman.

"Around 9:10. No, closer to 9:15." Kevin had asked me to hang out a little longer, and to be honest, I wanted to. Every time I looked at him, I thought, *This could be the last time.* We'd started reading Harry Potter together. We were on my least favourite book, *The Order of the Phoenix.* The one with the most evil antagonist, but the one I'd get to read to him in person instead of over the phone or Skype.

"Why were you driving to the lab, even though you told us your first day is tomorrow?"

"I wanted to figure out where it was and where to park, so I wouldn't be late tomorrow."

They didn't say anything, but I thought they understood. Cops are organized and rule-bound, more like the person I was trying to become.

They made me walk through finding the body and starting the code. I explained how I was torn about leaving the bag on his head as evidence and ripping it off as a doctor. We went over that several times. Then the questions got more bizarre.

The woman said, "Did you recognize the victim?"

"Recognize him? Of course not. I told you, I just came from Montreal."

"Had you met him before today? Maybe when you were visiting Ottawa on a previous occasion?"

I shook my head. "I don't think so. I didn't get a good look at his face. He had a bag on his head, and even after they cut open the bag, he was covered in vomit."

"You saw his features, though. His skin tone. His build," said the man. "Do you think you recognized him? Had you seen him another day?"

I shook my head. They stared at me, and I realized they wanted me to say it out loud, for the cameras. "No. I don't think I'd ever seen him before. I think he was black—I mean, it was hard to tell, it was so dark—but I didn't know him."

The man lit up. "Yes, he was of African heritage. Did that make him seem familiar to you?"

"No. I'm saying that I didn't know him at all. He didn't look like anyone from my high school or university that I remember."

"No?" The man looked disbelieving, but he said, "All right, then. How did you find work at the stem cell lab in Ottawa, when you were established in Montreal?"

"I set up a research rotation with Dr. Thomas Zinser."

"How did you know Dr. Zinser?"

"I, uh, one of my friends suggested him." My cheeks reddened.

The man raised his eyebrows.

"One of my fellow residents, Dr. John Tucker, knew him, or knew him by reputation."

The two officers grew still as soon as I said Tucker's name. They knew him. Of course they did. Tucker knew everyone. Seven point five billion people in the world meant 7.5 billion more friends for Tucker.

"Dr. John Tucker," said the woman.

"Yes."

"He was seriously injured during the hostage-taking at St. Joseph's Hospital in Montreal."

I closed my eyes. So they knew about that. I nodded. When I opened my eyes, they were watching me even more closely. The tone of the room, already sober, turned grim.

"You must have had an interview with Dr. Zinser at the stem cell lab before starting your work," said the man.

I shook my head. "Dr. Zinser and I e-mailed, and we Skyped together once. I never met him in person. We were both too busy." Dr.

Zinser was supposed to send me some forms, but he forgot. I decided not to mention that.

"You never came to the lab?"

"No. That's why I wanted to come early tonight, so I wouldn't get lost tomorrow morning. And because I tried to take a shortcut, Ryan and I were cutting through the park, in the snow, with the dog … "

My memory cast back to my boots sinking into the ground, our steps making muddy imprints in the snow, and I stopped right there. "The footprints," I said out loud.

The cops exchanged a look. The man leaned forward. "What about the footprints?"

"You can see our footprints in the snow. Me, Ryan, and Roxy. All the way from my car to the … victim. You know Ryan and I had nothing to do with this. Or at least you will in the morning, when you can see everything. You'll know we're all innocent."

I sagged into my seat with relief. The only way this day could've gotten any worse was if they picked me and Ryan up and slammed us in jail. Well, that wasn't going to happen. Science would save us.

"Hope," said the man, "no one is accusing you of anything, boot prints or not."

The woman reached her hand forward and said, in a too-gentle voice, "Do you want something to eat, Dr. Sze?"

I blinked at them. They kept asking if I knew the victim. They made me give an alibi, right down to my gas stub. Of course they were accusing me!

I dug my hands into the edges of the chair, which was made out of smooth plastic and didn't dent my fingers, but felt cool against my skin. That grounded me a little.

I said quietly, "I'm not hungry. I want to finish up here so I can see Ryan Wu." That, I was sure about. I needed to see him and John Tucker as soon as possible, with my own eyes, to make sure they were all right.

"Soon, Dr. Sze," said the female officer. "Very soon."

Human Remains

CHAPTER 4

"You found a body, Hope?" Kevin burst out of the living room on my left. "That's so cool!"

Good thing my little brother was fist-punching the air instead of jumping on me. My ankle was a bit sore. Not enough to complain about, but I'd be less nimble catching an almost nine-year-old. Kevin was shoulder-height on me now, and growing every day.

"God! You get all the good stuff, and I get the violin lessons." Kevin heaved a sigh.

"I'd rather have the violin lessons," I said under my breath, taking my glasses off and shaking them to encourage the condensation to evaporate. Even with my myopic eyes, I saw my dad's brow crease with concern as he examined my face under the yellow lights of the hallway. He said, "Are you all right?"

I shook my head, but my mother was already yelling from the kitchen, which lay directly in front of me. "We made bone soup. It's very good! At first, it didn't taste like anything, but Dad added some salt, and now it's perfect. I'll get you a bowl."

My stomach twisted. My parents' soup tends to be tasteless, greasy, and full of animal bones. The steamy, soup-laden air made me think of the wicked witch in Hansel and Gretel. I know this sounds weird, but I hadn't felt good about eating meat since 14/11, my secret nickname for the hostage-taking on November fourteenth.

Ryan called out something in Cantonese to my mother, but she said, *"Mo, mo, mo,"* and bustled into the hallway, nearly spilling a white bowlful of soup, and switching back to English for me because they never taught us Chinese. "You need your strength!"

"I need a shower." That, plus a gallon of water. I started walking to the bathroom, feeling Ryan's eyes on me. He needed a shower, too. I glanced at him over my shoulder, and I knew we were both thinking of past, soapy times, him closing his eyes against the spray, his body slick with water before he bent me over—

"It says here that bodies decompose more slowly in the cold. That makes sense," said Kevin, holding up his iPad and killing my buzz. "How long do you think the body was there? Do the cops know?"

"They know it's there. They interviewed us," I said, sighing. I couldn't even fantasize anymore. Was the rest of December going to be like this? Probably.

"Because rigor mortis starts in the first half hour or so. First the muscles get loose, and then they stiffen up after 30 to 60 minutes. It depends on the temperature."

My little CSI guy. I touched his hair, wanting to feel the dark spikes against my palm, but he twisted away. I guess he thought it was too babyish. I cleared my throat. "Good point. I'm not sure how much of that was the freezing temperature and how much was rigor mortis," I said, and my mother nearly spilled the soup again, while my dad said, "Hope—"

"What?" Kevin rounded on them. "I'm nine years old in eight days! Why should she get to have all the fun!"

"It's not fun," I said. It was wretched.

Roxy barked from the back of my car, clearly audible through the brick walls of our house. Ryan said, "I'd better check on her."

"Do you have a dog?" said Kevin, and obviously that beat researching a dead body, because he and my dad reached for their boots beside the door. I squeezed over—it's not a very big front hall, so we're supposed to put our boots in the closet to the right of the door, but no one wants

Human Remains

to bother—while my mom said, "I've got your soup! You need your strength. You're going to fall over. Forget about the dog."

Dad said, "We're going to help Ryan get his car. He left it at the hospital so he could drop Hope off."

"Eat some soup first!" Mom hollered at all of their backs, and then she rounded on me. "Where do you think you're going?"

"I've got to shower, Mom."

"Not before you eat soup!" She held the bowl aloft.

Was I supposed to slurp it standing up? "I'm not hungry," I said, shoving my boots in the closet. One of them toppled over, but I didn't care. It seemed fitting.

I finally made it down the hall, which led directly into the bathroom. My parents own a small, snug bungalow in Orleans, a suburb of Ottawa. My parents tell me the area started off as farmland, but now we've got schools, a grocery store, and even a wave pool and hockey rink a few blocks away, on Tenth Line Road. That shiny newness seemed so distant from the Death Star I figured must've been embedded in Montreal's historical stone buildings. I thought I'd be safe at home.

"But you have to eat soup!"

"Mom," I said, trying to soften my tone. My parents loved me. They welcomed me back, even though I was a serious downer who triggered Kevin to look up rigor mortis. "If I eat soup right now, I might puke."

Her eyes widened. She took an involuntary half-step back, sloshing the soup. A few spots drizzled on the parquet floor.

I took a right and grabbed a rag out of the linen closet. Opening and closing the wooden folding doors, the way I had since I was a kid, soothed me a little. I mopped up the soup and said to the wooden squares on the floor, and my mother's white and chartreuse polka dot slippers, "I'm sorry. I'll see if I feel better later. But I told you, Mom, I'd rather not eat meat right now."

"It's not meat. It's bone soup!"

I made a face at her. Bones made me think of the body's ribs breaking under my compressions, a detail that nagged at me. The skin I'd glimpsed on the man's chest had been smooth and young. We usually think about little old ladies' bones breaking during CPR, not young and

Melissa Yi   21

healthy males. There was no reason for his ribs to snap, unless he had osteogenesis imperfecta.

I popped into the bathroom, closing and locking the door with a satisfying *ping* of the tiny, fake brass door handle. My dad had renovated the bathroom himself, adding a grey pebble floor. I'd picked out the wallpaper in high school, white with tiny purple flowers, and I noticed it was starting to curl at the wall edges around the bathtub.

I didn't want to look at myself in the mirror over the sink, but I faced it. My eyes were bloodshot, although that's usually more a problem with my contact lenses than with my glasses. I'd gotten an avant-garde, spiky haircut post 14/11 that now hovered between laughable and insane. Your twenties are supposed to be this golden decade, but mostly, it's work, sleep, and crime for me. Except for my two guys. Them, I wouldn't trade for anything.

I tossed the rag in the wicker laundry basket and pulled my phone out of my pocket while my mother shouted, "I'll put your soup in the kitchen. When you come out, I'll warm it up for you. You tell me when you're almost ready!"

"Okay," I said, scrolling through my phone and smiling at the gajillion texts from Tucker, sometimes with snippets of Yiddish and other random languages. *So, nu? The stem cells rocking your world already?*

Let me know when you're free to Skype.

But the most recent one made me frown. *Okay, I see you're finally home. What happened to you?*

I texted him back. *Hi. How did you know I was home?*

Through the Finding Friends app. Remember?

Vaguely. I hadn't paid much attention when Tucker had mentioned there was this cool app he could help install on my phone. I typed back slowly, *Are you spying on me?*

No. I want to know where you are. Call me crazy, but after what happened to us, I like knowing you're not in a ditch somewhere. But why were you at the police station for an hour?

My throat caught. My heart fluttered in my chest, reminding me of a bird that got caught in a wood stove at my friend's cottage. The mother called, "Let it out! It's going to die in there!" The father said, "I don't want it to come out and crap everywhere! And maybe it's a bat, you ever think of that?" My friend was so embarrassed, not knowing how to make it look pretty for me, but she yanked a broom out of the closet to fight off the marauding bird or bat. In the end, they called the wood stove guy, so I never got to see it.

I felt like that bat/bird right now.

Tucker and Ryan were my two safeguards. I would trust them with my life.

And yet I didn't want them spying on me. Even if it kept me "safe."

Ryan had been right beside me, and what happened? We found a dead body.

Tucker was in Montreal, letting me go, letting me flee the crime-ridden city that I found so oppressive, but he was tracking me through my phone.

Said phone rang in my hand. Tucker's avatar glowed at me, the healthy, pre-hostage version, he of spiky blond hair, confident brown eyes, crooked grin. My eyes toggled between two buttons, green for accept or red for decline. Should I talk to him or not?

I hadn't known how to tell him that I'd found a dead body.

Now, I didn't want to.

More than anyone else in the world, I loved Tucker, and he drove me berserk, too.

I clicked Decline and turned my ringer off, even though it made me feel sick. Tucker needed to know that I was safe, that I loved him despite decamping to Ottawa with my other sort-of boyfriend.

I texted him instead. *I love you. I'll call you after my shower.*

And then I turned on the hot water tap. The pipes clunked before water gushed through the faucet. I stared at it, wishing it would wash me clean.

Chapter 5

Half an hour later, I felt less soiled and more human, especially after fried rice and a slice of pineapple that had been on sale at T&T. While my mother reminisced about other, better pineapples she could have chosen, I ducked into the hallway shadows to call Tucker. Again.

Tucker hadn't answered my post-shower calls or texts. He was so hyper, that was completely out of character.

Did he fall asleep, zonked on his pain meds? But that meant the dose was too strong, or he was on a dangerous drug combo.

It meant he needed me. Either that, or he was too mad to talk.

What if something had happened to Tucker?

I kept pressing redial and hanging up when I got his voice mail, like a psychotic ex-girlfriend with a restraining order.

I couldn't handle being away from him.

But I couldn't stand finishing my OB rotation at the hostage hospital, either. I would've cracked up. For real.

I don't want to be like this. I'd love to be perpetually perky and cute. *Who cares if people keep killing each other around me? I'm going to figure out whodunit and save a dozen lives while doing the splits!*

"Do you want an apple?" Mom called to me from the kitchen.

"No, Mom." My voice echoed in the hallway. I edged further away from her, past the main closet, toward the bathroom and my bedroom.

"I already cut it up for you. Red Delicious! Your favourite."

"Okay, Mom." I'd started eating other varieties while I was away at school, like Honeycrisp and Gala and Pink Lady, but whatever. I wasn't hungry. I needed Tucker. And Ryan. Ryan and Tucker. Tucker and Ryan.

"I put the bowl on the table."

"Thanks, Mom." It was easier not to fight her.

"Why are you standing in the dark? Turn on the light!" She flicked it on for me. The sudden brightness made me blink.

It was harder to worry about Tucker when my mother wouldn't leave me alone for one minute. I sighed and moved back toward her, glancing out the bay window of our living room en route to the kitchen. A pair of headlights beamed toward our driveway, followed swiftly by another.

Two cars with familiar outlines. Headed directly for my family's small bungalow.

My heart surged, and I stood at the window, my breath forming hazy circles on it, while my mother kept talking to me.

My phone buzzed in the pocket of my skinny jeans. I caught my breath.

We're back! U ok?

Even without the dozen emoticons that followed, I could have figured out that Kevin was texting me through our dad's phone. Not Tucker.

ok, I texted back. For once, I didn't write the whole word or bother with capitals. I closed my eyes in thanks. At least my family and one of my guys was safe.

"Oh, oh, Ryan's going to need some soup!" My mother clattered in the kitchen, and I was left in relative peace to watch our blue Honda Accord pull up our driveway, with Kevin dashing out to open the garage door manually because the electronic door opener got stuck halfway. Then Ryan's Nissan pulled up tight behind my car, which I'd left on the street. For some reason, that made me smile.

While Kevin described their car-seeking adventure in blow-by-blow detail, Ryan stood beside me and laid his hand on my waist, in the gap between my flannel shirt and my skinny jeans. I jumped slightly because it felt too good. Like, illegal.

I should feel somber after our brush with death. Dispassionate. Asexual. Especially surrounded by my family.

I shouldn't notice each imprint of Ryan's individual finger, or how the goose bumps rose on my forearms and my nipples jumped to attention.

Our eyes met. His nostrils flared slightly. His eyes narrowed.

Maybe I glanced down at myself, because he did too. A long, slow glance.

My lips parted.

My heart thudded in my ears, and I chanted to myself, *Tucker, Tucker, Tucker.* Trying to remind myself that I was at least partially spoken for.

And was any place unsexier than my family's living room, with my little brother jumping up and down in front of us?

Even so, my body nudged closer to Ryan's. My left arm crept up to touch his arm, stroking the hairs on his skin.

His fingers stilled for a second. He said, in a hoarse voice, "I should go."

"I'll be back later!" I hollered on my way out, even as my mother wailed about, you guessed it, soup.

We hurried into the cold, me with my jacket unzipped, Ryan with his boots unlaced.

One blink later, we were in his car, his mouth crushing mine, car doors barely slammed behind us, and Roxy's furious, back seat barks ricocheting in our ears. She tried to climb between the front seats to get to us.

I pulled away, laughing, but Ryan leaned forward, blocking that opening and keeping Roxy at bay. His body weight pinned me into the passenger seat, and I wanted him there, his lips hard against mine. Alive.

I needed the weight of his body. It brought me back into myself, forced me to feel something.

I couldn't get enough of the way he smelled. After being locked in hospitals for the past 4.25 years, he smelled like ocean breezes and clean laundry and a very healthy man, even without the evidence pressing under my navel.

His lips were hard, almost angry. He kissed me like he wanted to eat my mouth, and it excited me, even though my heart was breaking too. Because Ryan was my last good guy, the one who never had to rub his face against death and disease every day, the way Tucker and I did. Hell, Ryan was devastated when his grandmother died.

For the first time, Ryan had come face to face with a strange corpse.

Ryan wasn't a death virgin anymore.

He was hurting, and I could feel it in the tension of his shoulders, in the way he refused to take a breath when he plundered my mouth. He still slipped a hand behind my head to shield me from the car door, pinning his own hand, but he weighed me down with the rest of his body like he needed to do it.

He'd spent so much of his life playing by the rules, playing the perfect son and grandson and church-goer. He'd even tried to sell me on second virginity. Supposedly, even though we'd already had full carnal knowledge of each other, repeatedly and exquisitely, we could still save our souls by not having sex again until marriage.

I could feel rebellion in his mouth. He wasn't going to play by the rules anymore

And I gloried in it.

"I love you," I managed to get out, but the words were so distorted by our kiss, I didn't think he understood me, or cared, until his lips softened slightly. I felt his mouth move against mine, although I couldn't catch any puff of words.

It didn't matter. I knew he loved me. We'd loved each other for years, even when we'd broken up and were living on opposite sides of the province.

His tongue swept against mine, his fingers slid under the hem of my shirt, and for a second I tensed and thought, *No. We can't do this. My brother might be able to see us. We've got to—*

My body hollered, *DO THIS.*

Ryan's hips pushed against mine, through our clothes. Despite Roxy's frantic barks, my mind careened between scenes of break up sex and make up sex and sex sex.

When Ryan finally lifted his lips and hips off mine, the street lamp's glow dazzled my eyes.

I blinked, unsure if it was over, but he was sitting up, sliding his key into the ignition and saying, "Let's go."

My head buzzed. Even without him kissing me, I could hardly talk, could hardly program my fingers to reach for my seat belt. "Where?"

He said exactly two words. "My place."

CHAPTER 6

"I've never found someone dead before," said Ryan, as he exited the highway on to Woodroffe Avenue.

"I know." I stroked his hair, his neck, his ear. I couldn't stop touching him. Part of me was afraid that if I stopped, he'd remember that sex was verboten because Jesus said so. And part of me simply marvelled at the softness of his earlobe and the way I could feel the mastoid bone lying under the skin behind his ear. He was made so beautifully, Ryan was.

"I've never been brought to the police station, either." He hit the gas. He was gunning for his apartment. The streetlights periodically lit up his profile, so his face blinked in and out of darkness.

He was going a good 20 clicks over the speed limit. Every time we hit a stop light, he had to jam on the brakes. On the last one, the car skidded slightly on the snow, but he handled it easily, coming to a full stop before he turned right on Constellation Way.

As soon as we pulled into the deserted garage of his brick apartment building, Ryan killed the ignition and turned to me.

Before I unlatched my seat belt, he was kissing me on the lips.

Zoom. I kissed him right back. Our teeth clicked. My bottom lip split. I tasted the iron tang of blood.

It made me kiss him harder.

Tucker's face launched into my mind, his eyes blazing with betrayal.

I jerked my head back. My breath steamed into the air. *John Tucker. You love Tucker. Tucker saved your life.*

I turned my face toward the windshield, trying to think, while my breath condensed on the glass.

Ryan kissed my left ear.

I squiggled in his arms. He started kissing my neck, which was strictly unfair, because he knew how that short-circuited my brain.

I love Ryan, too.

I yanked Ryan's shirt out of his waistband and shoved my hands up his stomach and chest. I felt his abdominal muscles jerk in surprise, and I waited for him to say no, that he was Christian, that we had to save our souls from hellfire after all the sex we'd had two years ago.

Instead, he grinned and helped work his way out of his jacket and shirt. Then he sat in his car in his full, bare-chested glory, with more defined pecs than I remembered, under that smooth brown skin, and I was melting, melting, my tongue adhering to the roof of my mouth with longing.

Ryan moved back to kissing my mouth. This time, he was the one sliding his hands under my shirt, trying to unbuckle my bra in the back, only to realize that I was wearing a sports bra with an elastic band.

He growled and unzipped my jacket. Then he unbuttoned my flannel shirt before sliding both layers off my shoulders at once.

I flinched a little in the cool air of the car. Ryan and I hadn't been naked together in over two years. But I knew I looked pretty good in a plain black sports bra, not crazy-muscled, but slim and reasonably-toned, so I sat up straight while he devoured me with his eyes.

He reached for my bra strap, ready for the great reveal.

I crossed my arms over my chest. "Before we go too far, we should talk."

Ryan made an impatient noise. His fingers stilled, but didn't release the elastic band.

"I still love you and Tucker. Both of you. I'm not choosing only you. That would destroy him."

Human Remains

"I don't care." He looked at me, and I realized that he really didn't. He didn't give a fuck about Tucker, didn't care that the guy had thrown down for me during the hostage-taking. In fact, he hated him for it. Ryan wanted to be the one who'd protected me.

Ryan started running his hands over my back, which is only marginally less sensitive than my neck. I clenched my teeth, breathing through them, trying not to liquefy at his feet.

"Hope. Don't talk." His dark eyes burned.

I felt a twitch between my legs before I said, "Ryan—"

He kissed me. Ryan's always been a good kisser, but this was Ryan with a touch of Satan, my split lip, his tongue reaching in my mouth while his hand wound in my hair to make sure I couldn't get away.

That reminded me of the hostage-taking, and I tried to jerk my head to the side, even as part of my brain whispered *Yes, that's right*, and I kissed him back, rubbing myself against him, breathing his breath. I could have died last month. I'm sure, in most parallel universes, we did get blown away.

Somehow, that made it harder to say no. To think of the future.

Ryan's free hand ran down my back, feeling my curves under my clothes. I could tell it wasn't a cursory skimming. He really wanted to memorize my body up to and including my ass. He let go of my hair so he could cup and then squeeze both cheeks hard enough for me to feel each fingertip.

When I gasped, he sucked that into his mouth too.

Then he shifted to yank my bra off. It got caught on my ear— sports bras aren't meant for sexy unveiling, more to keep your boobs from bouncing too hard when you run—and we both laughed before he said, "Sorry" and kissed my right ear, sticking his tongue in it for good measure.

My body tilted toward Ryan.

He cupped my bare breasts, one in each hand.

I backed off right away, but when his hands followed me, one thumb on each nipple, my mouth dried up.

My breath came in quick, ragged puffs of air. Ryan was supposed to be my safety net. I hated his whole "no sex again until we're saved by the sanctimony of marriage" thing, but I realized that I'd sort of counted on it, too. He was safe.

Well, Ryan wasn't safe anymore.

He bent his head and licked each nipple. The second one, he bared his teeth and grazed me with his incisors. It was so erotic that my whole lower body clenched. He wouldn't hurt me, would he?

Ryan's dark eyes flashed. No, he didn't hurt me. But he was yanking my jeans off, my skinny leg jeans that tend to get caught on the calves. Nothing I'd wear for our great reunion sex. Some girls wear granny panties or don't wax if they want to remind themselves not to have sex that night. But I know at least one girl who broke that Odysseus contract with herself and told the guy to wait while she headed for the bathroom and shaved herself as best she could before climbing on top of him.

Rules were made to be broken.

I tried to focus on Tucker. My knight in rumpled greens. My hero of the ICU. That made me hotter, to be honest. I reached for my phone, reached out for Tucker, but since my jeans were around my ankles, it meant that I bent over the seat, ankle-cuffed by my jeans and trying not to hit my head on the dashboard, while Ryan shucked off my underwear.

I caught my panties as they slid halfway down my thighs and yanked them up hard enough that they folded up in all the wrong places.

Ryan laughed, and I felt like a '50s throwback, 99 percent naked and clinging to a semblance of virtue in the front seat of a car.

"I love you," said Ryan.

"I love *you*," I said.

He placed one hand between my legs, and the look in his eyes, enjoying the wetness, made me want to pass out. Especially when he started rubbing my clitoris through the fabric. I've heard some guys need a map. Ryan could write the map.

"Um," I said. I'm good at self-control. You can't do med school without discipline. Except it was all evaporating as I started to writhe over his fingertips.

Ryan's head bent over my breasts so that he could kiss each one before his tongue circled one nipple, synchronizing with a finger that had slipped under my panties.

Wait! I'm still holding on to my underwear! I thought, confused, just before I exploded.

Human Remains

It happened so fast, I hadn't finished shuddering and blinking away black spots, when he pushed two fingers inside me and started tapping my G-spot. My mouth fell open.

Ryan laughed, a throaty laugh, but I was too far gone to care. Dimly, I realized that he was using his free hand to unbuckle his leather belt. His left hand, so he was a bit more awkward, but he still had it off in seconds, and now he was unzipping his pants.

"You're going to ... fuck me ... through my underwear?" I managed to say, even though my eyes were rolled up in the back of my head.

"You're going to take it off for me."

I did.

CHAPTER 7

MONDAY

I'm kneeling on the snow. Snow seeps into the gap between my snow pants and the top of my boots, chilling my skin.

I hold a pocket knife in my hand. The blade catches the moonlight.

I'm leaning over the body. I'm alone, slicing open the bag on his face.

I hold my breath, waiting for the vomit to spill out of the hole, but the man's bulging eyes stare into mine, and his mouth drops open—

I snapped awake, a scream arrested in my throat.

The door creaked.

I batted aside the duvet, heart battering my chest. *Where was I?*

My head ached with every heart beat, and my breath choked.

One thing for sure: there was no Ryan beside me. The rest of the bed was cold, but smelled familiar, and I recognized these old snowman flannel sheets.

The white wood door yawned open while I groped for my glasses on the dresser next to the bed.

I jumped behind the dresser, crouching as I shoved the hooks behind my ears. A waist-high maple dresser wouldn't provide much cover, but it

Human Remains

was better than nothing. It could shield my head and body, if not my feet.

"Hope?" said a little boy's voice.

I exhaled, trying to tame my heart. "Kevin?"

"Why are you hiding?"

I straightened up from my scrunch, trying to look dignified while I checked that it was, indeed, my little brother barging into my bedroom. "I was practicing."

"Practicing what?" He tilted his head to survey me with curiosity in the dim, dawn light. He was only wearing underwear, and made no attempt to hide the curve of his belly. Kevin was a kid who shucked his pants as soon as he came in through the door after school. Not exactly terrorist material.

I breeeeeeathed before I answered him. I touched my duvet, which has this red fleece cover that my parents bought me as an early Christmas present or late 14/11 present. Either way, I love to lie in bed and make a nest out of it. I find it very comforting, especially when the feathers are as high and fluffy as possible.

Kevin grinned an evil grin from the doorway, his glance fixed on my duvet.

"Kevin, no!" I half-hollered. I didn't know what time it was, but I couldn't smell coffee or hear talking, so our parents might still be aslee—

Kevin took a running leap and belly-flopped onto my duvet, squishing all the feathers underneath him.

"Kevin!" I started spanking his butt.

He veered from side to side, evading my palm while extending his blanket-squishing area.

"Stop it! Get off! Get off right now, you little brat!"

Kevin grabbed either side of the blanket and folded his arms over his chest, swaddling himself from both sides before he shifted onto his back, squashing more feathers underneath him and laughing the entire time.

"You jerkwad! You Fangbone!"

"Fangbone! Yeah!" It's one of his favourite books. Not the best insult.

Through dint of greater height, dexterity, and years of experience, I flipped him onto his face and pried the blanket edges out of his little fists. I was smiling as I threw my duvet on my desk, where it would remain relatively unmolested. He was chortling his teeny little head off.

Okay, not his head off. That reminded me of the body last night, with the bag around the head. I'd been dreaming about it, that feeling of suffocation, the cold soaking into my clothes and into my bones ...

I shook my still-fuzzy head and rolled out my stiff shoulders. Then I remembered exactly what (and whom) I'd done last night, and my entire body seemed to flush.

I checked the phone lying on my dresser, but Tucker still. Hadn't. Answered.

Just as well. I couldn't talk to him with a straight face today.

Touching my phone reminded me, though: had I remembered to turn on my alarm?

Good thing Kevin had woken me up. I scowled at him anyway. "What are you doing here? Don't you knock?"

"Sorry. You've been gone so long, I got used to coming into your room." He widened his deep brown eyes, staring at me. He's a cute kid, the only one in our family who doesn't need glasses yet, with high cheekbones and a perpetually moving mouth, and he knows exactly how to mine his adorableness.

I swatted him again. "Liar. This is my room, and you know it. What's up?"

The duvet slumped half off my desk, onto the chair, and Kevin laughed.

I poked him, provoking another round of hee-hee's before he caught himself. "I was going online, checking news about the body—"

"You already found an article on it?" I sagged. Even though I knew the man had been mostly dead, I was sorry to hear he was officially deceased. Also, news outlets had suffered so many cut backs, the man could easily have slid under their radar.

Kevin snorted. "You're the top story for city news."

"Oh." I guess it's true that if it bleeds (or dies), it leads. Even so, I found that kind of suspicious. I prodded Kevin in the side again. He's getting a bit fat. If he slumps, the skin folds into rolls on his sides.

He giggled.

Human Remains

I smiled, but I had to ask him. "Did you tell the news outlets?"

Kevin shrugged and pressed his lips together the way he does when I tickle him.

I threw my hands in the air. "You did! You tipped them off!"

"Hope, you want them to know, right? It's a health issue."

"How is it a health issue? You're eight years old. You don't even know what a public health issue *is*."

Kevin ignored me. "They want to know if people are dying around a hospital. I'm helping them. I wish they'd paid me, though—"

I hadn't even considered the terrible PR of having someone die outside your hospital. The Ottawa Health Science Centre reps must be freaking out.

"—but it was easy! I wrote that you and Ryan found a body—"

"What? You *named* us? Holy sh—" I barely managed to bite back the curse. "Kevin!"

"They have Contact Us forms on their websites. They like if you have pictures, though. I wish you had a picture."

"Fuck!" I try not to swear in front of my brother, but this was epic. Our mother thundered down the hall, already calling, "What is it?"

"I'll take care of it, Mommy," said our father, heading toward us in his navy terry cloth bathrobe, looking bleary-eyed behind his glasses, but my mother pushed ahead of him, totally un-self-conscious about her hair wrapped around pink curlers and her feet stuffed into those polka dot slippers.

"Sorry. I didn't mean to wake you up, or swear," I said. I didn't want to worry my parents, but here I was, rousing them with not one, but two curses at the break of dawn.

"You said the F-bomb," said Kevin.

"I know. Sorry."

"And almost the S-bomb."

"I *know*, Kevin. Sorry."

He shook his head. "At my friend Sam's house, they've got a swear jar. If you swear, you have to put in a dollar."

"A dollar! That's nuts. You broke into my room. You squashed my blanket, you told the media about me and Ryan .... You're not supposed to do that, Kevin! You give tips anonymously for a *reason*."

"Why?" said Kevin, rolling onto his other side and playing with his belly button. "If I found a body, I'd want everyone to know."

"Because now everyone's going to track us down and ask us questions."

"Well, you don't have to answer them," said Kevin.

"We'll put the answering machine on," said Dad. It's true, we're one of the only households with a real, concrete, old-school answering machine, because my parents shell out for a land line but are too cheap to pay the monthly fee for voice mail. "Don't worry, Hope."

Now that the adrenaline had worn off, I felt pretty awful. I'd woken everyone up, sworn at my brother twice, and now reporters would descend on me.

"What's this? Are the reporters coming?" My mother touched her hair, where her white roots showed under her dyed-black hair. It was clear where her priorities lay.

"No, it's okay, Mom, I'll deny everything," I said.

"You can't do that. That's lying," said Kevin, and I'd already shocked him enough today, so I said, "I mean, I'll tell them 'No comment.' It always worked before."

"You never found a dead body before," said Kevin, which was true, but I said, "It's not as big a deal as being taken hostage. It'll all die down soon. I mean, it'll be over soon." I never realized how much I talk about death and violence until I started trying to censor myself.

Kevin said, "Anyway, Hope, I never got to tell you the good news!"

I raised an eyebrow. "There's good news?"

My dad stood up and yawned loud enough to crack his jaw, making his way toward the shower.

Kevin's eyes gleamed with excitement. "Yeah! They've already ID'd the body. And get this, Hope. It's a guy who worked at the same lab as you! His name is Lawrence something."

CHAPTER 8

I couldn't get into the stem cell lab.

It was locked.

I guess I should've expected security, but it still took me by surprise, because this is Canada, yo. After taking the elevator to the third floor of the Ottawa Health Sciences Centre, I was now flanked by two sealed, frosted glass doors on either side of the elevator.

My badge from Montreal's St. Joseph's Hospital was strictly ornamental here. I didn't even know which door to knock on.

Between the barred doors, they'd made a small, purple-walled welcome area with a chair, a phone, and a ledge holding the directory, a sheet of paper in a plastic frame. I quickly scanned for the name Dr. Thomas Zinser and called his secretary.

A plump, smiling, fifty-ish woman with greying brown hair pushed open the frosted glass doors on my right. "Hello, I'm Susan." She wore a navy wrap dress and wedge heels.

I looked down at my red rayon blouse and the plain black dress pants that probably cost less than her mani-pedi. My boots tracked dirty water everywhere, even though I'd wiped them upon entering the building.

Susan waved her hand and said, "You can leave your boots at the front." She pointed to a boot rack inside the doors.

I hadn't brought an extra set of shoes. My heart plummeted. You know that moment when, despite careful planning, you'll end up as the idiot on your first day, tromping around in your socks? "Um, I didn't bring shoes. Sorry, I don't know what I was thinking."

She said, "Don't worry about that today. We have other things on our minds. I don't know if you heard about Dr. Acayo—"

I cleared my throat, not wanting to reveal exactly how much I knew about Dr. Lawrence Acayo. "I heard. Did he work at this lab?"

"No, he was at Dr. Hay's lab next door. He was so charming."

That was an interesting word. Usually people would say "nice" or "intelligent" or "hard-working" or some other generic, academic compliment. I looked at her more closely, but she had stopped behind the first desk, which was naked except for a monkey tail plant, a computer, and a tray of papers. She started leafing through the papers. "You'll have to get your badge and parking pass today. You can do that during the meeting."

"Shouldn't I go to the meeting? Dr. Zinser said I should see what a lab meeting was like."

"Oh, it's not a normal meeting today." She met my eyes, the corners of her mouth turning down. The lip liner around her mouth was crooked on the left, exaggerating the effect. "We've decided to have a little memorial for Dr. Acayo." She gestured with her left arm toward the entire room, and over the warren of cubicle walls, I noticed a group of at least five people gathered around the doorway of the lone corner office.

Ah. The guy in the middle must be the lab head, Dr. Thomas Zinser. I'd only ever met Tom by Skype, but he was easy to spot because of his crown of white hair, white lab coat, the way people clustered around him, and the bank of windows visible through the open door of his corner office. He was patting a woman's arm consolingly.

"I'd like to pay my respects, if you don't mind," I told Susan.

"Oh, that's nice of you, dear, but it's only a small gathering for the people who work here. It's really not a good introduction to the group. You can meet everyone after lunch." She held a form out to me with a smile that didn't reach her mascaraed eyes.

I took the form and placed it back on the desk, messing up her piles. "I work here now." The words jerked out of my mouth.

Her eyes widened, so I tried to make my tone more compassionate than confrontational. "And I would have liked to know him. I—" I was going to play the card, shouldn't play the card, was going to play the card. "We were very sorry to find his remains."

Her body became unnaturally still. "You … "

"My friend Ryan and I found him last night."

For the first time, she looked at me. Really looked at me. Her chin wobbled. "You're not … oh, my goodness. Oh." She sat down so abruptly that her ergonomic chair squawked in protest.

"I was coming to visit the lab last night, to make sure I knew where it was," I said, more softly.

"Of course." She drew a paper clip out of a well on her desk. She fiddled with it, still staring at me in mixed fascination and horror.

I'd seen that look before. Avid eyes, repelled yet drawn to me, as if I had smallpox or measles or both pockmarking my skin.

"So I'd like to pay my respects." Ryan would want to know about this. He'd already texted me a few times this morning. And Tucker would practically neigh in excitement when I told him I'd almost worked side by side with Lawrence, if he ever answered his phone.

Still, this wasn't an investigation. It was about honouring the dead.

"I don't know. Oh, my goodness. I'll have to speak to Dr. Zinser," said Susan.

"No problem."

She glanced at the clock screensaver on her desktop. "The meeting's starting at eleven. I'll have to see if I can discuss this, and maybe you'll have time to get your badge before the meeting."

"At eleven?" I cheered up. I was early?

"We changed the time because of the … change in topic." She kept sneaking glances at me. My hands. My neck. She wanted to look at my face, but when I made eye contact with her, she dropped her gaze and reached for the phone. "Excuse me."

"Of course." I backed away from her desk.

After a minute, she glanced over my shoulder and nodded.

I swivelled. Tom waved at me from his entourage, and I started heading toward him. He wasn't much taller than my five-foot-two, and probably not older than his 40's, but he had the same kind of prematurely white hair that plagued my mother's side of the family, along with pleasant features and a ready smile.

I wiggled my way into his circle and half-waved at the rest of the crowd before I turned to the big dog. "Hi, Dr. Zinser, I'm Dr. Hope Sze, the resident doctor starting in your lab today—"

"I know who you are. Welcome, Hope, and please call me Tom." He glanced at the rest of the circle. "This is a crazy day. You should go get your ID card and parking pass." He ran a hand through the hair above his ears, looking distracted.

A very pretty woman with pale skin, Asian eyes, and a big rack said, "I still can't believe it. Are we sure about this? Is everyone sure?"

I pressed my lips together. Out of the corner of my eyes, I could see Susan closing in on me, ready to foist me on the parking pass people.

"It was on the CBC this morning," said a white guy in a ragged Strumbellas T-shirt and sweatpants. Unruly brown hair, sandals over socks even though it was December. He was cute in a pothead sort of way, except his brown eyes missed nothing.

"Yes, but did they ID him?" said the Asian-esque woman.

I reached for Tom's sleeve. He turned toward me, and I said, "I'm a physician. Maybe I could help more here."

Tom shook his head and signalled Susan, who led me back toward the door and said, "Everyone's very upset today, dear. It would be better if you got some of the administrative work done first."

I couldn't help feeling that they were blaming me. *She's a doctor. Why didn't she save him?* I opened my mouth to explain, or apologize, or defend myself.

Susan read my mind and pressed her warm, soft hand on my arm. "No one's blaming you, Hope. Now that you told me, I'm glad that a medical person found him. But we still feel responsible. We're going to take a few minutes to remember him now."

Right. That was exactly what this "medical person" wanted to do, too. Find out who Lawrence was, what he was like, and how he might've ended up with a garbage bag over his head.

Wait. No. I meant, I wanted to honour his memory. I swallowed hard. "Susan." It still felt weird to call grown-ups by their first name, but I fought the embarrassment, because this was important, and I wanted her to think of me as an equal. "I know this sounds strange, but I would like to stay for that. I won't say anything if you don't want me to. It's just, I couldn't do anything for him when I found him. The least I can do is listen to his story now."

Susan sighed and glanced back at Tom. "Dr. Zinser and Dr. Hay might find it very crowded in the conference room."

I was halfway in. I knew it. Sometimes, it's easier to charm the gatekeeper's gatekeeper. I smiled sweetly and let Susan return to Tom's side to do her magic. She returned, shaking her head, and said, "He said you could bring the Timbits. It's a tradition for students to take turns bringing the food to lab meetings."

Timbits are doughnut holes, cheap and ubiquitous food in the ER. "Should I get a box of fifty?"

"Maybe, to be safe," she said, and I rushed back out the door to the elevators. I'd have to phone Susan to let me in without a badge, but that and Timbits were a small price to pay. I should have brought some on the first day as a pre-emptive "thank you for having me." Shoot. I'm really bad at stuff like that.

Twenty minutes later, Susan got first crack at the box of Timbits. She bent over, wincing a little. Ouch. I never want to get old. I noticed that she chose the glazed strawberry cake ones that are one of my favourites. The jelly ones can get messy, and the chocolates don't actually taste like chocolate.

Susan guided me into a conference room on the left where maybe a dozen people milled around, holding cups of coffee and looking serious. Most of them were my age, or within a decade, so the older ones stuck out. Tom, with his white hair. A sixty-ish-year-old Chinese man wearing a shiny grey suit, whose eyes immediately went to the box of Timbits before he shook his head, dismissing them. A slim white lady, of about the same vintage, in a white pants suit, classy and intimidating, with sharp brown eyes. When she saw me, she frowned, Timbits notwithstanding.

Susan murmured, "Dr. Judith Hay is the head of virology. I'll introduce you."

We made our way toward the pantsuited Dr. Hay. I could hear Susan breathing heavily beside me, and I slowed down my walk for her. We weaved through the crowd as Dr. Hay watched us, a small wrinkle between her eyebrows. Like Tom, her hair was pure white, but hers was cut into a severe bob. In contrast to her white separates, she was wearing well-polished black shoes with a low heel. I moved to shake her hand, belatedly remembering the box in my hands, which I set on the oval faux-mahogany table, along with a small pile of paper napkins.

Dr. Hay shook my hand firmly, but she was studying my face and listening to my name. She said, "Doctor Sze." She pronounced it like the letter C, which was close enough. "You were the one who found him."

"I did," I said, fighting the urge to cross my arms behind my back.

She tilted her head. Unlike Tom, her knee jerk response wasn't to banish me. She thought I was an interesting specimen. "We'll have to talk," she said. "Thank you, Susan."

Dr. Hay shoved the box of Timbits toward the centre of the table and clapped her hands. "Is everybody present? It's eleven o'clock."

There weren't enough seats, so I stood against a wall while most of the people got a chair at the table, Tom and the older Chinese man among them. A few more sank into the chairs against the wall, including the half-Asian woman, who got a chair that was too close to the screen. The Strumbellas guy got a better chair, off to her left.

Dr. Hay raised her voice. "This was supposed to be a lab meeting, but today we'll hold a memorial. As most of you know, we lost one of our members most tragically yesterday."

She touched the laptop next to her, and the projector sprang to life, showing a picture of a handsome young man, probably in his late twenties like me, although sometimes it's hard to tell with black skin. As one of my black friends put it, "Black don't crack and Asian don't raisin."

Lawrence's hair was cropped close to the skull. He had direct brown eyes, espresso skin, a broad nose, and an elegant neck. He wasn't smiling, but he was handsome in a "can't touch this" sort of a way, which is like Kryptonite to some women. Even I found it hard to look away from his picture.

"Dr. Lawrence Acayo was born in Uganda. He had obtained his undergraduate degree from Oxford and a Ph.D. from Stanford University. He had begun post-doctoral work at Sunshine University in Miami before we recruited him. You may be familiar with his research with Dr. Kanade involving the pathologic avian H5N1 influenza viruses."

Hang on. "Pathologic" meant deadly. And "avian" meant bird. Dr. Acayo was working on bird flu? I didn't know that. Of course, I didn't know who he was until this morning.

"He was also extremely proud to be part of Dr. Kanade's team as they generated new viruses combining the H5 haemagglutinin gene with the pandemic 2009 H1N1 influenza virus's remaining genes."

My brain fuzzed out as soon as she said haemagglutinin, but I did remember that outbreak of "swine flu." Six people died in the Ottawa area, including a brilliant chemistry professor.

My neck prickled. Dr. Acayo wasn't a random Ph.D. He was someone who'd researched deadly viruses. Coincidence, or something that had caused his death?

I didn't get up and yell about it, because not only was that deeply uncool, but everyone else was nodding like this was par. Yeah, yeah, killer viruses, whatevs. One of the guys started rummaging in the Timbit box.

My heart rate slowed down a tad while I surveyed their faces. There's a study showing that most of us respond to a situation based on other people's reactions. In that study, they simulated smoke, and if you were alone, you would report a potential fire, but if other people in the room seemed calm, you would subconsciously assume it was okay, even if the smoke was so hazy that you couldn't make out their faces. By the same token, if this group thought killer viruses were normal, I couldn't help thinking I should chill out.

Dr. Hay was still talking. "Lawrence arrived in September. He said he wasn't looking forward to his first Canadian winter."

Everyone laughed politely. I remembered the sheen of his jacket. He hadn't had a chance to wear it much before he'd died.

"In the spirit of diversity, Ottawa University chose Dr. Acayo as part of their Students of the World campaign. They made the following video and said we could play it in his honour."

I had to smile when she cued up the cheesy music and intro, but I sobered when Lawrence looked at the camera and said, "Coming to Ottawa University is a dream come true."

It was the first time I'd seen him alive and moving. He was better-looking than in his picture. He was one of those people who wasn't only the sum of his facial features. His animation, his personality and intelligence, made me sit up straighter, especially when he cracked a smile.

A male narrator intoned, "Ottawa University is thrilled to welcome Lawrence to our virology lab, headed by Dr. Judith Hay," while the video showed Lawrence suited up in the lab with safety glasses and a lab coat, using a pipette, which is sort of like a fancy needleless syringe used to measure liquid precisely and transport it within the lab.

Then the video switched to Lawrence accepting an award from an older white guy wearing ceremonial robes, probably Lawrence's Ph.D. graduation.

Now Lawrence stared at the camera directly. "When I was a little boy in Kampala, I dreamed about doing this kind of research while making a safe home for my family."

I sat up straighter. He had a family? Did he mean his family of origin, or—

Nope. The camera cut to a black woman with a good-sized 'fro, a look I love. She beamed at the camera and said, "We love Canada. It's so safe."

I flinched. That's the stereotype. But it wasn't safe for Lawrence. Did she regret coming here? What was happening to her? Even if she wanted to work here, she might not have the right visa, and now her husband was dead.

I heard a murmur from the doorway and turned. People were whispering and glancing at a figure less than fifteen feet away. Two people got up and blocked my view, but I glimpsed a black woman advancing slowly but purposefully toward us.

CHAPTER 9

The woman didn't look like an obvious threat, but Susan was hurrying toward her, trying to catch her arm and slow her down.

The audience glanced at the scene behind us rather than at the video.

Dr. Hay's phone buzzed. She reached for it to read a text. Her shoulders stiffened. She swivelled around in her chair and stood up.

I edged toward the back of the room. Toward the door. True, it meant I was moving closer to the intruder, but I was also three steps closer to freedom. A crucial difference when you've been trapped with a lunatic before.

Someone stopped the video. Another turned on the lights.

The intruder woman reared back on her heels at the fluorescent beam, but she leaned forward again, glaring at the entire room from the doorway. I was close enough that I could see the sheen of sweat on her face, and I thought, *Angry*. No, that word wasn't strong enough.

She was clearly Lawrence's wife. Her onscreen face was frozen with her eyes closed, but the resemblance to the live woman was unmistakable: round face even rounder in real life, big, beautiful eyes, chocolate skin (lighter than Lawrence's, but not an extreme difference, if you care about that kind of stuff). She was wearing a long, loose midnight blue dress that covered her arms and trailed the ground, but her salt-stained black boots poked out the bottom, which gave me a jolt of recognition.

Susan reached the doorway a minute later, mouthing her apologies, although we were all watching Mrs. Acayo, who said, in a loud, rolling, musical voice, "*Thank* you."

No one replied. Why was she thanking us, when she was clearly one step away from going postal?

"Thank you, Dr. Hay, for inviting me to this tribute you set up for my husband. Of course, I didn't receive the invitation until only forty minutes ago."

Dr. Hay walked across the room and reached for Mrs. Acayo's shoulder, although her hand fell away before she made contact. "I apologize for that. We decided to turn this lab meeting into a tribute, as you say, but it took a while for my assistant to find your contact information. Would you like to join us?" She gestured toward her own seat, her red nails catching the light, and Tom, the pothead guy, and half a dozen other people immediately stood up to offer her theirs. Chair legs scraped across the linoleum floor in a blunt chorus.

Mrs. Acayo surveyed the room, studying our faces. She paused on mine, startling me. I was a no-name lab temporary worker standing against a wall. Why would I interest her?

Her eyes narrowed, gauging my reaction, and I remembered how transparent I'd felt in front of the police officers. I would have to learn how to mask my feelings if I was going to survive.

I took a deeeeeeeeeep breath, squared my shoulders, and tried to look sympathetic, respectful, and like I had nothing to hide.

Mrs. Acayo inspected me for another beat before she analyzed the next face. And the next.

Some people's hands twitched as she scrutinized us. Pothead and DemiAsian exchanged a quick side glance. Mrs. Acayo was making us all uncomfortable, but you can't stop a widow from doing whatever she wants on the day after her husband dies.

Tom gestured at his chair again, but Mrs. Acayo tromped toward Dr. Hay's and held on both chair arms as she sank into it, her breath escaping in a soft sigh.

Tom offered his chair to Dr. Hay, which made me like the guy. Still, I felt a bit uncomfortable when he migrated toward the back wall to stand closer to me.

I sidled over to make room for him.

Tom smiled at me. I tried to smile back.

Mrs. Acayo reached for Dr. Hay's Mac laptop, which gave us another collective shudder—*thou shalt not touch thy neighbour's computer without permission*—and pressed play on the video.

Mrs. Acayo's onscreen image opened her eyes and smiled before to/she said, "I heard you can go skating on the river. Lawrence and I can't wait."

I bit the inside of my lip, where I thought no one could see. Of course Lawrence could and did wait. Forever. Lawrence would never lace up a pair of skates and glide on the iced-over Ottawa River, and even if Mrs. Acayo made it there, she wouldn't be holding hands with her dead husband, unless we were speaking figuratively.

While the closing credits sang a chorus for Ottawa University and diversity, Mrs. Acayo shut off the video and plunked back into her seat. Her spine slumped before she yanked herself upright.

Dr. Hay did her best to pat her on the shoulder. "Would you— would you like a Timbit?"

Someone laughed and tried to stifle it, but Dr. Hay glared around the room so ferociously that we all fell silent.

Tom cleared his throat. "Refreshments would be a good idea. Perhaps some coffee?"

DemiAsian rose to pour a cup for Mrs. Acayo. A short, Middle Eastern-looking guy laid a napkin out for her. The older Asian man opened the Timbit box and placed it in front of her without actually forcing her to take one. I stood by the wall, waiting for it to be over, until Mrs. Acayo said, "I don't understand what happened."

"It does seem to be a mystery," said Dr. Hay, who looked like she'd rather be researching frog spawn.

"He was supposed to come home. He was working here. He texted me to say he'd be late. He never came home." The hurt in her voice transfixed us. DemiAsian stood by her side, not wanting to interrupt by setting the cup of coffee down.

"I made supper for him. He loves to eat, even though he's so skinny. He told me he could buy some Creole food on his way home. I said, 'Don't be silly. I make food that is better and more healthy and cheaper. Just come on home.'" She pushed against the table. Her voice rose plaintively on the last word.

I was calculating. If she was making supper for Lawrence, she probably expected him home anywhere from five to eight p.m. It was possible that they dined late, but probably not around 9:45, which was when we found his body.

How long had he been missing?

Were the police interviewing Mrs. Acayo? I've heard they always ask the partner first, and she did seem a little off, although grief can make you deranged. I should know.

"My friends want me to stay home and drink tea." As if that were a cue, DemiAsian placed the coffee in front of Mrs. Acayo and stepped backward. Mrs. Acayo gave her a level look that was neither thankful nor accusing. More assessing.

DemiAsian blushed. She was paler-skinned than me, so the vasodilation was more obvious. I noticed her slightly sharp nose, another inheritance from her white side, before she crossed her arms over her most impressive asset, her D-cups. (I had to guess at the measurements, but they were certainly at least four times my size.)

Mrs. Acayo shook her head and turned back to Dr. Hay, sagging into her seat again. "I can't stay home. I want to help."

Of course her husband was beyond help, but I sympathized. When I wasn't completely drained and numb with shock/grief/PTSD, I got these weird bursts of energy. Agitation, my therapist, Denis, called it. I tried to explain to Denis that I was always like that, that was how I got through med school, but mostly, he told me to breeeeeeeeeathe, which sounds even funnier with a French accent.

Tom said, "Maybe you could meet some friends. Or there might be a bereavement organization through the hospital or university."

Dr. Hay stood up. "Excellent idea. I'll contact them immediately." She cut out of the room so swiftly that I felt the breeze on my skin. She did not make eye contact with me or anyone else.

I shifted my weight from one foot to another. Presumably Ottawa did have some sort of bereavement program, but how fast could they get here? In the meantime, were we all going to sit here with Mrs. Acayo? It was only 11:22, but felt like aeons.

"Perhaps," Tom said slowly, "one of our members could stay with you and make you feel more at ease."

I stopped shifting. There was only one superfluous person at his lab. The one who'd already been told she should go off and get her passes instead of working.

I understood his logic. There was no point in keeping two entire labs stuck in a meeting room. Better to have one person play babysitter.

Did he know I was the one who'd found Lawrence? Only if Susan had passed him the memo.

First Tom looked at DemiAsian, who shook her head minutely.

Pothead coughed; he didn't look too nurturing.

Next was a white guy with what I call Jesus hair, long and wavy and brown and past his shoulders, as well as eyes set a little far apart and a slightly blank expression. He didn't seem to recognize what Tom was asking for.

The Chinese man, who looked to be in his sixties, pushed his glasses up his nose. His grey suit had an unfashionable sheen to it, but that and his neatly-knotted red tie seemed to declare a lack of interest even before he gave a short but definitive head-shake.

The short, handsome, Middle Eastern-looking man stood up. He wore a kind smile, and I liked the way his purple tie contrasted with his black suit. "I can help. My name is Dr. Samir Al-Sani. I work at Dr. Zinser's laboratory, next door to Dr. Hay."

Mrs. Acayo grabbed the table so hard that her fingertips blanched. "Who are you?"

"I'm Dr. Al-Sani. Samir," he repeated, but he was glancing at Tom, uncertain. "I'm a post-doctoral fellow and recent recipient of the Banting and Best Postdoctoral Fellowship for my work on Lymphangioleiomyomatosis."

I wanted to laugh. Poor guy. Even with a widow, he had to trot out his academic credentials. But I'd stayed silent long enough. I might be the only person in the room who knew what it felt like to have death stalk people on either side of me.

I crossed the floor to Mrs. Acayo's right side, the side with the cooling coffee. I took my time and made noise so that she could hear me coming.

She turned slightly toward me, her hands falling off the table and into her lap.

I said, "We're very sorry for your loss. My name is Hope Sze."

Her eyes homed in on me. She slowly observed the landscape of my face, noting my brow, my eyes, my lips, my chin. I wasn't sure what she was searching for, but I let her examine me in silence. I had nothing to hide.

At last, when her eyes returned to mine, I said, "I started working at the lab today, so I hadn't met your husband here"—I stumbled a little on the last word. I hadn't met him alive and in the lab, was what I meant—"but that was a lovely video you did with him. I bet you would have liked to skate on the canal together."

She opened her mouth. I braced for her first words, like, *I know who you are. Why didn't you save my husband's life?*

I could practically feel the rest of the room eavesdropping. At long last, she said, "Do you know my name?"

"No." Now that she mentioned it, her name might not even be Mrs. Acayo. Do most Ugandan women change their name after marriage? "Sorry."

"My name is Immaculate Joan Acayo."

Wait. Her name was *Immaculate?* I sometimes groaned at my parents for naming me Hope, but this was light years worse. Even Joan makes me think of Joan Rivers or Joan Crawford or some other poor, old, and perhaps deceased American celebrity with her face yanked up by plastic surgery.

"You can call me Joan." She rubbed her belly underneath her shift dress.

"Thanks." I didn't know if I could call her Immaculate with a straight face. I felt sorry enough for the kids from Immaculata High School. I decided to change the subject while everyone else filed out of the room past Tom, who kept an eye on us from the doorway.

"Your name gives me great comfort. I think God is giving me a sign, Doctor Hope."

Human Remains

Uh oh. I'm not religious, although Ryan is, and plenty of people have tried to convert me since 14/11. I swerved around the subject. "You can call me Hope. Unless you want me to call you Mrs. Joan?"

It sounded silly, and we both laughed before she shook her head again. "I am a widow now. I prefer not to be reminded of my status."

"Yes. Naturally. Of course." I'd started imitating her formal way of talking. I'd have to stop, or she might think I was making fun of her.

"Are you Christian?"

I'm not used to people being so up front about it, but maybe this was a cultural thing. Plus, she'd probably have been in recent touch with the clergy. I shook my head.

"That is too bad. My church is wonderful, such a help. I can bring you on Sunday, and you can meet everyone."

"No, thank you." This was absolutely surreal to me. Her husband died yesterday, but her first priority was to recruit me for her church?

"Maybe next Sunday," she said.

I stifled a laugh and shook my head again. "If I ever want to go to church, my boyfriend has me covered," I said, before I realized that it was a pretty slang-y way of putting things, and I might have to explain better. Leaving out the part that I had more than one boyfriend, and was therefore pretty much the opposite of what she was looking for.

Her forehead crinkled. She said, "Is his church born-again?"

"No."

"Ah." She smiled at me and reached for my hands with both of hers. Her plump hands felt slightly damp. "You should be born again. It is not enough to go to any church. You must accept Jesus Christ into your heart, as your own personal saviour."

OMG. I knew it was almost Christmas, and her husband had died yesterday, but this was too much. My cheeks flushed, and I knew I couldn't fake a smile for one more minute. "I'm so sorry for your loss. Please accept my condolences." I stood up and spun away from her. Everyone else had left. Even Tom had begun migrating back into the lab.

She said, "Doctor Hope. Doctor Hope!" Joan's booming yet musical voice halted me and drowned out the buzz of the departing people's conversation.

I locked in place, hunched over my plastic chair.

Everyone in the doorway, including Tom, wheeled around to stare at us.

I sank back into the chair, letting its metal legs take my weight. I couldn't abandon the grieving widow. "What is it, Joan?"

Her grip tightened. The strength in her fingers reminded me of Lawrence's cool, stiffening hand, though, and I tried not to let my face betray me before she said, "I like you."

"Oh." I couldn't honestly say that I liked her back. I didn't even know the woman. I struggled to come up with the correct response. Among everything else, 14/11 had destroyed any aptitude for witty banter.

"You are different. You are supposed to cry with me, or ask me how I am going to make it back to Uganda. Instead, you are a doctor who asks me to call you by your first name, and you get angry when I offer to bring you to church to thank you. You are a very different woman, Doctor Hope."

I could see what she meant. "Um, thank you?"

Her smile widened. She had perfectly straight, white teeth. I bet she didn't even bleach them. Did they do bleach in Uganda? For sure they did in Miami. Distracted by her dentition, I almost missed her next pronouncement: "I am going to bring you to dinner. You and your Christian boyfriend."

"Oh. No. Ryan doesn't want—"

"His name is Ryan. Good. What kind of food limitations do you have?"

It took me a second to realize that she meant food allergies or preferences. "Well, I'm sort of vegetarian right now."

Joan raised her eyebrows at me. I realized that was a wussy way of putting it, so I said, more loudly, "I'm vegetarian."

"Is he vegetarian also?"

"Ryan? No."

"Good. I will make a variety of foods. It is no problem. In Uganda, many people eat a vegetable diet, and I know many tasty dishes."

"No, Joan, I don't want you cooking for us. Your husband passed away. I want you to rest and … " What the hell are you supposed to do when your husband dies? Wear black, veil optional, and weep a lot over the flowers your friends send?

Joan shook her head. "I am a woman of action, Doctor Hope. I refuse to sit idle. You and your Ryan will come to my house and eat delicious food. I can even serve drinks. I, myself, don't drink alcohol, but I have no objection to those who do."

"I don't drink much either," I said, relieved that we had something in common.

"Then it is settled. You will come to our apartment. It is small," she added, after a moment, "but it is comfortable. Give me your phone. I will add myself as a contact."

Bemused, I passed over my iPhone, and she did, even adding a thumbnail selfie before handing it back.

"Now. What is your number? I would like you to come over tomorrow evening."

Well, I'd like to, but I'd be too busy wanting to rip my own skin off. "Won't you be busy, ah, making arrangements?"

"Lawrence would want me to have you over. I have already spoken to the police and the funeral home. We will be having a ceremony on Sunday, and I would like you to come to that, too, with your Ryan."

My Ryan. I liked the sound of that, even as I protested. "Oh, but you'll be so busy. You'll want to be with your friends, perhaps go to church, getting ready for the … memorial."

Her face burned with some sort of emotion that made me take a step back, but soon she was smiling again so brightly that I must've been mistaken. She said, "One way I keep my sanity is through cooking, Doctor Hope. I want to cook for you and Ryan."

"You want me to make something? Or bring drinks?"

She shook her head. "If I am too tired to cook, I will serve casseroles. People are bringing casseroles that are—" She shook her head, and I laughed in recognition. I ate a lot of cafeteria casseroles when I was a student.

It was official. Ryan and I had a date with Lawrence's widow tomorrow night.

Chapter 10

"Do you know what CRISPR is?" said Tom, once we'd returned to his office. He had the biggest, U-shaped desk I'd ever seen. The side closest to him was stacked in papers, but the visitor's side was completely clean.

I perched in the visitor's chair. "Yes. At least I understand the concept of cutting genetic code with 'scissors' made of clustered regularly interspaced short palindromic repeats."

"And do you know how CRISPR is revolutionizing research?"

Not much. "I know that this technique is a faster, cheaper, and more precise way to cut a gene sequence than we've ever had before. I know that once you cut out the sequence you don't want, all you have to do is plant another sequence you do want, and the bacteria will help mend it by replacing the bad sequence."

"That's fair. What articles have you read?"

"Some basic ones." I wondered if I should admit that I'd mostly listened to a Radiolab podcast about CRISPR, pronounced crisper. They'd explained how bacteria used CRISPR like a mug shot of their enemy viruses, and now humans were using CRISPR for their own needs.

"I'll send you some links. You're going to fit in fine." Tom stood and reached for the doorknob of the pale wooden door behind his desk. It opened directly into his lab, a large room filled with black lab benches. He waited for me to enter, so I did, and he said to my back, "Next time, you'll have to tell me about finding Lawrence, though."

I whirled around, my mouth gaping.

He gave me a slight smile and closed the door.

My heart still beating erratically, I checked out my surroundings. Like my high school chem lab, it had black lab benches made out of some sort of plastic-y material that resists chemical spills, set up in rows for people to work on.

But the room was a lot bigger than my high school's. Like the size of a big swimming pool—not an Olympic pool, but a nice, big rectangular pool that you could swim decent-sized laps in. And the whole wall on the left was made up of windows, which meant everyone had a window office, and was significantly nicer than working in the fluorescent-only dungeons of an emergency department.

The lab wall on the right had two doors that led to the hallway, both locked with card-scanners, which was higher-tech than my high school. They also seemed to have significantly more storage. Every lab bench was stacked with open shelving that could be accessed by people working on either side of the bench, and seemed to hold a lot of glass flasks, labeled boxes, and other equipment I couldn't identify, although the person with the closest lab bench had a Domo-kun stuffed animal on an upper shelf and a name plate that said Summer.

The wall behind me, the one shared with Tom's office, was covered by a fume hood and some refrigerators. The far wall opposite us opened into another, smaller room, and I could make out another fume hood, refrigerator-like things with electrical panels, and freezers along the most distant wall.

So, my high school chem lab, but with a ton more equipment, and people who actually knew what they were doing. Nice.

One of the hallway sensors flicked green. A door was cracking open. A man's voice drifted in.

"He made a lot of enemies."

"Enemies is a strong word." Another guy's voice. Lower. More controlled.

Interesting. But probably something they didn't want overheard. Where should I go? The lab was filled with rows of black benches, yet I belatedly realized that Tom hadn't assigned me one. He'd quizzed me on CRISPR and drop-kicked me into this gigantic room.

Susan had handed me a folder on lab safety and told me to run some computer modules on the subject for the next two days, but she hadn't shown me which computer to use before she'd gone to lunch.

"Come on. You know he did." The first guy raised his voice.

"No—"

I was standing a metre away from the door into Tom's office, between the glass-fronted fume hood and the first lab bench. I took two steps forward, beside a white refrigerator, and then Pothead and Jesus spotted me from the closest hallway door.

Jesus, the one with the long hair and the softer voice, immediately shut his mouth. His real name was Chris, which was pretty easy to remember because it was so close to Christ. Jesus Chris shot off to the other end of the lab, furthest from Tom's office, without another word.

Pothead stood in the doorway, studying me from underneath his long eyebrows. His rumpled appearance didn't mean he was dumb. As a matter of fact, it probably meant he was one of the smarter people here, because he didn't have to prove himself. His badge said Mitch Lubian.

I stared back, trying to look professional and aloof.

"What's your name again?"

"I'm Hope Sze, a resident in family medicine from Montreal. You can pronounce it like the letter C—"

"Sze," he said, with a pretty good inflection. "I know who you are."

I tried not to take a step back, but I blinked.

"You're the doctor who found Lawrence and messed up the crime scene."

Now my face was flaming, and I was on the defensive. "I was trying to save his life. One of the causes of pulselessness is hypothermia, and you have to do CPR until you know that he's warm and dead. So I started CPR. I wasn't trying to mess up the crime scene."

He held up his palms at me. "Hey, I'm not a medical doctor. I'm not going to tell you how to do your job."

Like hell. I switched subjects. "And how do you know all that, anyway?"

"I know a lot of things," he said, and smirked.

Human Remains

The smirk did it. He was a pretty good-looking guy, but a know-it-all sets me off. "Yeah? Like the fact that Lawrence had a lot of enemies?"

His turn to draw back. The calculating look returned. His brown eyes were intense under a heavy forehead. The fact that he had a little stubble growing on his face, and heavy sideburns, didn't endear him to me. "I could have been talking about anyone."

"Give me a break. He died under bizarre circumstances. Of course you're talking about him."

After a second, he walked forward and clapped his hand on my shoulder.

His hand felt like warm meat through the thin cotton of my shirt. My brain jumped back to the memory of another sweaty, unwanted hand on me, circa 14/11, and bared my teeth like a wolverine before stepping away so that his hand fell toward the ground and off my shoulder.

He said, "You're strange. I like you."

Right. "Thanks," I said. I could have told him likewise, but I try not to lie, and I definitely felt lukewarm about him. "Did you know Lawrence pretty well, then?"

He said, "Hey, who didn't know Lawrence?" His voice was much lighter, and louder, like he wanted Chris to hear. "Dr. Hay considered it an honour that Dr. Acayo made it to our humble town. He could have stayed in Miami, 'making important contributions to the body of knowledge about the Influenza A virus, or embarking on a new course with the Zisa virus.'"

From his mocking tone of voice, I could tell Pothead was probably quoting Dr. Hay.

Chris made a sound from the back that was somewhere between a laugh, a snort, and a grunt.

"The Zisa virus?" I said, because that was the new bit I hadn't heard about. "I thought he was working with Dr. Kanade on influenza and bird flu."

"He was, as far as I know," said Mitch, "but he wrote new proposals about Zisa, too. Judith thought his ideas were 'magnificent.'"

Yep, bitterness. Something I'd have to unpack later. "Well, Zisa is the next big thing, right? I can understand wanting to work on that right now." The Zisa virus hardly causes any symptoms in 80 percent of infected people, who bop around, spreading the infection, mostly via the *Aedes aegypti* mosquito, but occasionally through intercourse or non-sexual close contact, since there was a case in Nevada over the summer where an elderly man with a high viral load spread it to his son, possibly through sweat or tears. The other 20 percent of people think they've got the regular flu's fever and achiness, with the extra bonus of a rash and conjunctivitis, and may not think to wear mosquito repellent before they act as a food source for more hungry mosquitoes.

Mitch looked sour. "Yeah, but why work on it here? All the resources are further south. If you want to be cutting edge, you either have to go to a big centre—John's Hopkins proved the link to Guillain-Barré—or you head right to Brazil or Columbia, where they don't have the funding, but they do have the patients."

"You'd go to Brazil if you wanted to study the children with microcephaly," I said. The true tragedy is that pregnant women pass Zisa on to their babies, who then go on to develop microcephaly, joint problems, and other congenital defects. "That's the sort of clinical study that I would do." Clinical basically means "study on people" as opposed to working with cells like they do here. Both of them are important. You have to start off with molecular genetics to figure out what works and how to do it, and then you move on to animal studies (I know, not my favourite thing, either, but a necessary evil) before testing it on humans. Doctors tend to do the clinical trials that are at the tip of the iceberg, as opposed to stem cells, unless they're M.D./Ph.D.'s.

I added, "Like you said, though, the money is in North America. What little money there is." The U.S. government balked at approving emergency Zisa funding, even though Puerto Rico, supposedly part of the U.S., was already hard-hit. Like George Orwell pointed out, some animals are more equal than others.

Pothead's eyes narrowed. "Don't kid yourself. The money is always in the U.S."

That, I couldn't argue with. As our former Prime Minister Pierre Elliot Trudeau pointed out, when the U.S. sneezes, Canada catches a cold. The reverse is true as well: when money boomed, it was in the States; when the oil wells dried up, Canada started crying first. And

Human Remains

since Miami was ground zero for Zisa's entry into the continental United States, you'd think Lawrence would have stayed.

One of the hall doors beeped. DemiAsian pushed it open. Her eyes immediately met mine, then Pothead's, before flicking back to my own. She marched up to me and held out her hand. "We haven't officially met. I'm Summer Holdt, Tom's research assistant."

Holdt, huh? So her mom was Asian and her dad was white. "Nice to meet you. I'm Hope Sze." I didn't bother explaining the pronunciation. She'd probably heard the name before.

"Welcome. If you have any questions about the lab safety training, let me know. We don't want you spilling DMSO everywhere. You'll be shadowing me for most of the first week." She turned to Pothead. "Mitch, are you harassing Hope already?"

Mitch shrugged. "Just saying hi."

Chris snorted again.

I was still trying to figure out what DMSO was. Something bad, obviously.

"I thought so," said Summer, putting her hands on her hips. She turned to me. "Have you been able to log onto the computers to figure out the lab safety courses? Or have you been too busy getting set up with payroll and your lab access card?"

"I haven't done any of that yet," I said.

"Time to get started." She gestured for me to move further into the lab, and I realized that she was a mother hen sort. This might come in handy in trying to figure out what was going on. Mitch/Pothead was a prickly guy, Chris didn't seem to interact much with people, and Tom was busy doing whatever a lab head does. Probably writing grants.

I needed someone who would talk, and Summer was her name-o.

I all but batted my eyelashes when I said, "Could you point me in the right direction? That would be awesome."

CHAPTER 11

"That was really nice of you, to make friends with Lawrence's widow," said Summer, taking the hospital stairs carefully beside me. She'd volunteered to show me the way to my passes, but she was wearing scarlet high heels, which made navigation more difficult amongst the throngs of scrub-clad workers and at least one elderly woman wearing a Fitbit. Personally, I only wear high heels for Christmas formals, and I kick them off after a few hours.

"She kind of made friends with me," I admitted.

"I'll talk to Tom about raising money for her situation. I mentioned it to Susan this morning, and she suggested I bring it up at the meeting, but—"

I nodded. Awkward to bring it up in front of Joan.

Summer lifted her hand off the rail. "It was good of you to reach out to her. I'm glad you're here."

"You are?"

"Yes! I'm the only woman. It gets lonely."

Working in medicine, I'm used to being surrounded by guys. Even though med school is over 50 percent women now, there are still plenty of times where I'm the only one with ovaries. But she was working with Tom, Chris/Jesus, Pothead/Mitch, the Middle Eastern guy who worked

Human Remains

on something unpronounceable, and the Chinese man I still hadn't met. "What about Dr. Hay?"

Summer laughed. "You must be joking. She's in the lab next door."

True. And yet, still only forty feet away.

When we reached the foot of the stairs, Summer pointed to the left and then paused. "I know you must be getting a lot of questions about this, but are you sure it was Lawrence?" She took a deep breath. "Especially if he had a bag over his head?"

It was a strange question. Not the ones I expected, which were more visceral: what did it look like, how did it feel. I said, "I didn't identify him. I—we—happened upon him. It was someone else who identified him later, probably the police."

Summer twisted away from me. When she turned back, her face was carefully neutral. "Of course. Sorry I bothered you."

"You didn't bother me," I said. "I mean, it's not like you're the media. I've had some of them calling me, especially this one guy, Jonathan Wexler. The police asked me to keep quiet, though. I guess it's like, if we have a case of sexual assault in the emergency department, we try not to interview them multiple times. We leave it to one person on the sexual assault team, so the story doesn't get told and retold in a way that looks bad in court." I paused. "But if it were the other way around, I would totally be asking you questions."

She smiled for what felt like the first time.

My turn to be intrusive. "Were you good friends with him?"

"Oh." She turned red and averted her eyes. "I didn't know him that well. He worked with Dr. Hay."

And yet that was not an answer. "Did you meet him at lab meetings?"

"Of course. Plus, we had a party in September, kind of a mixer, where I met his wife." Her eyes met mine again, guileless, but there was obviously something she wasn't telling me.

"Did you know what he was researching?"

"Sure. Dr. Kanade's work on influenza A is pretty famous. Or infamous."

"Is that your area, too?"

"No, I'm the research assistant at the stem cell lab, not virology. They've got their own R.A. I'm a jack of all trades, depending on what needs doing. Right now, I'm working on transplanting mesenchymal stem cells to reduce age-related osteoporosis in the mouse model. Dr. Hay is a virologist. She recruited Stephen Weaver from the University of Southern California, Davis."

"Hang on. Who's Stephen Weaver?"

"You don't know about his work on Rift Valley disease?"

Hell. I'd never even heard of Rift Valley disease. You don't have to know much about infectious diseases to pass med school in a very cold country where people don't travel or emigrate a ton. "Was Stephen Weaver at the meeting?"

"Yes. He's the guy with glasses. Tall, skinny, very short hair, in his 30s, kind of looks like Steve Jobs but with a plaid shirt?"

I scanned through my memory. I couldn't remember anyone like that. It bugged me. I like to at least look at everyone in the room. Part of my control freak OCD since 14/11. I feel like I'm safer if I've sussed out the danger. Of course, her description wasn't exactly stand-out.

I wanted to pull out my phone and look him up, but first I turned sideways to avoid a bunch of students with hot coffee in their hands. "Did Stephen know Lawrence before coming here?"

Her eyes widened. "I'm not sure. Why do you ask?"

"They were both in California, right? Lawrence was at Stanford." I didn't know state geography well, but I knew that much, and that virology probably isn't that big a world.

She made a face. "I have no idea. I guess they knew each other pretty well after working together for a month, especially with the funding—" She bit her lip.

I gave her a questioning glance.

"I shouldn't have said anything."

"What happened to the funding?" I said. I'm not good at beating around the bush.

"Well, I don't know much about it. Lawrence was supposed to have independent funding when he came here, but it might have dried up. Dr. Hay was going to look into using some of her overall lab funds to make up the difference." Now she was seriously chewing her lip. "I'm not supposed to know anything about it."

"I won't gossip. I don't even know anyone here," I said, but my mind was whirling. The little I knew about research is that funding sucks. It was never great—governments chip away at things that don't have big voting power and don't pay off immediately—but it's gotten so bad that some scientists have taken to Kickstarter and other crowdfunding sites to get work done.

Was that a motivation to kill someone? I didn't think so. None of the lab people struck me as murderers. But then, of the killers I've met, almost none of them looked wacko from the start. It's kind of like a pulmonary embolism: you have to keep a high index of suspicion because they can be silent killers.

In fact, I found myself looking at Summer a little differently already. She was a few inches taller than me, a bit more muscular, and nimble enough to navigate in high heels. I couldn't imagine her overpowering a full-grown man, but maybe that was part of the point. How had someone managed to incapacitate Lawrence and possibly suffocate him?

It was a bit like a chicken and egg. Which came first, death or the bag? Did someone kill Lawrence and then put a bag over his head, or put the bag on first and wait for him to die?

Or was it all suicide?

That would be tragic. Heartbreaking. Eviscerating. But it didn't necessarily mean another person was responsible and had to be held to account.

Was he drunk or on drugs when he ended up in the ditch? That was the most likely explanation. Then it wouldn't take a whole lot of strength to incapacitate someone. I remembered knocking a teenager out with Propofol. She slurred, "*That* is some *good* shit." After I popped her shoulder back in its socket, she sat up and said "Thank you!"

With Ketamine, they don't thank you. Their pain is not their own. They may have their eyes open, theoretically watching you, but their focus is somewhere over the rainbow in Wonderland, and they don't care what you're doing to their arm or leg.

Personally, I like to give both Ketamine and Propofol together. Some people call it Ketofol.

"Did Lawrence like to party? Like drink or take drugs?" I asked. If anyone would know, it would be another young person. Maybe not a work colleague, but it didn't hurt to ask. Also, I'd better change the subject away from grants and revisit it another time.

"Oh, yeah." She laughed before she caught herself. "Well, I don't know."

Which one was it? Instead of arguing, I said, "What did he take?"

She shook her head. "I don't know. He asked, but I'm not really into the club scene."

I didn't believe her. She seemed like she could party to me. Which meant that she wasn't telling me the whole truth. I couldn't take anything she said as gospel, but at least she was willing to talk. There's a fairy tale about the princess who lies all the time, the princess who tells the truth every time, and the princess who only lies about her family. I was pretty sure I'd met the one who lies part-time, but I'd have to compare stories to make sure.

Summer glanced around and said, "I'll tell you later. You'll have to buy me a drink first."

A small price to pay. "After work?"

"Yes! We usually go out on someone's first day."

So they must have gone out on Lawrence's first day. That made me feel bittersweet. I pushed it aside, along with the fact that I was already feeling slightly poor after the Timbits. "Where should we go?"

"Petra's. It's a tradition."

"Okay." So I looked at an agenda like this: 1. Go out with Summer and possibly the rest of the crew, 2. Drag Ryan to a dinner party with the widow tomorrow, plus the omnipresent 3. Worry about Tucker.

I paused. It felt like the breath got sucked out of my lungs and bronchial tree.

I was doing it again.

I'd left Montreal and Tucker and detective work, but as soon as I came across a dead body, boom. Back to my old tricks.

"Are you okay?" said Summer. "We're almost there."

Like my problem was walking for ten minutes down a hospital corridor. I nodded, unable to speak for a second. We'd ended up next to the gift shop selling balloons, so I stood there for a minute, studying the Mylar "Get Well Soon!" rainbow bubble and the "It's a Boy!" and "It's a Girl!" blue and pink circles like they were ancient scrolls.

Breeeathe.

Summer still looked concerned, but slightly eager. *I met the new girl, and she was so nuts, let me tell you …*

My phone rang. I seized it. Tucker?

No. It was an unfamiliar 613 area code number. A local caller, but not my parents or Ryan. Still, it was better than the pity and curiosity mingled on Summer's face, so I pushed on Accept. "Hi, this is Dr. Hope Sze." I'm used to identifying myself because I get so many calls from the hospital, and most of them don't pronounce my name right.

A woman's voice said, "Hello, Dr. Zee. This is the coroner's office."

CHAPTER 12

"The coroner?" I repeated, in a strangled voice, and Summer pivoted toward me, nearly sparkling with excitement.

I took two steps backward, so I was now beside the display of wide-eyed stuffed animals. I lowered my voice and turned away from Summer. "Uh, yes?"

"Dr. Koja would like to interview you about your experience last night."

"Dr. Koja," I repeated. It's a stalling tactic, and not a great one.

"Yes, Dr. Koja is the coroner taking charge of this case."

"The coroner—" Of course this was a coroner's case. It was a suspicious death. My throat tightened. I couldn't speak anymore.

The secretary sighed. "Dr. Koja is a medical doctor who has special training in death scene investigation. She would like to speak to you as soon as possible." The secretary obviously thought that I was questioning Dr. Koja's credentials, which was better than impeding the investigation, but not by much.

"Um, I'm at the research lab near Ottawa U this month."

"She can meet you there. It shouldn't take more than half an hour."

Half an hour! That sounded like forever to me. If I spent half an hour with an ER patient, the staff doctor would knock on the door and ask if I'd drowned in there. Unless I was trapped with a psycho hostage-taker. That's a different skill set.

"I'm doing my orientation today. I won't be able to meet her."

Summer watched me, her eyebrows dancing. *A coroner wanting to quiz Hope! O Happy Day!* "You can take time off from lab safety. Most of the stuff is online," she said, but I shook my head and tuned into the tinny voice.

"Dr. Koja can adapt to your schedule. She can even meet you, since you're located close to the scene. How about Thursday at 1 p.m.?"

"I'll have to talk to the lab supervisor."

Summer was making faces to show that I didn't need Tom's permission, but I waved her away.

"I'll pencil you in, and you can call me at this number to cancel, should the need arise." Someone had obviously told Dr. Koja's staff it was a better strategy to book an appointment than to let the interviewee waffle around.

I felt like holding my head in my hands, but I finished my errands with Summer and beat it back to the office so I could do my lab safety modules.

While Summer strolled back to her Domo-kun bench, I sneaked a look at my phone.

I'd missed a text from Tucker: *Don't worry.*

I barraged him with replies. No answer, and I couldn't call him to yell at him because Mitch was working two cubicles down, almost in straight sight of me.

I texted Ryan before I started pestering Tori Yamamoto, another St. Joe's resident and actual sane person. I needed my trustworthy doctor friends right now. The Volvos, Hondas, and Toyota friends. The ones who had the wherewithal to answer me, *I'm fine. How are you, Hope?*

I wrote right back. *I'm worried about Tucker.*

After a short pause, she texted, *Yes, he wanted me to tell you that he's fine.*

Fine is a boring word. A tea and crust of bread word. Tucker would never use that word. *What happened to him?*

A longer hesitation before *He doesn't want you to worry. He says he's handling it.*

I glanced up because I heard footsteps. Mitch was heading toward the door to the lab. When he saw me watching him, he looked away, but I said, "Hey, are you coming to Petra's tonight?"

"Probably. If I get my work done."

"What about the virology lab? Are they coming, too?"

He shrugged. "Not usually."

"I'd like to invite them. Could you let me in?"

"You want to talk to them in person?" He looked surprised, but I said, "It'll only take a minute, and I don't have their e-mail addresses."

He shook his head. "I don't have access to their lab, but you can call their R.A."

I felt dumb as I scooted back to the little purple-walled alcove. No answer from Dr. Hay's secretary, so I called the lab instead. A young, brown-skinned woman wearing a white head scarf and blue robes pushed open the door for me.

I showed her my ID badge. "Hi! I'm Hope Sze. It's my first day at the stem cell lab. Do you want to come to Petra's at seven?"

She shook her head and hurried into the hall, toward a woman's bathroom across from the elevators. I didn't even catch her name.

Oh, well. I'd already wedged myself into the door, so I headed into the lab. I wasn't invited, but I wasn't not invited, either.

Dr. Hay's lab was smaller than Tom's. It was the same layout, in a mirror image, but more like a kiddie pool instead of a full-sized swimming pool, reflecting her smaller number of students. Because of this, the office section and the lab both shared part of the frosted glass wall facing the elevators, whereas the Zinser lab was so large that the office took up all of that front glass wall, with the lab behind it. It meant Dr. Hay's office had more light, between the frosted glass hallway and the wall of windows on the opposite side.

It also seemed more spare. The shelves weren't crowded with as many things, and the lab benches held less equipment. There was a central aisle between the lab benches as well as an aisle on either side of them, instead of the two lab benches squashed cheek to cheek in Tom's lab. Dr. Hay had fume hoods, fridges, freezers, and what I now recognized as incubators and shakers, like Tom, but it felt emptier and colder, somehow.

Human Remains

People always say that you look like your pets, and vice versa. Well, I'd say Tom and Dr. Hay looked like their labs. One a busy, crowded little town bursting with personality, the other a small oligarchy or dictatorship.

Even at half the size, Dr. Hay's office section seemed empty except for one guy working on the far right, even though it was only four o'clock. I glanced over the cubicle walls and saw that the door to the corner office, presumably Dr. Hay's, was closed.

Dr. Hay's door swung open in front of my eyes, revealing an office wallpapered in framed degrees of all sizes as well as a black poster with a green virus on it. I tried to read the closest degree, but it seemed to be from McGill, which does its degrees in Latin. Dr. Hay glared at me and my box of Timbits.

"Sorry to bother you, Dr. Hay, but I was wondering if your lab might join my lab in a get together tonight at Petra's." Inside, I was quaking. She sure didn't seem like the party type, but this was my chance to check out Lawrence's lab bench, if she stopped looking down her nose at me like I was a butterfly she'd pinned onto a block of wood.

Dr. Hay gave a tiny shake of her head. "Who let you in here?"

"Oh. I knocked on the door, and a young woman with a head scarf—"

Dr. Hay's nostrils flared. "I'll have to speak to Ducky."

"I don't want her to get into trouble. I kind of insisted." That was an exaggeration, but better I took the hit. I really didn't like the vibe from Dr. Hay. "Are we talking about the same person? I didn't catch her name, but she looked Middle Eastern or something like that. I'm pretty sure her name isn't Ducky."

"Her name is hard to pronounce. She said we could call her whatever we wanted."

I licked my lips. Asians are no strangers to taking on new names for assimilation. My parents didn't give me or Kevin a Chinese name at all.

The hall door swung back open, and the person in question scurried to the closest bench, fussing with her flasks. I said, "Well, I should invite her, too. Thanks for talking with me," and marched through the lab, to her side.

"Ducky" cringed when she saw me, and I could feel Dr. Hay watching both of us. I said, "Hi. I'm Dr. Hope Sze, the medical resident from the stem cell lab next door. Would you like a Timbit?"

She shook her head, looking down at her equipment. She touched her pipettes, one after the other, like she was counting them.

"What's your name?" I said.

"Ducky," she said, almost too softly for me to hear.

Even though I didn't look up, I could sense Dr. Hay stirring in her doorway.

"Do you have another name?"

"Safar."

That didn't sound anything like Ducky, so I presumed it was her last name. "Oh. And do you have another given name? First name?" I didn't want to say Christian name, since I was pretty sure she was Muslim. In French, you say *prénom*, which would also translate as first name.

"Dahiyyah. Excuse me, I can't find my condenser. I think someone moved it."

I blinked. It sounded sort of like da-HEE-yuh. Ducky was easier to remember. I opened my mouth to ask another question, but her shoulders lifted, as if to block me out, and I knew she didn't want to talk to me. Not in front of Dr. Hay, and maybe not ever.

Dr. Hay crossed to our side and said, in a ringing voice, "Ducky is very busy. I don't know how this lab would run without her!"

"Yes," I said, but I was looking at Ducky. "You're the lab research assistant? Or are you an undergraduate or graduate student?"

"Ducky has a bachelor's of science and will be applying for a Master's degree next year. She is absolutely invaluable to me. I can't live without her," intoned Dr. Hay.

"How long has she been working here?"

"Over two years now, I'd say. And treasured every single day."

Dr. Hay was a Ph.D. who worked with oncogenes. And yet she couldn't pronounce the name of the woman who'd worked for her for two years? "Okay. Nice meeting you both. I only have one more person to invite. I see him in the office." I knew Dr. Hay was watching me and wanted me out, but ignored her and pushed open the door to the office area.

Three out of four desks sat empty. I cut through the central aisle, between the pairs of desks, to the one guy typing at the computer with his back to me, at the front left corner of the room. The sign on the grey fabric cubicle wall said Stephen Weaver, so I'd come to the right place. His desk was the one closest to the office hall door, so he was sort of on my way out.

"Hi."

He didn't look up. He kept typing, frowning slightly. He didn't need glasses, unlike most academics. He was okay-looking, if you like the rude, silent type.

In addition to his name, he'd printed out blow-ups of a few organic molecules. He also displayed his undergraduate degree from Duke in chemistry, his Masters from Stanford, a Ph.D. from USC Davis, and a poster on Rift Valley disease.

The most striking poster photo depicted an animal lying on its left side, a miniature cow with brown and white skin.

Its eyes were closed. A sliver of pink tongue protruded from its mouth. Blood spilled from the stump of its umbilical cord onto the ground, near a ruler conveniently located to show how big it had been, maybe three feet head to tail.

This calf reminded me of Lawrence Acayo.

For a second, I couldn't speak.

Instead, I read the caption: *Bovine fetus afflicted with Rift Valley disease emphysema. The skin is stained with meconium.*

I swallowed hard.

I guess if your mission is to eradicate Rift Valley disease, some visible reminders around your cubicle might keep you motivated. I've seen worse in my embryology textbook, which I once abandoned in the bathroom, leading my housemate to yell, "Hope's leaving textbooks of dead babies in the toilet!"

But I didn't pin pictures of dead babies on my office wall.

Behind us, I could hear Dr. Hay ordering Ducky to make her some rooibos tea.

I'd better get a move on. "My name is Dr. Hope Sze. I'm the medical resident who started working at the Zinser lab."

"I know who you are." He spoke to his computer monitor. His tone was even. Matter-of-fact.

I couldn't tell if he knew I was a doctor, the new research grunt, or about my notoriety as an amateur detective, so I decided to keep cheerleadin' on. "Oh. Well, great. I was going to invite you to the get-together we're having at Petra's—"

"I can't leave my work." After a pause, he said, "But thank you."

Someone had obviously beat some manners into him, although not without a great deal of difficulty.

"That's too bad. I was hoping to get to know you." I tried to turn on some Summer-like charm, even though it felt leaden.

He snorted. "You want to solve the case."

My stomach dropped, and not only because Dr. Hay was taking in every word from Ducky's bench twenty feet away. "It could be both."

For the first time, he looked at me. Not checking me out in any sexual way. He was cataloging my hair, my expression, the smear of dirt on the cuff of my red blouse, the baggy waist of my dress pants, my boots, my hands clenching at my sides. He was assessing me.

Well, fine. I checked him right back. He was probably medium height or taller. Hard to tell while he was sitting down. Black hair buzzed short and square, wire-rimmed glasses (not hip, not throwback; unmemorable). His requisite lab coat covered his clothes. Square jaw, slight bump in the nose, brown eyes. Again, nothing to swipe right or left over.

Except the feeling I got from him. He was cold, like Dr. Hay. Still, I forced myself to keep talking. "I hear you're working on Rift Valley disease."

He continued to stare at me in a way that made me uncomfortable, so I opened up the box holding the last few Timbits. "I have a bribe for you, if you come."

He didn't even glance at the box. "No one's going to eat those."

"Well, they're still good." My voice faded. I had a tendency to inhale anything that was even faintly edible. One day during my surgery rotation in med school, none of us had breakfast, so a resident managed to scare up a few digestive cookies and pieces of cheddar cheese, and convinced us to eat them like a sandwich. "Sweet and savoury," he told us. For once, I balked—I nearly choked on the salty cheese mixed with the sweet cookies—but all that happened was that I ate first the cheese, then the cookies as dessert. Food does not go to waste around me.

Human Remains

"They're garbage," he said. "Now, Ducky's almond cookies were almost edible. But for the most part, I prefer a fruitarian diet."

I blinked at the little dough balls rolling around in the bottom of my cardboard box. I considered telling him that in the hospital, any food is ravaged, including the next day. When you're working around the clock to save lives, food is a precious commodity. You're not going to subsist on fruit alone.

But when I opened my mouth, his eyes burned at me so fiercely that I took a step back.

For the first time, the corners of his mouth flitched in a smile. "That's right. Some of us have to work." He turned back to his computer, already dismissing me, even though I was still in the room.

That pissed me off.

I stomped toward him. Good thing I'd kept my boots, because he couldn't ignore the clunk of my heels on the linoleum.

Stephen raised his eyes to study me again.

My heart bashed around in my chest, but I stared right back at him in a silent challenge.

The ungraceful part was that I did have to leave. It wasn't a movie where we could cut away. This was his study, not mine.

My phone buzzed.

I straightened involuntarily from the vibration.

That was enough for his tiny smile to flicker to life again. "Go home." He started typing on the computer again, and this time it was over.

Except I had to have the last word. I was born in Ottawa. Ryan and my family lived here. True, my mailing address and at least part of my heart were registered in Montreal, but over my shoulder, I informed Dr. Stephen Weaver, "I am home."

CHAPTER 13

My exit was marred by the fact that I needed a key card to escape, and I didn't want to ask Stephen Weaver for help, so Dahiyyah had to release me through the lab while Dr. Hay glared at both of us.

My cheeks were still burning by the time I hit the hallway. Wow. Did I ever deserve a drink.

Only the fact that I'd survived worse kept me marching toward the lab while another memory side-swiped me. No, not 14/11. That was a day of rage. This was a day of burning humiliation.

The Fateful Day of Burning Humiliation: November 26th

I'd fallen asleep in Tucker's hospital bed, and the nurses hadn't kicked me out. What can I say, near-death has its privileges.

But when I woke up, instead of meagre sunlight and a lukewarm breakfast tray, a white, narrow-faced blonde girl—she reminded me of the singer from Walk off the Earth, only as a teenager—stared at me with dark, avid eyes.

"Eek," I said, raising the thin, flannel blanket over my face.

Her hand reached for the edge of the blanket, so I tightened my grip, shrouding my hair, shrinking down into the soft mattress, nudging

Human Remains

closer to Tucker's warm body. Unlike me, his head was still exposed above the blankets.

Tucker woke up. His arm slid around me automatically, which made me smile, despite the current horror. It was like I fit there. Against him. Against the world.

"Sissy, what are you doing here?" said Tucker. "It's not visiting hours."

Sissy? I calculated the near-whiteness of her hair, the eager intelligence of those brown eyes, plus her sharp nose and thin upper lip, and I realized yup, she was Tucker's sister. He once told me he had two of them, but this was not how I wanted to say how de do.

I'd hide here until she went away. She looked like she was maybe fourteen, or a young sixteen. You can get away with looking weird in front of young people.

Of course, she'd tell the rest of her family in approximately 2.2 seconds, if she hadn't already texted them a picture.

"Mom talked to the nurses, and they said it was okay. Because you're a *hero*." Sissy burst out laughing, but I was realizing that a girl this young might not have driven herself—

"Good morning, John," said a woman's voice, and now I really wanted to die. No, not die. but at least conveniently re-materialize in another plane, instead of getting caught in Tucker's bed.

A man's voice. "Heyyyyyy, Buddy."

"Hi, Dad." I felt Tucker's stomach tremble with laughter. Yes, he would find this funny. Fucking hilarious, actually.

"We brought you a breakfast sandwich," said another girl's voice, from further away.

Fantastic. The entire Tucker clan was here. I'd miraculously avoided them through my misanthropic ways until this very moment.

Tucker said, "I'm not hungry yet."

"He's got a girl under there!" Sissy told her family.

Heat flamed in my face. I tried not to breathe. I pressed my body against Tucker's. I'm not too big. I wouldn't make that giant a lump under the blanket.

Or I could brazen it out. Act like this was an ideal way to introduce myself to the Tucker clan. I was a medical doctor. I'd confronted murderers. I'd escaped a hostage-taking. Some people said I was a hero too. But I felt ill, breathing in the warm blanket air while Tucker's family hemmed us in.

"What are you talking about, Cecilia?" said the mother.

"Hope! You know, that girl he's always talking about? At least, I think it's her. She's Chinese!"

Tucker's core muscles tensed. He said, "Sis, it's none of your business."

"But you're supposed to be recuperating." The way Sissy pronounced the word, I could tell she was imitating her parents. "Does that mean sleeping with girls?"

"It means you can take your Egg McMuffin and leave us alone," said Tucker, but inside, I groaned. *Us.* He'd admitted I was there, hiding in his bed.

"John Roderick Tucker," said the mother. "Is that how I raised you?"

Tucker's body shook with laughter. "Yeah, pretty much."

I suppressed my own grin. Roderick? I don't know why, I never thought to ask him his middle name. I knew Ryan's already, because it was his Chinese name.

"We're going to leave now, so that Hope can have some dignity," said the mother.

I wasn't crazy about the dignity part. In the twenty-first century, shouldn't Tucker be as embarrassed as I was? But I fully adored the "leaving now" part. If I could ever look his mother in the eye, I'd thank her. Like, in a decade or two.

"But Moooooooom! I want to see her. I never met her. She's famous!"

"I want to meet her too. I can give her the sandwich!"

The first one was Sissy and the second one was the younger sister. Already, I was getting to know his family, even if I had only laid eyes on one of them.

Tucker stroked my hair under the blanket. He was still laughing, but I could tell he didn't want me to go. He wanted me to stay bundled against him, despite the fact that his family had destroyed whatever vestiges of romance we'd managed to kindle the night before. He couldn't keep his hands off me. I pressed my hand on his warm, quivering chest. I loved him so much that I could almost feel it surging out of my body, even though I was simultaneously dying of awkwardness.

"Mom's right, Sissy. Let's go." The dad's voice brooked no argument, even though Sissy said, "I'm not going. This is the best thing that's happened all day!" and the mother answered, "It's only 7:45 a.m., Cecilia. I'm sure you can find something else to do today."

"I have to give him his sandwich!" protested the younger one. Her feet tapped toward us before they receded.

After an eternity of a few minutes, Tucker murmured to me under the blanket, "The coast is clear. I can have my evil way with you."

I didn't trust him. Or Cecilia. I clawed the blanket away from my head to take a quick peek. No additional Tucker clan eyes lingered at the doorway. But what if they hovered outside? His sister(s) would love to ambush me.

Tucker rolled his chest over mine. "You think I'm joking?"

We were so close, I had to alternate looking into one of his eyes or the other one. Both of them were bright with amusement. He had morning breath. But none of it bothered me as much as the fact that his entire family had CAUGHT US IN BED TOGETHER. "This is not the time for joking, Ryan."

Tucker's body stiffened, not in a good way.

My own words echoed in my ears. "I mean—"

Tucker said, "I know what you mean," and rolled off me. The mattress shifted with his weight.

Suddenly, we were left feeling like used 4x4 sponges. When I sat up and leaned forward, he didn't meet my eye. I didn't try to kiss him.

I blinked back sudden tears. He *was* a hero. He deserved better than my waffling heart.

On the other hand, calling him Ryan was an honest mistake, and now I had to do the walk of shame away from his room and potentially into his family's hands. That was punishment enough, wasn't it?

I heard wheels trundling down the hall, and the nurse calling out good morning to the patient next door. I leapt out of bed and said, "'Bye, Tucker." I wanted to say more than that. You know how some people say "Never go to bed angry"? I've never really subscribed to that. Ryan and I left each other mad before bed plenty of times, before we broke up. Okay, that wasn't the best example. But the point was,

I didn't want to leave Tucker. He and I knew better than most that life could turn evil in the blink of an eye.

But it took courage to say, "I'm sorry." The words clutched in my throat. New esophageal spasms at the age of 27.

He still didn't look up, but his fingers played with the covers.

I added, "I love you, Tucker" before I hurried out of the doorway. I was already around the corner before I thought I heard him say, "Love you too."

My heart was thundering. I blinked back tears. I didn't want to leave him like this, in a hospital, post-gunshot wounds and mentally screwed up, even if he'd technically survived.

A black nurse rolled a blood pressure monitor down the hall. She paused when she saw me. I nodded at her.

She said, "Spent all night with him, did you, girl? Good for you."

With an agonized look, I confessed, "His family's here."

She stared at me before a grin broke over her face, and I realized that I'd gift-wrapped the gossip of the day. Now it would be all over the nursing station that I'd slept with Tucker and that his parents had caught us. I sprinted for the stairs, praying that his entire family had withdrawn far, far away. As I pushed open the door at the bottom of the stairs, I checked my watch and thought, *Okay, gotta brush my teeth. I've got teaching in five minutes. I don't have anything to eat, but I can drink water. I think I've got some gum in my bag. That'll give me sugar and sort of brush my teeth at the same time.*

From behind me, Sissy called, "Booyah," and I almost screamed.

CHAPTER 14

By 7:45 p.m., after three shots of the alcoholic persuasion, I was feeling mellow. Yes, I'd found a dead body, I'd been deserted by my two boyfriends (Ryan was at work; only Yahweh knew what had happened to Tucker), and I never wanted to face Sissy again, but it all just meant that I should buy my new friends some more drinks!

"What are you all having? My treat!" I called. The Tragically Hip sang "Courage," which seemed like a good sign.

Summer held up her half-finished Bollywood Diva cocktail. "I'm good!"

"You shouldn't be," said Mitch, waggling his eyebrows. He'd polished off two Heinekens already.

Chris flipped his hair over one shoulder. He seemed comfortable in Petra's, an underground bar panelled in dark wood and red brick with gleaming brass rails. I liked the cute waitresses wearing black tuques even though it had to be almost 30 degrees Celsius inside.

Stephen Weaver and Dr. Hay had boycotted us, as expected. Tom had some sort of function with his wife. The Middle Eastern guy, Samir Al-Sani, had said he had to work, and Dr. Wen, the older Chinese scientist, had stared at Summer and me and said, "Many Asian people

Melissa Yi

fail to metabolize ethanol because of a lack of alcohol dehydrogenase and aldehyde dehydrogenase."

Now I held up the chocolate martini Summer had bought for me and said, "To alcohol dehydrogenase!"

"And aldehyde dehydrogenase!" she screamed back, and we burst out laughing.

My phone rang with a 514 area code. I grabbed it in case it was Tucker borrowing someone's phone, even though, when I'm eating and drinking, I try not to touch my hospital germ-laden phone. A man's voice said, "Hope, it's Jonathan Wexler of the CBC."

"Hey, Jonathan." Egads, one of the media hounds. I tried to sound normal. Should I hang up? Summer caught my eye, and I had to choke back a laugh.

"Hi, Hope. Thanks for taking my call. I understand you found a dead body in Ottawa yesterday. Tell me about it."

"I can't. I'm with my coworkers." There. That sounded nice and official, even though Mitch had wandered to the bar and was gesturing at a banjo mounted on the wall, trying to persuade the bartender to let him play it.

"That's a shame. Let's discuss this another time. Could I have your e-mail?"

"How did you get my phone number?"

"It was listed."

"My cell phone number?" I wasn't that drunk.

"On our tips line."

God damn it, Kevin.

"What was that?"

Did I say it aloud? I was pretty sure not, but even Chris was staring at me now. I pushed my martini out of arm's reach, across the smooth oak table, and said, "I can't talk to the press."

"Sure you can. You're doing a fine job of it already."

"Jonathan, shouldn't this go to your Ottawa colleagues? You're horning in on their turf." The words spun out of my mouth. My head felt light and airy. Definitely a welcome change from previous paranoia, but still rather disconcerting.

Mitch wandered back with a small plate of salsa, nacho chips and a menu, which he slid in front of Summer.

Chris gulped from his bottle of Keith's Pale Ale while staring at his phone. I could not imagine getting jiggy with someone like that. His head would always be somewhere orbiting the planet.

I told Jonathan Wexler, "Sorry." Not sorry. I hung up.

When the phone rang again immediately, I pressed Decline. If he kept calling, I'd have to block him. It was easier than trying to rig up a new cell phone number before Christmas. And I still wanted Tucker and Ryan to get a hold of me ASAP.

"You're a popular girl," said Mitch, popping a nacho in his mouth.

"Not really." Because I'd touched my phone, I'd have to wash my hands before I ate any nachos, or figure out how to drink without using my hands. That might be kind of fun.

Summer pretended to pout. "Sure you are. It's hard to get attention around you."

I couldn't help glancing at the relatively gigantic special attractions under her low-cut sapphire shirt, and she laughed.

I blushed. Now even the females were teasing me. But I felt bulletproof. No wonder Denis had cautioned me about falling into drugs and alcohol. I'd told my counsellor, "Dude, I don't even drink coffee, unless it's iced Vietnamese coffee, and even then, it's only been twice."

Shots were better than Vietnamese coffee. Way better.

My phone buzzed again. I smiled at Ryan's name and then read his message.

Where are you?

I picked up my phone and crowed, "The last time this happened, I found a dead body!"

Mitch leaned over the table toward me. Too close, but instead of withdrawing, I patted his hair. The curly ends were soft, and he smelled like beer, which is normally gross, but I didn't lean away. He said, "Who's that?"

"Ryan."

"Your boyfriend?"

I nodded and wondered if I should explain about Tucker. Wonder-Tucker. Tucker, my love. I wanted to break into a mournful song, like a beagle howling at the moon.

Did Roxy howl? I started to text back, *I'm here.* I was trying to be responsible and quickly answer the people I loved. Unlike Tucker.

Mitch said, "What about the guy who was in the hostage-taking with you? His name wasn't Ryan."

Damn, these guys were smart. Too smart. I hiccupped and covered my mouth. "Tucker. He's my boyfriend, too."

"You have two boyfriends?" Summer leaned in my face. Her skin was so pale. I reached up to pat her cheek with my non-phone hand and said, "You're pretty."

"What, you want a girlfriend, too?" said Mitch.

"No." I tried to speak with dignity. "I can appreciate beauty without wanting to hit it." Oh, another violent image. Damn. Well, I was drunk. I didn't have to censor myself.

"I dunno," said Mitch, grinning at me.

"I do. But you are pretty," I assured Summer. I managed not to look at her breasts. It must be even harder for straight men to resist the lure. I pressed send on my text. "Whoosh," I said fondly, listening to the noise of it reaching its target, before I remembered to add, *Petra.* I gave up on the apostrophe. Too much work.

"Where's Tucker?" Mitch wanted to know.

"In Montreal."

"Why isn't he here with you?"

I could feel my face stiffening. Congealing. The alcohol couldn't protect me from this. "He needs more surgery."

"Why?"

I didn't answer.

Summer touched my arm. It felt like a warm weight, and I stared at her pale skin against the red fabric shirt. "What happened to him?"

My face flushed. I said, "You can probably look it up in the news. The Montreal papers covered it pretty thoroughly."

"I want to hear you say it," she said, dipping her head, and for a second I understood what it must be like to be a guy, when a pretty girl asks you to do something, and you're like, *Dooooh, okay.*

"The first shot hit him in the chest. Got his right lung. It collapsed, and the lung cavity started filling up with blood. A hemothorax and a pneumothorax." My hands clenched. I'd wanted to jam a chest tube in him, but I hadn't had the tube, God damn it. I had the knowledge and the capability but no fucking chest tube, and the officers had yanked me back from trying to install one with my bare hands.

"The second shot got him—" I took a deep breath and forced myself to continue. "—in the left lower quadrant of his abdomen. It hit his small bowel and nicked his sigmoid colon. The circumference of the wounds weren't big—they did a primary repair—" Even drunk, I could tell that they weren't following me, so I said, "They stitched the holes in his colon back together. I was so happy. He's young. He's only 27. Healthy guy. It should've healed together perfectly. He said he was going to go home and move in with me, since we were both on sick leave." My eyes filled for a second, but I blinked that back and made my voice hard. "But I knew something was wrong on post-op day five. He was nauseous, and then he sent me out of the room because he started puking. We got a scan, and it turned out his sigmoid was leaking. They tried to repair it, but he ended up having a sigmoid colostomy. It's temporary, until he heals up, but … "

They were all silent for a moment. Well, Chris was always silent, but he put down his phone.

Mitch dropped his chip without eating it.

Chris spoke for the first time since ordering his beer. "What does that mean?"

"It means his bowels were shot up and they sewed them back together, but it got infected, and right now, he has a bag that collects his stool hanging outside his body." I grabbed my martini glass and emptied it. Fuck my iPhone hands. This called for serious drinking.

Summer tried to hug me. I held myself rigid, counting the seconds until she pulled away. She smelled like orangey perfume (I know that's not a real smell, but it reminded me of spray tans and Snooki, if you know what I mean) and a little bit of sweat, which wasn't terrible, but wasn't what I wanted, either.

Tucker's story was in the newspapers and radio and TV, at least in Montreal. He was a hero, and that meant we were everybody's business now. It wasn't a secret. I just didn't like to talk about it, or think about it. Neither did he. We pretended that nothing had changed, except now we were together.

"It's not the end of the world," I said. That was what we kept telling ourselves. But it did suck. No two ways about it. No one wants a bag of shit affixed to their bellies. The background music, still on a Tragically Hip kick, softened to "Ahead By a Century." "They're trying to hook him back up again, but he went septic, he was on antibiotics for weeks—" I didn't want to think about it. It made me want to carve into the table with my nails, until my blood marked the wood. "They don't dare discharge him on home care now. He's stuck in the hospital."

This is what bites about being a hero. Everyone likes the pretty part, the defeat-the-monsters-and-get-the-girl part. But no one wants to end up with one lung collapsed and bleeding and a left sigmoidectomy before they hit 30. A guy with Crohn's Disease who'd gotten an ileostomy at age 21 suggested that Tucker might look at message boards for veterans, not to be an imposter, but to find other people who'd been injured at a young age, because on Facebook, everyone seemed to dance around him, saying, "You're so awesome! We value your sacrifice!" but in real life, they're like, "Ew. A colostomy."

Not that it stopped Tucker. Not really. My entire body heated up, remembering what we'd managed to get up to.

"That blows," said Mitch. "Is there anything we can do to help?"

I shook my head. "He's doing better. Now he's waiting for the leak to stop so that they can reattach him. I was going to stay with him, but … " I borrowed Summer's drink, swirling the glass to make sure I got a good amount of alcohol with each sip. "It was time to start our next rotation. There was no way he could work, physically, but he really wanted me to go. He said I was mouldering and I had to get out."

Summer raised one well-groomed eyebrow.

The alcohol burned my tongue and made my eyes sting. "At first, I thought we could do a research block. We'd write a paper on trauma, or hospital security, you know? We could do it together. No one would stop us. We'd get a pass. But he'd, like, fall asleep over the articles, or he was a bit foggy on what he'd read the day before, and all of a sudden, he was like, 'Nope. Look. I'll keep going with this, and you go do a formal research block. I've got contacts. I'll set you up.'" It was terrible, seeing him so vulnerable. I'd taken it for granted that Tucker was always quick on the uptake, with a joke per second, but post-op and post-fistula and post-op again, he was neither.

"Yeah, I get it," said Mitch. He looked more serious than I'd ever seen him, almost noble in the dim light of the bar. "No one wants to be seen like that."

Summer turned on him. "There's nothing to be ashamed of. He saved her life!"

Chris glanced down. I realized my nails were cutting into my palms, so I slowly unclenched my fists while Mitch said, "That makes it worse. He went from hero to gimp. I'd send my girl away too. Better for her to come back and find me whole."

"He is whole," I said, and when they all looked at me, I realized that my teeth were locked together. "I'll take any part of him I can get. But he won't let me in right now." He said, *I love you, Hope, but I don't want you to see me like this. Get out of here. I'll tell you when I can see you again.*

I was so pissed off, I left him like that.

And when he called me after we found Lawrence's body, when he let me know he was watching me, but not letting me close, I wanted to make him suffer.

So his payback was ignoring me for the past 21 hours. *Oh! What a tangled web we weave, when we cannot give reprieve.*

Summer squeezed my hand. "I feel so bad about this. Seriously, how can we help?"

I looked at them each in turn. Chris met my gaze, steady and straight. I couldn't read anything more in his dark eyes, but I didn't get a malignant feeling from them.

Mitch leaned back, holding the edge of the table. After a second, he nodded at me.

Summer had tears in her eyes and wouldn't let go of my hand.

I said, "Well, I know it's sick, and it has nothing to do with Tucker, but I still want to know how Lawrence died. Will you help me?"

And one by one, they nodded.

CHAPTER 15

"Is there some way we can get the security footage?" I asked the Scoobies, a.k.a. Summer, Mitch, and Chris. I know "Scoobies" is a weird name, but that's what Tucker called anyone who helped me with my cases, named after Buffy the Vampire Slayer's cohorts. And Scoobies seemed kinder than lab rats, which is what my med school friend Ginger affectionately nicknamed her lab colleagues

Summer and Chris shook their heads.

Mitch said, "Well, maybe. I know one of the security guys. We're always saying we should go out for a beer."

Summer wrinkled her nose. "That doesn't mean he'll let you look at the footage. The police will want to see it, right?"

Mitch nodded. "As long as we sweeten the deal for him, he might be willing to play it for us like a movie. Hell, he could tell his boss he wants to review it, and that way he gets paid to watch it, and I'll bring the beer."

He reminded me a bit of Tucker in that he knew everyone, regardless of status, and he was willing to bend the rules. It worked to my advantage for now, but I'd have to keep an eye on him.

"It'll help if you come, though," he said to Summer.

She pulled a face. "No."

Human Remains

"What? He's a nice guy."

"You mean the one who's always sucking on his cheeks? No. No way."

"Harold's a nice guy."

"Harold should stick to other sixty-year-olds."

"I'll go," I found myself saying. If Harold liked Asian girls, I could use that to my advantage. And Mitch would be there. It wasn't like I'd be stuck with a nasty old letch by myself.

"We'll all go," said Mitch. "Summer's being a pain in the ass."

She threw him a filthy look. "Just because he's not staring at your ass."

"Maybe he is." Mitch stood up, arms in the air, and did a shimmy.

"Stop!" She shoved his butt away.

Chris drank his beer and ignored both of them.

Okay, they were a bit nuts. But so nice. (The obligatory Canadian compliment.) I found it tough to believe that they'd kill anyone, and I needed to trust people. "All right. Let's meet Harold. The sooner the better, because the police will be coming for the tapes, if they haven't already."

"I'm on it." Mitch picked up his phone.

Summer stared at him. "You text Harold? I don't believe it."

"Naw. I'm going to call security and see if he's working. He does a lot of evenings. He's always complaining about it." Within minutes, he was winking at us. "Hey, Harold, it's your buddy, Mitch."

I glanced at my still-silent phone. I wanted to call Tucker, but not while all this was going down.

"Not much. Hey, do you think a few of us could come visit you tomorrow morning? See how the other half lives?" After a few minutes, Mitch said, "Yeah, she's coming. She wouldn't miss it."

Summer stuck her tongue out at him.

"How about 10 a.m.? How's that sound?" He glanced around the table, and we all nodded. I wanted to be in the lab enough that Tom thought I was a hard worker, especially in the first few days, but this was too good to miss.

Summer was about to buy a round of shots when I felt laser eyes land between my shoulder blades. I stopped laughing and spun in my chair.

Ryan.

Even from across the room, I felt a shock wave radiate up my chest. My face flushed, studying him. Again. Always.

He was letting his hair grow out. Not a lot, but enough that it touched his collar in the back, and it wasn't as spiky on top. His eyes were still the same: clear sclera, brown irises almost as black as his pupils. Straight nose, medium brown skin, a pointed chin. And lips that looked as good as they felt. Somehow, it added up to sheer excellence.

Ryan cut past three girls trying to line dance. He swept around a server with a full tray of drinks. He moved toward me like a shark. Silent. Gorgeous. And hazardous to my health, given his set jaw, tight shoulders, and those dark eyes that electrified me from twenty feet away.

"Who's that?" Summer finger-combed her hair, her chest thrusting forward. Then she glanced from me to him and back again and said, "Is he yours?"

"Ryan is mine," I said, unable to keep the pride out of my voice, especially when he arrived and slid both hands on my shoulders.

"Hi, Ryan. These are my friends, Summer, Mitch, and Chris."

"Nice to meet you. I'm Ryan," he said, but when Summer asked him what he was drinking, he shook his head. "I'm driving. And so are you," he added, when I opened my mouth.

"You could drive me," I said, raising my eyebrows to make the double entendre clear.

"I've got Roxy in the back."

"That never stopped you before," I murmured in his ear, kissing his cheek for good measure.

He half-smiled, but every time I angled for a drink, he blocked me. Like cock blocking, only for alcohol, to the point that my pleasant haze evaporated in less than half an hour. I sighed, zipped up my coat, and bid my new friends adieu.

Ryan pushed the door closed on Nickelback's "Rock Star" while we stood in the wind at the foot of the stairs and I fumbled for my gloves. My left pocket zipper was stuck. I sighed.

"Why are you drinking, Hope?" Ryan said.

Human Remains

I waved at my new friends through the glass in the door. Summer twinkled her fingers in response. Mitch raised his beer stein at us ironically.

The cool air on my cheeks felt good, even though I was almost sober now. I got my gloves on and twinkled my fingers at him, like Summer. "They're going to help me figure out who killed Lawrence."

Ryan stopped tugging me up the steps to Elgin Street. "You don't even know them."

"Yeah, but they knew their colleague. It was Dr. Lawrence Acayo, who worked in the next lab over. Mitch is friends with a security guard. We might be able to take a look at the card swipes and video tape and see who was in and out of both labs yesterday."

Ryan lowered his voice, but it still echoed in the stairwell. "Okay. And how is drinking going to help you figure out how Dr. Acayo died?"

I shrugged. "Um, bonding?"

He didn't smile back. "Weren't you the one who told me that 75 percent of people with PTSD can end up as alcoholics?"

I sighed. I could hardly remember the study myself. "Only the ones who were abused or had violent trauma—"

"Did you have violent trauma?"

"I guess so." My buzz officially withered and died. *Good-bye, martinis. Farewell, shots. I can't have a relationship with you because I like you too much.*

"Babe." Ryan swept my bangs out of my eyes so he could see me. "You scared me. I don't want anything to happen to you."

I sighed. "Fine. I'll hold off on EtOH until I'm not a human wrecking ball. Happy now?"

He shook his head. "I'm not happy until you're okay. But when the coroner drags us in for questioning—"

"Us?" I'd texted him about my call. He'd sent back sympathy, not mentioning any summons.

"The secretary called me afterward. I was going to tell you in person. They want to see me tomorrow. It's cutting into my work, Hope."

I twisted my hands, which felt very cold. The staircase seemed to capture the wind, whipping it into my eyes and creating turbulence out of my hair.

I knew his work was important. He'd tried to explain the software things he did, and he'd even showed me some hacker tricks like using Metasploit, but all I really knew was that he loved his work.

Ryan took my hands in his, sandwiching them between his warm palms. He couldn't stand to see me cold. We looked into each other's eyes. "What's going on with you, Hope?"

I loved the way he said my name. Simple, but with a long O that conveyed tenderness.

I told him the truth. "I don't know."

"You never drink."

"I do, a little. Less than you, though." Ryan likes the occasional beer. I'm not against alcohol, but I do more dancing than drinking to celebrate the end of midterms. I smiled. "I made sure to drink a lot of water so I don't get too dehydrated while I'm at it."

He shook his head and kissed me, pressing my hands together while he did it. I could feel his breath on my face, warmer than the wind. And I thought I heard a bark.

I pulled back, laughing. "You really brought Roxy?"

He nodded. "Rachel said she was in a bind, so I stopped on the way. I thought she might cheer you up."

"You always make me feel better," I said into his neck. Our hands were getting squashed between our bodies, but I didn't care.

Ryan started pulling his shirt out of his jeans.

"What are you doing?" I knew already, but any minute, someone could come in or out of Petra's and knock us down the stairs. I could still hear people talking inside the building, and the faint strains of Lenny Kravitz's take on "American Woman." If the Scoobies cared, they had a good view of our play-by-play.

Ryan took my wrists in his hands and lay them on his bare stomach, not flinching at the temperature of my fingers or the wind that must be drifting up under his shirt. He was wearing a long, black wool coat, so he swept the edges around both of us.

Tears pricked my eyes. He always used to do this, let me warm up my hands and feet on him. I'd kick off my boots; he'd grab my ankles and place my bare soles on his abdomen, slowly warming them up, as we wedged ourselves between the front hall closet doors and the wall at 288 Silver Lane.

Human Remains

He didn't have to lecture me about the dangers of alcohol. We could recite them and the Serenity Prayer for good measure. But it felt so darn good. I'd been happy, even joyful, for the first time in recent memory. So what did that make me? And what would I become?

For the first time, I understood how tough marriage could be. If I wasn't the same person as I was when we broke up two years ago, then how could a marriage last forty years? Both of you would change until you were almost unrecognizable. It was almost like that fairy tale, Tam Lin, where you have to hold on to someone fiercely, even if he becomes a lion who bites you, or a burning bar of iron that sears your skin. How do you keep holding on?

Ryan would hold on. He would be there for me.

It didn't matter if I solved this case. It didn't matter if I got thrown out of residency. It didn't matter that I was a godless heathen who was always trying to get her hands on his body.

Ryan loved me.

The whole thing with Tucker pushed him to his limit, but Ryan was gritting his teeth and doing his best to drag me out of the darkness.

Ryan was saving my life right now, one day at a time, as surely as Tucker had saved mine last month.

If you think of life like a Dungeons and Dragons game, where we have certain talents that are more apparent than others, one of Ryan's strengths is loyalty. It's not flashy, but it's strong and deep. And that was what I needed. If you asked me to answer most objectively, *Hope, do you need a guy who tosses you off balance and keeps you entertained, or do you need someone who holds you down? Someone who can anchor you when the rest of your life whips around faster than the girl's head in Poltergeist?*, I would have to answer, *I need Ryan.*

I looked into his eyes, and neither of us had to say a word. We made our way to his car, me shuffling behind him, my arms still looped around his waist, my bare hands on his skin.

CHAPTER 16

TUESDAY

I had a bit of a headache, but nothing I couldn't handle when I woke up. I drank two gigantic glasses of water, then texted Ryan from the warm duvet and snowman sheet cocoon of my bed. Two evenings in a row with Ryan's mind, heart, and body. #livingthedream

I felt newly grounded. The fact that Tucker still hadn't answered didn't shake me. He knew where to find me. And if he didn't, I'd head back to Montreal Friday night, or Saturday at the latest, to chase him down.

In the meantime, I had Ryan.

I'd also extracted the Scoobies' Sunday whereabouts while I was drinking at Petra's.

Summer had the weakest alibi. She'd met her sister for lunch downtown, and then she'd gone for a run around 2 p.m., made a kale salad and some noodles for supper, and watched *Big Little Lies*. In other words, she was unaccounted for after about 3 p.m. Although I didn't consider her the killer type, she did have the opportunity.

Mitch and Chris had both been at the lab during the day. Then Mitch had gone to Petra's until 10 p.m., which put him out of the running if the bar staff could vouch for him.

Chris had driven back to his apartment and fallen asleep after leaving the lab around suppertime. "I was tired," he said, shrugging. The other two Scoobies had nodded like this made perfect sense, instead of the next-worst alibi.

I rolled out of bed and shook out a pair of jeans. It was almost 7 a.m. I'd have to boot it if I wanted to get in two hours of the lab safety course before we met the security guard at ten.

I managed to finish three short modules on an office computer before all three of the Scoobies had trickled into the lab. Everyone was muted after a night of drinking. They clinked glass and scrolled through stuff on their computers or tablets. Tom popped in and out a few times and asked me how it was going.

I gave him the thumbs up.

He disappeared into his office, but the door had barely closed behind him before I heard the guys' raised voices coming from Chris's corner. I wandered from the office to the lab.

"You should know. You're a winner," said Mitch, from the back of the lab. He was at Chris's bench instead of his own, two rows away. The way that he spoke, there was a shadow behind his words. A probing.

Chris shook his head and refused to answer.

After a long moment, Summer called to Mitch from the front of the lab, "You need to let that go."

Was it some sort of relationship thing? Like, maybe Summer had gone out with Chris instead of Mitch? Although she seemed closer to Mitch.

Maybe it was a research thing, like the guys had been going for the same grant.

Summer waved her hand at me. "Hope doesn't want to hear about that stupid e-mail."

That only made me want to know more. "What e-mail?"

"It was spam." It was the first time that Chris had spoken. His stool scraped on the linoleum floor, and he stood up and shoved it back under the bench instead of looking at any of us.

"Eighty-eight spam," said Mitch, jingling the change in his pockets.

"What are you talking about?" I asked. Gotta admit, this was more interesting than filling out quizzes about how I wasn't allowed to wear contact lenses in the lab.

Mitch started chanting, "I got ninety-nine problems, but the *blut* ain't one."

"Shut up," said Chris.

"What's a bloot?" I asked, making Summer laugh, but Chris swung out of the lab and would've slammed the hall door if it didn't have some sort of hydraulic hinge.

Mitch stopped singing and shook his head. "Damn."

"What happened there?"

Summer bit her lip.

Mitch said, "I better go," and hustled after Chris, although he gave us a peace sign before the door closed behind him.

I looked at Summer, who shook her head and said, "Do you want to get one more safety module done before we go meet the security guy?"

"No. I want to know what that was all about."

"That was Mitch being an idiot, as usual." She shook her hair out. She was wearing it loose today. It fell to below her shoulder blades, shiny and soft, but I was not about to get distracted.

"And an e-mail," I said.

"Yeah. Chris should never have showed it to Mitch. He should've deleted it. That's what I would've done."

No one could answer a straight question around here. But I couldn't yell at them. I needed them. I breathed in and out before asking, as nicely as possible, "Can you show me?"

Summer shook her head. "I never got a copy. I might be able to find the website, though. I mean, I don't think it means anything, but if you really want … "

"I really want."

She sighed and glanced at the door, but the guys weren't coming back in anytime soon, so she walked over to my computer in the office, in the corner furthest from Tom, and started poking around half-heartedly before she showed me a website for The White First Movement.

It opened with a picture of a stereotypically cute white baby. Crudely lettered above it was the slogan, Endangered Species. Save Our Nation.

Dear White Brothers and Sisters,

Its time for us to Act. Pure White people make up only 8% of the world population.

Join The White First Movement, a non-violent, progressive religion that preserves the White race.

Contact us now before it's too late.

They even had a logo, a fancy "WFM" topped by a cross and a crown.

I felt the hairs raise on my body. Not only on the back of my neck, but on my arms and forearms.

Summer glanced at me and said, "It's not so bad."

"How is this not bad?" I flipped through the website. "They're saying white people are better than everyone else, and that dating other people is 'miscegenation' and 'genocide.'" *That's you, in case you hadn't noticed.*

She sighed and clicked another tab. "Well, this is about how they don't condone violence and won't accept anyone with a criminal record. They say they're peaceful."

"And that makes them okay? I thought Canada had a law against hate speech. We should report this."

Summer didn't say anything.

"You reported it, right? I mean, this is a white supremacist site. And they're sending out spam to people like Chris. They're *recruiting.*" I spat the word out. I don't like people coming to my doorstep and trying to convert me to their religion. But it had never occurred to me that a racist would try and brainwash me through my e-mail. That seemed insidious and wrong. Meanwhile, people like Summer would say, *Oh, it's okay. It's only* wimpy *white supremacists.*

Not okay. Not fucking okay.

I suddenly remembered finding Lawrence's body. Roxy had gone ballistic, running away from us and barking.

Lawrence's body had been faintly warm.

What if the killer had still been in the area?

What if he'd been watching us?

Now I was glad the police had taken us into custody after the code. My God. What if I'd been busy resuscitating Lawrence and someone had come up behind us and attacked us, too?

CHAPTER 17

I struggled to breeeeeathe instead of shooting fire out of my pupils.

Don't jump to conclusions, Hope, Denis had told me. *Stay here. Stay in the now. You're safe.*

Safe is a relative term.

If you're not white, no matter where you go, even "nice" Canadians are constantly barraging you with questions. *Oh, you speak such good English! Where are you from?*

Canada.

No, really, where are you from?

Or some guys think you're an easy lay.

Some guys (and girls) think you're a vomitous, loathsome sub-species not fit to lick their plantar warts.

And some of them want to kill you.

Doctors joke about how every shooting/stabbing/crime victim says, "I was just standing on a street corner, minding my own business, when this guy … "

But what if Lawrence really *had* been in the wrong place, at the wrong time, like me on 14/11?

Was that better or worse than a targeted killing, where someone attacked the immigrant, or the black man?

My panic wasn't infectious because Summer, the only other person in the room, shook her head and tsk-ed at the website. "How come no one knows the difference between *it's* and *its* anymore?"

I covered my eyes, thinking of Lawrence's body, lying on his side, crumpled and vulnerable.

After a second, Summer said, "Sorry. I guess it's not really funny."

"No. But more funny if you're white."

She looked wounded. "I'm only half white. Lots of guys scream 'Ni hao!' when I walk down the street."

I ignored that. "Or if a black man hadn't died."

"Wait." Summer held up her hand. "You think maybe this is linked to *Lawrence?* You think—"

"I think you should find that e-mail, forward it to the police and let them decide."

She shook her head. "But I don't even have that e-mail. It was something that Chris got because some random sent it to him."

Mitch spoke, startling me. "What's this?"

He must've come through the lab door to the office. While I tried to control my heart rate, he gazed at the computer screen and snorted. "The detective doctor thinks that racist spam caused Lawrence's death? Seems a little far-fetched, doesn't it?"

"We're looking for reasons someone might have killed him. That's a reason, isn't it?" I stood up and rounded on him, my fists balled at my sides.

Summer broke in. "You'll have to talk to Chris about it. He's the only one who got the spam, so far as I know."

Mitch snorted. "Look. No offence. Lawrence seemed like an okay guy and all, but I don't want to get caught up in this stuff. I've got work to do." Mitch pushed open the door to the lab.

I followed him back to his lab bench, where he picked up a round-bottomed flask, ignoring both of us.

I said, "You've got work to do. How about he had *living* to do?"

Mitch sighed and put a pipette back in his drawer. "I know I said we'd help you. I'm bringing you to the security guard in fifteen minutes. But I'm not going to chase down every crackpot theory."

"Right. A man died, so we should chill out and smoke some weed."

"I'm not saying that, although it's always a good idea."

Summer laughed.

I didn't. "The police are supposed to investigate every angle. This is an angle. If you don't cooperate, you're impeding the investigation."

Mitch closed his drawer. "Look. I know Chris pretty well. I'm betting he doesn't have anything against Lawrence, or against black people—or any other colour, for that matter. He doesn't want to get sucked into this, and who can blame him? We work up to 70 hours a week here, and if someone publishes before us, bam. We're doomed."

I knew the whole publish or perish thing. I knew grants were going the way of the dodo bird. I knew that tenured professorship was now more of a mirage than reality, with course work off-loaded on to underpaid and overworked teaching assistants. I took a deep breath, a real one, and felt my heart rate de-escalate for a second.

Mitch said, "All Chris did was get spam, something everyone does. Let the first person among us who is spam-free cast the first spam." I felt the corner of my mouth tugging upward.

The lab's hallway door yawned open. Chris slouched back toward into his corner without acknowledging any of us.

"But you can tell people about this." I faced the first two Scoobies, ignoring Chris for the moment. "Ottawa University must have some sort of diversity group, and the police might want to know."

Summer's eyes widened. "I think you're taking this a little too seriously, Hope. They haven't bombed anyone. It's a *blog*. Mitch said they were more pathetic than anything else."

"Hate is hate is hate." Summer looked puzzled, and I explained, "The campaign slogan for gay marriage in the U.S. was 'love is love is love.' They didn't see a connection between two people loving each other and having to prove what kind of genitals those people had. They said love is love is love. Well, hate is hate is hate. You can bet that these guys have ties to more radical white supremacists."

She muttered something.

"What?" I said, sharp. I was not in a good mood. I would not have chosen to come to this lab if I'd known they were being targeted like this.

"White nationalists. That's what they call themselves now. WN."

"And you know this how?"

She glanced at her phone. "It doesn't matter. Listen. It's almost time to meet the guard. We've got to head over to security, if we're going to do it."

"We'll meet you there," said Mitch. "I've got to finish up."

"You're useless," she said, and while they argued, I walked back to the office and sent the website address to myself so that I could access it later. Then I shut that mess down. No reason for Tom to stumble upon it and think I was in love with Hitler.

"This way," Summer said, opening the door to the hallway and pointing at the elevator. We rode it down to the basement with her on the phone, studiously ignoring me. So it was a perfect time to send the website address to Ryan and Tucker and see what they made of it.

What? Ryan texted back.

One of my colleagues got spam from this site. Can you check it out?

No problem.

My kind of guy.

Tucker didn't answer. But he would eventually, if he was conscious. Tucker's brain is insatiable. He's almost attention-deficit, the way he bounces from thing to thing, saying, *Ooh! Shiny! Wait! Did you know Spiderman is el hombre araña in Spanish, but they call Batman Batman? My new wallpaper is the surface of Pluto. Did you see this paper on Ect2 lung adenocarcinoma?*

While I was on my phone, I started paging through my apps. Finding Friends popped up.

Ah. Dr. Tucker's favourite weapon.

If he could use it to spy on me, wasn't the reverse true?

I loaded up the app. Sure enough, John Tucker was listed as my only friend. I clicked on it. It started loading. It took forever. Wi-fi wasn't the greatest in an elevator.

The door pinged.

"We're here," said Summer, stepping through the opening, but I was still staring at my phone.

If Finding Friends had it right, Dr. John Tucker was no longer ensconced in Montreal.

He was in Los Angeles.

CHAPTER 18

There is no stealth way to enter a security booth, so it was good that Mitch had decided to turn it into a party. It was a room not much bigger than a generous walk-in closet, surrounded by Plexiglas, with a bank of black and white TV's built into the desk.

Harold was less grotesque than I'd imagined. Old, glasses, bald, but he fit into a uniform okay, and he seemed to memorize our faces, so he wasn't some wizened remnant putting in his hours until retirement. He did seem to linger when he held Summer's hand, but she withdrew it and took a step back, and he seemed to handle that all right, turning to Mitch and saying, "What can I do you for?"

Mitch looked solemn. "Harold, we're worried about safety at the lab ever since Dr. Acayo died."

"We all are," said Harold. He placed his palms together as if he were praying, the points of his fingers aimed toward his chin. I've seen other old people do it. I think they were trained to control their body movements so they looked more poised, instead of slopping all over the place the way we do now. "How can I help you with that?"

"We wanted to make sure the security in the lab was up to par. We know we have to swipe the cards to unlock the doors."

Harold pointed at his monitor. "Every time someone swipes an access card, it comes up on my computer. See?" A yellow bar popped up, showing that Nathalie Ouimet had entered the radiology department.

I'd never really thought about it before. I'm like this: swipe card, door opens, run inside. But Big Brother was watching us and recording us every minute.

Mitch nodded. "Yeah, that's what I thought. But we've never checked the doorway security cameras. Do they even work?"

"Of course they do." Harold gestured for us to gather around the TV's, and I ended up on the end, where I couldn't get a good view of the grainy little black and white figures moving on the screen.

"What are these shots of?" I asked.

Mitch gave me a look, and I realized that he wanted to run the show. Grr. That was a safer bet, though, so I smiled and said, "Never mind."

"No problem," said Harold, putting him higher up in my estimation. "Of course we have security footage of all the main entrances and exits and the parking lots." He gestured at the TV's.

I counted them. Seven views on split screens. Not exactly comprehensive, and how were one or two people supposed to keep an eye on them, plus patrol the grounds?

Answer: they couldn't. But if anything happened, they could go back and watch it. That was a sobering thought, that maybe security was more for reassuring us than actually keeping us safe in real time.

Mitch said, "Hey, I recognize that one." He pointed at the screen on his end.

I squinted. I thought I recognized Susan's hair and figure navigating into the lab.

Harold smiled. "That's my boy."

"So do you have footage from Sunday?" Mitch asked.

Harold said, "Of course." He liked to say that a lot, but it made him sound confident, which was probably useful in a security guard. "The police have already spoken with me about it." He puffed out his chest. Summer nodded and tried to look enthusiastic, but Mitch was the one who spoke. "Yeah? It's all digital?"

Harold nodded. "We only save 36 hours' worth of data, so the police called us immediately to tell us what they wanted, and we were able to accommodate them."

Human Remains

"So you have a copy," said Mitch.

"Ottawa University and Health Sciences has a copy," said Harold.

"Yeah? And did you happen to look at it?"

Harold rubbed his chin. "I could hardly call myself a security expert if I didn't."

A security expert. Is that what they're calling themselves nowadays? I didn't dare look at Summer, or we might start giggling.

"Cool," said Mitch. "Did you see anything interesting in the lab?"

Harold smiled. "It depends what you think of as interesting. I did see Dr. Acayo at the lab, if that's what you're asking."

"Was he alone?"

"For part of it." Harold nodded in agreement with himself. His Adam's apple stood out in his neck.

"Did anyone else go in on Sunday?"

"Oh, lots of people. The lab lady is always there."

I raised my eyebrows, and Mitch said, "You mean Dr. Hay?"

Harold looked uncomfortable. "I think that's her name. The boss. You know." He twitched. It was clear that, unlike on TV, he was not going to whip out footage to show us, so Mitch tapped his phone for a minute and brought up a picture of Dr. Hay.

"Yeah," said Harold, losing the wrinkle between his eyebrows. "She comes on the weekends all the time."

Well, I guess that's how you end up becoming the head of the lab.

"But the other guy plays a close second. The guy with the dark hair was here until one a.m."

I caught my breath.

Harold nodded at Mitch's picture of Stephen Weaver, only to jerk his head away. He didn't want to tell too many tales. We'd have to tread carefully. Would Mitch know how to do that?

Mitch scratched his chin. "That's cool. Did you see me, too?"

Harold's jaw relaxed. "Yeah, I always see you. That's my job. You were only there until 4:30, though."

Mitch pointed his thumb and index finger like a gun. "I can never get anything past you, man."

Harold beamed. He glanced at Summer out of the corner of his eye, and she ground out an insincere smile that looked pretty enough that Harold rearranged his shoulders.

"Anyone else?"

Harold nodded. "Except Miss Holdt, your whole lab was in and out that day. Dr. Zinser doesn't always come, but he was there in the afternoon."

Mitch laughed. "I must've just missed him. That's how it goes. Awright, man." He offered Harold his fist.

Harold managed the fist bump. He seemed non-plussed when Mitch made an exploding noise and spread his fingers out, saying, "Later, man."

CHAPTER 19

Ryan was meeting with the coroner right now.

I didn't want to text him and distract him, but in between lab safety modules, I squeezed my eyes shut and wished him good thoughts. Like, *please let it be short. Let her believe you. And let her go easy on me on Thursday. Amen.*

My phone vibrated on the lab bench. Immaculate Joan Acayo had sent me a photo of what looked like rice, trying to get me psyched up for her dinner party tonight. I sent back a smiley face and figured that was it, until my phone started playing Kanye's "Gold Digger."

What? I never chose that as a ringtone for anyone. I picked it up.

John Tucker was trying to Skype with me.

I hit the green button immediately. "Hello?"

"Hope." Even on a blurry, pixelated video call, he looked good. Relaxed. Not as pale, not as tight around the eyes. He was wearing a white T-shirt that said BOY-O. He'd even spiked his white blond hair in the front, which he'd let fall flat when he was super sick. He looked the best he had in weeks, which was both a relief and infuriating.

"Where are you?"

He smiled "Sorry I didn't answer you before. I wanted to get everything lined up first."

"What are you getting lined up in L.A. while your bowels are hanging out of your body?"

After a pause that wasn't entirely due to the Internet lag, he burst out laughing. "I wouldn't put it like that, but okay. How'd you figure that out? Sissy? She was threatening to tell you."

"No." I felt like giving him the finger. His little sister wanted to keep me more in the loop than Tucker did. "The Finding Friends app works both ways, you know. I can see you tooling around L.A. What are you thinking?"

"Ahh." He smiled and saluted me. "You're a smart woman, Hope Sze."

I didn't tell him I'd only figured that out this morning. "If you're a smart man, John Tucker, you'll tell me why you flew to the other side of the continent."

He raised his eyebrows. "I want a reanastomosis."

"You flew down to L.A. for *surgery?*" My voice cracked. I almost dropped the phone.

"Yeah. We both know I need it."

"But your team said you had to wait. They wanted to make sure your fistula had healed, so that you don't rupture your primary repair again."

Tucker waved his hand. "Yeah, I know what they said. They told me that every time they rounded on me. They were worried about screwing up because the first surgery went sour. So I talked to my friend Ken, the one who's doing a trauma fellowship at USC, and he said the guys in Montreal are a bunch of pu—uh, pansies."

I was trying very hard to breathe through my nostrils without making too much noise.

"You remember how we read a bunch of articles by Panikos Catrakilis? He's the medical director here. Ken pointed out I'd be a lot better off in a place where they do trauma surgery all the time. They've got gang bangers coming out of their … colostomy bags, you know what I'm saying?"

Yes. Tucker was making jokes, even if they made no sense. I almost smiled. He was feeling better. The trip to L.A. made him feel like he was doing something besides lying in a hospital bed, trying not to die.

"I get what you're saying," I said. "But does it really make sense to fly all that way? The Quebec government won't pay for the surgery."

"Fuck the Quebec government. This is for me. Ken showed them my scans and my record, and they had no hesitation about hooking me back up again. None. And you know who's going to do it?"

"Panikos Catrakilis."

"Nah. He's old now. Does more R&A—research and administration. But you know Hiro Ishimura."

"No way! From EM Chat?" That's my favourite emerg podcast.

Tucker chuckled. "Yeah. I thought that would get you."

Hiro is billed as the world's best and nicest trauma surgeon. He appears regularly on EM Chat to discuss everything from REBOA (sticking a balloon through the femoral artery into the aorta to try and prevent someone from bleeding to death) to the best way to handle neck trauma.

"Hiro's going to do your reanastomosis?"

"That's the idea. He said he's going to try and give me a break on the price because we're both Canadian. He was born in Montreal. Did you know that?"

"No. Well, I knew he was Canadian, but mainly they're asking him what to do for pediatric seat belt signs." I fought my way back to the task at hand. "Why did you cut me off? I texted you, I called you … "

"Well." His brown eyes bore into mine. "I was on a plane, for one thing."

That was true. But he hadn't been on a plane a hundred percent of the time. The airports have Wi-fi. Hell, his hospital probably has free Wi-fi for all its patients paying three thousand bucks a day. I stared at him.

"And the other part was, everyone told me that I should flip the ratio."

I raised my eyebrows, but my heart was jigging like a Riverdance revival. Whatever he was about to tell me, I wasn't going to like it.

"I've been chasing after you one hundred percent of the time, Hope. From the first second that we met, I've wanted you. I've told you you're the one. I threw down my life for you."

I could hardly hear him over the pounding in my ears. I knew it. This was it. He was going to break up with me. What a horrible way to do it, over Skype.

"And ninety percent of the time, you've been running away."

I opened my mouth.

"Not all of the time. I know that. You were there for me in the hospital. I'm not saying you weren't. But this whole thing where you want to have Ryan too—"

Yes. The death knell. I stared at his image, willing myself not to cry. If this was the last view I had of him, I wanted to see him. His brown eyes. His cheeks were more hollow, but he still had colour in them. His hair was shorter than usual, and I stared at the tips of his ears.

His earlobes were harder to see on-screen, but I'd memorized them. You know how some people have earlobes that are completely separate from their heads and some people's earlobes are attached? His are attached, and a bit red, and covered with blond fuzz. I liked to kiss his earlobes and lick them sometimes, trying to feel the hair on my tongue.

"—I'm having serious trouble with that. Are you crying?"

I started to shake my head before I realized that my face was wet. I guess the tears came after all. I said, "I love you."

"I know you do." He closed his eyes for a second.

I forced the words out, even though he wasn't looking at me. He found me too ugly, inside and out. "I want to be there for you, Tucker. I don't want you to do this. Flying away from me, going to L.A. without telling me—what were you thinking?"

He didn't say anything. Now he was watching my face. I could tell that it made him sick to hurt me, but that was exactly what he'd done. And we both knew why: he wanted me to know what it felt like, to be on the outside. To have the other half of your heart take off on you and not tell you what was going on.

"I get it." I breeeeeathed. Denis would've been proud of me. "I'm fucked up. You had to get away from me. Okay."

"No." He half-laughed. "You're getting it backward. *I'm* fucked up. Look at me. I'm the one who's got my bowels hanging out in L.A."

I could feel my tears in real time now. "That's not what I meant. I'm sorry."

He raised his voice. "I don't want to be like this. I can't do it anymore."

I covered my face. I was sobbing, and I didn't want him to see me.

"I've got to get rid of this bag, so you can take me seriously and not pick me out of pity."

That, I heard. I yanked my hands away from my face. "Tucker. I have never—"

He kept talking over me. "I don't want you here. I don't want you to cry over me and argue with the surgeon over when it's time to extubate me. You do your thing, and when I come back, I'm back. I'm winning."

You're a winner. The words floated into my brain, for no apparent reason. I shook them off. "Tucker—"

He took a deep breath. "Hope, I love you. That's all I wanted to say. I'll call you when it's over."

"No!"

But he'd already cut the connection.

I was staring at the still-warm phone in my hand, with only the picture of Tucker's avatar smiling at me.

Chapter 20

On the stairs up to Joan's apartment, Ryan tossed over his shoulder, "I started working on your mission."

"What mission?" I chose each tread carefully. My feet seemed to stick to the stairs, and the walls needed a paint job. I was not looking forward to this dinner party.

"You want to know if there's a white supremacist in the lab. I made up a website so I can check the IP addresses of people who click on it. It's called the White Birthright."

Charming. I tried to sift through my rudimentary knowledge of the Internet while the sound of Arabic music wafted through the walls of a nearby apartment. "But even if you know the IP, that doesn't necessarily tell you which person—"

"There are ways of figuring out what you need to know. The referrer, the search term, the GPS latitude and longitude. Whatever it takes."

"The latitude and longitude would show the lab, or the hospital, right? That could be hundreds of people." It was hard to think. Another resident had cranked up the news. There had been an earthquake in China, hitting 6.9 on the Richter scale.

"I can use first-party tracking cookies to figure out which person it is. Even behind a firewall."

"Can they figure out who you are? Does it go both ways?"

Ryan laughed and tugged me by the hand to the top of the stairs. "I'll cover my tracks."

"I don't know." I chewed my lip. "You saw Lawrence. I don't want the same thing to happen to you."

He shook his head and took my hand, brushing his thumb over the back of it. "Hope, that's ridiculous. You take risks all the time, but you don't want me to build a website because it's putting my life in danger?"

I smiled a little. "You got me. But I'm serious."

"So am I. If you really want to pursue this—and I can see you're not going to let this go—you've got to diffuse the risks. I'm going to build a website, the White Birthright Movement, and see if I can get some traffic to it. It's not that big a deal. I just don't know if I'll get any hits when they already have big sites like 14-88. Okay, this is it." He stopped at apartment number 9 and knocked on the door, which opened immediately.

Joan's apartment smelled terrific, full of steam and unknown spices.

She beckoned at me and Ryan. "Come in, come in!"

I lurked behind Ryan, staring at Joan's belly, which protruded beneath the fitted cut of her patterned dress. The fabric's bright yellow splotches on royal blue satin reminded me of Christmas lights or rioting potatoes, but I was fixated on the size of her belly, which hadn't been so obvious under her tent-like dress the day before.

She was a big woman, so it wasn't a slam dunk baby belly. But there had been other clues the day before: her broad-based gait.

The way everyone tried to give her a chair.

Her plump face.

I blurted out, "Are you pregnant?"

"Yes, of course. I am 28 weeks along." She beamed at me.

My face sagged in horror. I was supposed to be on the second month of my obstetrics rotation, but after I started hyperventilating around fetal monitors and dreaming about guns and placentas, they'd swapped me out for a research rotation.

Now who was waving me inside her apartment? A pregnant woman.

My personal ultimate PTSD trigger. The one thing guaranteed to make my vision blacken at the edges and make me want to claw through anyone and anything that got between me and the nearest exit.

I averted my eyes to gaze at the black marks on the narrow hall's white paint. I knew those kind of marks. I'd made a few of them in my previous buildings, when my bike tire bashed into the walls, or we couldn't quite make the corner up the stairs with my futon.

Ryan gave me an *Are you okay?* look.

I shot him one back: *Of course not.*

There was a pregnant woman making me dinner. I was about to enter her abode voluntarily.

I breeeeeeeathed.

Was that curry in the air? No, maybe not. But something deep and rich, anyway.

My stomach rumbled.

As part of this whole PTSD/depression thing, I haven't been eating as much. But I used to devour food. I could out-eat guys who were a foot taller than me.

I missed that Hope.

From the hallway, Joan's apartment looked dark and claustrophobic. I should've anticipated that. When was the last time you saw a student with luxurious accommodations?

Still, I hadn't braced myself for a bachelor's apartment with the bathroom immediately to the left of our doorway and a kitchen feeding to the right off the main room.

No way I wanted to be trapped in a box that small with a pregnant woman. It was easily twice as big as the hospital room from 14/11, but it still felt like it was squeezing my lungs from the hallway.

Breeeeeeeeathe.

While I balked, Ryan said, "Hello, I'm Ryan Wu. Thank you for inviting us," and handed Joan our gift basket.

A frown flitted across her face. She reached for the basket, but only after a second's pause. The plastic wrap crinkled in her hands. "I told you not to bring food."

Ryan smiled and pointed at the crackers, pretzels, tea, and whatnot tied with a red ribbon. "It's food that you can serve later, or offer to people who drop by. We could have gotten you a fruit basket, but I thought it might go bad if you don't eat it soon enough. Hope said you had too many casseroles." He took my hand. His skin felt warm, which meant that my hands were icy.

"Thank you," she said, and craned her neck to look behind Ryan, at me. I was still standing in the hall, mute.

I smiled, even though it felt like my cheeks were splitting. I knew that my eyes looked dead from the dismay splayed across her face. I said, "Thank you for inviting us to your home."

Upstairs, someone banged a door, and a woman shouted. Little kids' footsteps skittered.

Joan set the gift basket on a table near the kitchen, under an eye-catching, somewhat Impressionistic painting of a black boy playing at a water faucet.

Ryan took a step inside the doorway, but I drew back, so we ended up holding hands in mid-air, across the threshold.

Joan gestured at me with one hand. "Come in, Doctor Hope and Doctor Ryan!"

My mouth jerked.

Ryan laughed outright. "I'm just an engineer."

"Oh, engineers are very important. In my country, they make sure you get things done." Down the hall, someone started playing "Stressed Out," by Twenty One Pilots, and Joan had to raise her voice as she made her way back to us. She was subconsciously rubbing her belly, which made me want to tear off down the hall and try to make Tucker talk to me.

Breeeeeathe.

I squinched my eyes closed. I was being rude. She was pregnant, she was a widow, and she had made us supper.

Also, I was hungry.

I took a deep breath and crossed the threshold. *We who are about to die, salute you.*

Ryan exhaled in relief.

Joan moved to close the door, but I didn't budge. I wasn't ready to be cornered with a pregnant woman yet. I said, over the music, "I'm getting some air. Is that okay?"

Joan looked at me, at the bathroom door by her right elbow, and back to me. "People usually close the doors in this building."

Ryan squeezed my hand.

I took a deeeeeeeeeeeeeep breath and stepped past the doorway. Light-headed. Palpitations. But doing it anyway.

She had to jiggle the door to fit it properly in the door frame. I tried not to flinch when she locked it. Or maybe I did, because Ryan placed his free hand on my shoulder before lining his boots by the front door and offering to hang my coat on a hook on the back.

"Thanks." I handed him my blue parka, one my mother had bought for herself and passed on to me. I kicked off my boots and told Joan, "It smells delicious. I've never had Ugandan food before."

She laughed and started back into the kitchen, which was a little cut-out on the other side of the narrow wall that kept the fridge and stove visually separate from the entrance. She stopped and seemed to gather herself.

"Are you all right?" I said.

"Oh, fine, fine. I love to cook. My man loved to eat. We were the perfect match." Her smile didn't reach her eyes. She turned to the kitchen.

I said, "I want to help you. I can … " What could I do? I hung my purse on a hook and followed her, Ryan by my side.

Food steamed from two burners on the stove. The table was set with three places and a plastic carafe. Our gift basket squatted uncomfortably in the centre, in lieu of a flower arrangement.

"Do you want me to cut up vegetables?" I turned to Joan and caught her rubbing her back.

Uh oh. My heart thudded, but when I moved toward her, she made a point of straightening up and saying, "Everything is ready. You make yourselves comfortable."

Ryan and I exchanged a look. His said *Get me TF out of here.*

"We can come back another time, when you're feeling better," I said, edging back toward the exit so quickly that my socks slipped on the vinyl floor. "I'm sorry that we intruded. We'll let you—"

Joan threw her hand out. She couldn't reach me, but her intentions were clear. "You're not going anywhere, Doctor Hope, until you try my banana juice, followed by my vegetable curry and my *matoke.*"

I quaked. I didn't know what *matoke* was, but I really didn't want her to go to so much trouble. Honestly, my North American ass would have been happy to take her to a restaurant and try and make her see Canada as something besides the country that killed her husband. The only thing that made me happy was that I was right about the curry.

"As for you, Mister Ryan, did you know that Uganda is home to the Ankole Cattle?" Ryan shook his head, and she said, "Our meat has the lowest cholesterol levels of any in the world."

I smiled a bit to myself. Every country has pride. I'd never heard of the Ankole cattle, but if I were eating meat, I'd definitely give them a try.

"I was unable to procure any Ankole for you tonight. You'll have to be satisfied with what I found at Loblaws. That's the nearest grocery store."

Ryan pressed his lips together. I said, "You don't have a car?"

Joan waved her hand like she was swatting a fly. "I took a taxi."

Oh, God. The pregnant widow was taking a taxi so she could make us a traditional Ugandan meal, for no discernible reason. "Joan, you need to be resting."

"That's what my church keeps telling me. 'Joan, you need to rest.' 'Joan, let us know if you need anything.' They bring me casseroles and pray for me. I tell them the prayers are good enough." She waddled to the table and poured a dull, opaque, yellow liquid into three wine glasses.

When I took mine, I realized the "glass" was made of plastic, and that it was a bit cloudy. She might have picked it up from a dollar store, with an unknown BPA status. I tried not to grimace.

The liquid smelled like bananas, so at least that was one mystery solved.

"It's banana juice," she said, catching my expression. "Of course it's not the real *omubisi* because it's a different type of bananas here in Canada. I had to do my best."

"Sure." It never occurred to me that there were different varieties of bananas, but it makes sense, like different varieties of apples.

Joan held her cheap glass in the air and waited until we followed suit. The three of us stood with our glasses aloft while she said, "Thank you so much for coming, Mister Ryan and Doctor Hope. May God bless you for the rest of your lives."

Argh. Church talk even before we sat down. My fingers tightened on the plastic stem while I did my best to smile.

"May the Father, the Son, and the Holy Spirit protect my husband's immortal soul. May they bring comfort to us and our families in this time of deepest sorrow and greatest need. May Lord Jesus bless us all!"

"Amen," said Ryan.

I murmured along with him, trying not to let my face betray my thoughts. A pregnant woman, an enclosed room, and praying. Could this night get any worse?

Joan's eyes glittered. Her lips stretched around her large, white teeth. My stomach twisted, even before she raised her voice, filling the empty room. "Let us drink to the health of the two fine people who found my husband!"

CHAPTER 21

Ryan had already bent his head, eager to sample the juice. After that little bombshell, he yanked the glass away as if it were arsenic.

My hand slipped. I would've dumped my entire serving, but the juice was so viscous, it only had time to slide sideways before I righted the glass in the air, my heart hammering in my chest.

Gotta get out of here.

Gotta get out of here.

I set the glass back on the table, untasted, and said, "Excuse me."

Joan's mouth tightened, even though it was still stretched into a parody of a smile. "It's all right. I know who you are. You are the ones who found my husband's body."

Ryan cleared his throat and took my right hand. I squeezed back hard, wanting to feel his muscles flexing against mine. It anchored me in reality.

Joan kept talking. "The police wouldn't tell me, but I was able to put the pieces together, especially when one officer said you were both Oriental."

Damn it. I guess that was enough of a giveaway at the lab meeting. DemiAsian was half-white. I suppose the older Chinese researcher could have been Ryan, but I couldn't imagine Dr. Wen poking around a park after 9 p.m. There might be other Asian people in the lab, but not many wearing a guilty expression. No wonder she'd homed in on me immediately.

And no wonder we had to leave.

Without exchanging a word or a look, Ryan and I started to back up toward the door in synch. I felt proud of our mind-reading, even though the execution was imperfect. My right ankle reminded me to land squarely on my sole if I didn't want a twinge in my ligaments.

"But you haven't had your juice," said Joan, spreading her large hands. "Where are you going?"

"We should go," said Ryan. "Thank you so much for inviting us. We shouldn't have intruded on your grief. It was very inappropriate of us."

I nodded and tried to look abjectly inappropriate while inching my body toward the door. Ryan had stopped moving in order to talk. *Can't talk. Leaving.*

Then I saw Joan's face.

Like we had hit her. I rarely use the word *stricken*, but now I realized where it comes from. Her shocked eyes. She didn't even breathe for a second. Her mouth worked a few times before she managed to speak again. "Your supper."

That was something my mother would say.

Joan said it again. "You didn't even have your supper."

She didn't look so scary anymore. Still a big-boned, solid woman, still pregnant, but deflated somehow. I felt like we'd kicked a puppy.

A mini puppy, smaller than Roxy.

Her husband had died. She'd spent all day cooking for us. And now we were fleeing.

True, she'd scared the stuffing out of me. But most things did right now.

I used to have an excellent gut. I could tell, at a glance, if you were harmless or a psycho. Experienced ER nurses have sharpened this instinct to an art form. If, say, Dr. Bob Clarkson starts blathering about how he's going to make the St. Joe's Family Medicine Centre so good that aliens will cross the galaxy to gape at its awesomeness, they'll maintain a *Mmm-hmm* expression while he digs himself deeper into the earth's molten core.

I missed that instinct. Post 14/11, everyone and everything seemed like a threat. It was only a question of how much. Minor dread vs. full-blown terror?

Ryan glanced down at me and pressed his thumb against my palm. He'd sensed my hesitation and was letting me take the lead.

It was a simple decision. Should we stay or should we go?

Ever since I'd seen how fast the life can drain out of a bullet hole, the smallest choices paralyzed me.

"I'm sure it's delicious." My voice disappeared on the last word, but I fought to get it back. "You went to so much trouble. We don't want to … intrude." Ryan had already used that word. *Intruder alert. Intruder alert.*

"I made it especially for you. I invited you to our home." Her eyes glistened. She was going to cry any second. I was making a pregnant widow weep. "You said you'd come. It was a sign, you two finding my husband. It meant that he didn't have to be alone. You're a doctor. You tried to save his life."

That was a pretty fancy term for moving his arm around, palpating his radial pulse, and starting CPR. "I did my best. Ryan was the one who called for help. But—"

She reached forward, as if to clasp my hands, but I was already holding on to Ryan with one of them, and the other one felt immobilized, even though my brain knew what I ought to do.

Her hands fell back to her sides. She rubbed her eyes and blinked hard.

Oh, no.

The first tear dripped down the curve of her brown cheek. "Please. I'm sorry if I scared you. I only want to know what happened to my husband. I can't sleep."

I couldn't sleep, either. I'd lie there with my eyes closed, listening to myself breathe. Waiting for the sun to rise again. Either that or nightmares.

"Mister Ryan. Doctor Hope. I know you didn't hurt my husband. I can trust you. And you can tell me what you saw and … what he looked like when you found him." She swallowed hard. She ignored the tears cascading down both cheeks, even though one of her hands had fluttered back to her belly.

She wanted to know. She had to know the truth, no matter how ugly it was.

That meant she was like me.

Sure, I didn't have another person gestating inside me, and we'd grown up on opposite sides of the planet, but we were both freaked out and alone right now.

So I did the only thing I could.

I took a step forward, tugging Ryan along with me, and I touched the bare skin of her arm with my free hand. "Of course."

CHAPTER 22

"Sit down. Drink. Please."

We obeyed, which made it seem more like a party and less like an inquisition. I'd never tasted anything quite like that banana juice. It seemed to hit the back of my throat before I registered the taste of bananas and something darker.

Joan threw her head back and laughed at my expression. She had a rich, deep laugh. The chair squeaked underneath her rotund form, which made her laugh harder.

Ryan smiled. "I like it. What do you put in it besides bananas?"

"I had to improvise, Mister Ryan. Not only was it the wrong type of bananas, but Loblaws didn't have any banana leaves to put in it."

"Please, call me Ryan."

"And Hope," I said, although my mind was lingering on banana leaves. While I'd seen some banana trees with wide fronds on a trip to Costa Rica, it had never occurred to me to throw them in a blender.

I placed my goblet on the table, careful not to shake it—it was a wood veneer table with skinny legs—and smiled too.

"Would you mind if I said a prayer before we eat? It's customary in my culture," said Joan, looking straight at me, the heathen sitting next to her, instead of Ryan, the Christian directly across from her.

I flushed. "Of course," I said again. I'd repeat that all night, like Harold.

I was surprised when she reached for my right hand. Hers was big and soft and warm, like dough, only much firmer. Her sleeveless dress left her arms bare, so I could see the muscles flex.

I reached for Ryan's right hand with my left, glad for the excuse to touch him. The painting of a boy drinking from a faucet hung close to me. I liked his face, and the colours, and the hexagons the artist had used over the canvas, like making big, beautiful pixels.

"Dear Lord in Heaven, I know you're looking after my darling Lawrence. We miss him very much, but we know that You are holding him in Your hand, close to Your Heart." Joan's voice broke. Her hand tightened in mine, and I pressed back, trying to comfort her. "We love him and You with all our hearts. Please bless our little gathering with Mister Ryan and Doctor Hope and most especially the new life I am carrying inside me. Amen."

Ryan murmured, "Amen," and I chimed in.

Part of me still wished we'd left, or that I'd refused outright as soon as she'd issued the invitation. But how could I say no to Immaculate Joan and her precious little baby? What kind of monster would that make me?

Joan opened her eyes. "I'm sorry if I frightened you, Doctor Hope. Sometimes I … I don't know what to say. I'm afraid I'm saying it wrong. We are new to Canada. I thought it would be more like the United States."

Ryan and I both laughed because we usually get told how we're basically Americans with more hockey.

"How is it different?" I said, even though I knew she wanted to talk about her husband. Her eyes were still scanning us, and her hand trembled as she let go of mine. Some chit chat might help, though.

I could tell Ryan wasn't liking any of this, but he clasped my hand and waited politely for her to answer.

She leaned back in her chair to think. It creaked again. "Miami is loud. So many people, so many cars, the music, the pushing, but it was full of life."

I could picture it in my head. I haven't been to Florida since I was a kid at Disneyworld, but as an adult, I would be all over the Cuban food and the lilac suits I'd seen on *Dexter*.

Joan bit her bottom lip. "Ottawa is cold."

I wasn't sure if she meant the temperature, the people, or both. And, of course, I couldn't blame her. "Did you want to stay in Miami?"

Her mouth twisted. "It was a dream job for Lawrence, working with Dr. Kanade. No one else in the world is doing that kind of research on Influenza A. Lawrence wanted to stay there forever."

So why didn't they? If both of them wanted to stay, why would they leave?

It could be the U.S. government. Even Canadians can have trouble getting working visas, but from the look on her face, I doubted that. "Would you go back?"

She stared at me with her wide, brown eyes. "It is too dangerous now, Doctor Hope."

Miami has a lot of guns. The five year FRCP(C) emergency residents often said that there wasn't enough trauma in Montreal and that they had to go to Miami for it. I was allergic—you might even say anaphylactic—to guns, but most residents weren't five alarm scaredy-cats.

Joan rubbed her abdomen in a slow, clockwise motion. "Lawrence wanted us to get out as soon as possible. He told me everything was fine, but I would wake up at night and hear him clicking on his computer, looking at the latest research."

What? No one stays awake at night researching guns. Well, I might, but we all agree that I'm not neurotypical.

She pressed on her lower abdomen with the heel of her hand. "He said I should go without him, but he has—had—a student visa. What am I supposed to tell immigration, that we're living apart because of a virus? A virus that started in our own country?"

And then it finally smacked me in the brain. They weren't worried about urban warfare, unless you counted microscopic terrorists.

She was talking about the Zisa virus, which started in a forest in Uganda.

This summer, we started to hear rumblings about it in Montreal. Pregnant women were petrified. But at the time, we had fewer than six hundred cases in Canada. The vast majority of them came from travelling to more southern countries. I kept telling my patients, *We don't have the* Aedes aegypti *mosquito in Canada. It's too cold.*

Them: *But what if the mosquito comes here?*

Me: *It probably won't be until after your pregnancy is finished.*

Them: *But what if a mosquito comes here, and bites someone, and then bites me, and my baby ends up with microcephaly?*

That was the especially vicious effect of the Zisa virus. It attacked neurological tissue. Especially fetal neurological tissue.

This summer, the Center for Disease Control and other agencies had formally announced the link between Zisa and microcephaly.

My eyes dropped to Joan's belly, cradled between her hands.

CHAPTER 23

I licked my lips. Ryan might not understand what we were talking about, but I didn't dare break eye contact with Joan now. Our rapport was too delicate.

"Is your baby okay?"

Her shoulders sagged.

Oh, no. Oh, God.

When Zisa started making the news because of the microcephalic babies in Brazil, we assumed that infection during the first trimester was the most dangerous. That's true of most of the TORCH infections (Toxoplasmosis, Other, Rubella, Cytomegalovirus, Herpes), and it makes intuitive sense: an embryo still forming its brain, lungs, heart, and guts can make more devastating errors in cell division compared to a 39-weeker ready to enter the world.

Then we started getting reports of fetal death with Zisa infections. Not limited to miscarriages at six to eight weeks, which we often see in the emergency department, but fetal death right up until birth.

Stillbirth is one of my nightmares. I glanced at Joan's stomach and made a quick prayer. *Baby, be okay.*

Compared to those better-known diseases, Zisa seemed relatively innocuous. When most Zisa-infected pregnant women gave birth to babies with a normal head circumference, we celebrated until some of those babies developed other abnormalities. They cried all the time. They seized. They had cataracts. They had trouble feeding.

Suddenly, it seemed like nothing could protect you. Not the miracle of conceiving a baby. Not giving birth to a normal skull-sized infant. Nothing. Zisa invaded cells and vessels in the brain not only in utero, but in a newborn.

Now I knew why they'd left Miami.

I asked, "Did you or Lawrence test positive for Zisa?"

Ryan sucked in his breath, but even out of the corner of my eye, I could see that he hadn't shrank away or started screaming. He was a good egg and a rational being. He probably knew that the vast majority of people only get Zisa via a mosquito, though you can also get infected through sex, in utero, or through a blood transfusion, none of which were likely to happen to us at a dinner party.

Joan's lips twisted. "Oh, Doctor Hope, I am the last one to know anything."

That was a strange response. She didn't add anything, but she maintained steady eye contact with me. I decided to change tacks. "Did you have a rash or red eyes or aches and pains?" I was speaking more slowly now, the way I did with patients who didn't speak much English. Joan spoke English, but I wanted to be extra-clear, even if it made me look like a colonialist.

She shook her head. So if she had Zisa, she was one of the eighty percent of people who didn't develop any symptoms. Like I said, it's part of the reason that the disease is spreading so fast. People don't even know they're sick. But she must have had prenatal care in Miami, right? And they would have tested for Zisa, especially since there was such a hullaballoo over the summer. I tried to remember exactly when the first reports hit that Zisa was being spread in the Miami-Dade area by local mosquitoes. August, I decided. I'd barely started my psychiatry rotation.

Even if Joan had been asymptomatic, they must have tested her. Or had they? So many pregnant women had jumped at the free Zisa testing, overwhelming the system, that the Center for Disease Control had to step in and help with the backlog.

But surely, if you worked in a lab, you would figure out a way to have your wife tested for Zisa. Maybe you could even test for it yourself.

I remembered Lawrence's body in the snow, and I shivered. What happened to this couple? How did they end up in Ottawa, and who killed one of them?

Time to back up. "You were tested for Zisa, right?" I said.

She nodded.

Okay. That was something.

"What did the test say?"

She didn't meet my eyes. At last, she murmured, "It was positive."

Ryan set down his cup and pushed it away a few inches.

Right. Zisa was spreading faster than it should have, for a purely mosquito-borne infection. Zisa might be transferred through saliva or tears.

I stared at Joan's tear-stained face, smelled the food she'd prepared for us in her own kitchen, wishing we'd never come.

CHAPTER 24

Ryan excused himself to go the bathroom, probably so he could discreetly rinse out his mouth.

I pushed the banana juice across the table, out of arm's reach, and tried to figure out when Joan might have gotten infected. Twenty-eight weeks was about seven months along. In mid-August, she would have been three months pregnant. Terrible timing, because even though fetuses can become sick any time, first trimester infections may still be the most dangerous.

"What do you know about your pregnancy so far?" I tried to phrase it delicately, asking if she knew about birth defects.

She placed both hands on her belly. "I'm so worried, Doctor Hope. I feel kicks, and I think, 'How will you stay alive? What are we going to do now that your daddy is with Jesus?'"

"We'll help you," I said. "You're not alone. You saw the group today. We'll band together." Summer wanted to raise some funds; Joan's church was on casserole duty; add in me and Ryan, and that might be enough.

"So many terrible things have happened. I need to know what happened to my husband. You understand, don't you, Doctor Hope?"

Human Remains

"Yes, I do." That feeling throbbed inside me again, that she and I were the same at heart, plunging head-first into danger when everyone else said *Stop, Drop and Think.* "What do you want to know?"

When Ryan walked back toward us, I could smell the soap on his hands. Poor guy. Now he knew how I felt touching Lawrence—

My breath seized.

Touching Lawrence. I'd already had skin-to-skin contact with him. Zisa is transmitted back and forth between the mother and fetus continuously during pregnancy, maybe through the placenta. We're not sure about the mechanism yet. The mother can't seem to develop antibodies until after she delivers, usually a week post-partum. And Joan had told me she had Zisa.

It's also sexually transmitted. Zisa is a persistent beast. It seems to hide in men's testicles, where the immune system is less likely to find it. They've found Zisa RNA in mouse tears and vaginal fluid.

Couples are supposed to use condoms or abstain from sex during pregnancy so as not to transfer it back and forth, but when was the last time you heard of a pregnant couple using condoms?

Joan had Zisa. Lawrence probably had Zisa. And now I'd been in close contact with both of them.

Breeeeeeeeeeeeathe.

There are no guaranteeeeeeeees. I'd touched Lawrence and sipped Joan's food. Still, chances were, I was not infected with Zisa. Yet.

"Where did you find my husband?" Joan was asking.

I opened my mouth, but Ryan was already telling her about Roxy running away and finding Lawrence's body.

"In the ditch beside the road?" Joan said, her eyes alert.

Ryan and I exchanged a look. It sounded so indelicate. *Yes, your husband's body was in the ditch.*

"I guess that's what you could call it," I said. "We did everything we could, though. I started CPR, which the police took over, and the paramedics got an airway and a monitor—"

Joan pressed her lips together and shook her head. "What was he doing there? He was supposed to come home for supper."

I held my breath. I wanted to piece together what had happened to Lawrence. This was what I'd been waiting for. And I didn't even have to ask.

She began to pick at one of her nails. "He said he had to work that afternoon. I wanted him to come with me to look at a crib, but he said he had to work. He said it was a matter of life and—" Her face crumpled. Her voice shook, and her hand drifted to her back.

"He was happy about your pregnancy, wasn't he?" I said.

After a moment, Joan said, "We were his family. He said he would do anything to protect us."

That wasn't an answer. I understood about work. Believe me, it's the closest thing my parents have to a religion. *Work hard. Look after your family. Are you tired? Work harder.*

But if Ryan or Tucker blew me off when our baby and I had motherfucking Zisa, I would stomp on them.

To be fair, Lawrence was a Ph.D. who specialized in virology. He understood the disease better than I did. Hell, maybe that was why he had to go in.

"Was he studying Zisa?" I asked, even though I knew I should let her ask the questions.

She sighed. "He was trying to get funding. The CDC had promised him, but because he moved to Canada ... "

Sure. The Center for Disease Control wanted to help Americans, not Canadians. And most cases were in the US instead of here. There was no good reason to move from the epicentre of the disease in the continental U.S., unless your wife was pregnant.

"That's just wrong," said Ryan, and while they commiserated over bureaucracy, I studied her kind, round face and thought, *Lawrence must have loved her.* I wasn't sure I liked him, based on the little she'd said, but he'd cared about her enough to move her to one of the safest countries in the world, Zisa-wise. Chile doesn't have the mosquito either, but Canada must have more job opportunities and a more solid health care system, although it couldn't protect Lawrence.

How on earth did he end up with a black bag over his head? Why hadn't he pulled the bag off himself?

You hear about infants suffocating in a bag, but not young, strong adults. I'd vaguely heard of committing suicide that way, but why would he bother bringing his pregnant wife here and killing himself? Unless he felt like, "My work is done, see ya. Canada will take care of you." But from all indications, Lawrence had been fighting for Zisa funding, not giving up. And suicide by bag, a block away from the hospital? An educated man could come up with a dozen better ways to kill himself.

In medicine, you're supposed to chase down every possibility with the caveat that "When you hear hoof beats, think horses, not zebras."

It made no sense that Lawrence had killed himself in such a stupid way. Therefore, this was a suspicious death. Therefore, the police were right to question me and Ryan. Therefore, I should try and unravel it myself.

"More banana juice?" said Joan, slowly rising to her feet. She pushed her hips forward as she did so, keeping her belly balanced in the air, her right hand supporting her back.

Neither of us had touched our cups after the first toast. We stood up to help her.

Ryan said, "My stomach is a little unsettled."

"Me too!" I sounded too enthusiastic, so I added, "Why don't you rest, and we'll talk instead of worrying about food?"

Joan's lower lip jutted forward. "Food will settle your stomachs. My delicious vegetable curry has been simmering all day."

Ryan winced. He hates the way my parents leave food out all day, even though my family is hardly ever sick, and I tell him we must have really good gut flora.

"Honestly, I'd rather talk," I said, but Joan made her way to the stove, placing each foot as if she were the one with a mildly sprained ankle, not me.

She said, over her shoulder, "The police asked me to come to the station. They have new information for me. I told them I couldn't come, I was cooking for you."

Oh, God. More guilt. I hurried to her side and glanced at Joan's face, shiner than it had been a few seconds before. If I reached out to touch it, I bet her forehead would feel clammy. "Joan? Are you—"

"Excuse me for one second," she said, spacing each word apart and pronouncing each one carefully. She rotated her body to the right like she was redirecting the Titanic.

Ryan and I exchanged a look.

"Joan, I can help you," I said, but she was already eking her way to the teeny bathroom beside the entrance. It was a bit like watching a turtle make its determined way across a beach. You know it has to get there on its own, but you really want to pick it up and make its life ten times easier. It felt like two decades before she breached the entrance and shut the door, vibrating the doorknob as she locked it behind her.

Ryan angled his head at the main door. I nodded and pointed at my watch to indicate that if we waited a few minutes, we'd try and make a graceful exit.

I braced myself for the sound of number one or two hitting the toilet bowl, but aside from a rustle of clothes, everything was quiet.

Ryan's face relaxed until Joan's urine started splashing. Ryan looked like he'd rather fight his way out of a biker bar than sit here and listen to that soundtrack.

"How was your day?" I said, raising my voice to cover the noise.

"Not bad. You?"

I shrugged. "I don't feel like they expect too much from me."

"Well, it was only your second day." Suddenly, Ryan stiffened.

A low moan came from the bathroom.

CHAPTER 25

Ryan stopped breathing.

Joan moaned again, a low, throaty sound that seemed to permeate the room.

The apartment walls seemed to fold in on me. My heart battered my ribs.

The last time I had a pregnant woman in a bathroom, I had to deliver her baby literally at gunpoint. What are the chances of that? Like, one in a million? Ten million?

This wasn't happening.

I heard Joan gasp through the door.

Somehow, I could tell she was trying not to cry.

This was happening. No matter how improbably.

I sucked air in through my teeth.

I was the only doctor in the room.

(I'm getting Punk'd, right? Is this Denis's new version of therapy?
Shock therapy.
#FML.)

If I was getting Punk'd, I'd better put on a good show for Ashton Kutcher or whoever was directing this reboot. I touched Ryan's hip, suddenly calm. This was the world's version of tossing me into the ocean even though I'd forgotten how to swim and had recently developed hydrophobia.

At least no one held a gun to my head.

I could handle this.

Ryan reached for his phone, ready to call EMS. They should give us a frequent caller discount.

I held up my finger. I wanted to assess what the problem was. Joan was alive. The baby, I sincerely hoped, was alive. If Joan was in early labour, we could drive her to the hospital and save her the ambulance charge of $200.

I crossed the room and knocked on the door. The wood was so thin, it jounced under my fist, although the lock held. "Joan?"

Even without my ear pressed to the door, I could hear her breathing hard and fast.

Joan was pregnant. I did not want to deliver her baby in the bathroom. Or deliver any baby, period, until I got the PTSD under control. I repeated, my voice higher-pitched than I'd like, "Are you having the baby? You want us to call 911?"

"Noooooooooooo." Another moan, more than a word.

I glanced at my watch. I should be timing these in case these were contractions, but it couldn't be more than two minutes between moans.

Bad sign.

I touched the doorknob. It didn't move. "Immaculate Joan"—it suddenly seemed right to call her by both her first names, to try and lift her out of her pain or panic—"are you having contractions, or not feeling well in general? I might have some Tylenol in my bag." My mother had pressed a giant bottle into my purse. If Joan wasn't vomiting, she could take a tablet. You can also administer it rectally, but it wouldn't be my first choice.

I jiggled the doorknob. It was locked, to my secret relief, backfilled with exasperation. "Joan, if you don't open the door, Ryan is calling for an ambulance. You have a high risk pregnancy, and you won't let me in. I'm a doctor, Joan. I've delivered babies before." Although not premies with Zisa.

She sobbed once, a high note that thrilled the air. Then she was silent.

"I'm calling 911," said Ryan, phone in hand.

I nodded.

Human Remains

"No!" Joan shouted.

Ryan and I stopped. No, she did she not need help, or no, she was too scared to go to a hospital after her husband had died?

"What's happening, Joan?" I said.

"I'm okay!"

She sure didn't sound okay a few minutes ago.

On the other hand, she'd said two words, which was better than groaning. Ryan started pushing buttons. I touched his arm.

"I'll go in there," I told Ryan, under my breath. "I'll get her to let me in. I'll take a look first. She might not need the hospital. She might be ... having a panic attack, or Braxton-Hicks contractions."

Ryan raised both eyebrows, clearly thinking, *And that's better?*

"She wouldn't need an ambulance for either of them. Braxton-Hicks are practice contractions."

"That didn't sound like an anxiety attack to me," said Ryan, meeting my eyes head on. Most guys would've already hit the parking lot, but Ryan would always stand by me in a crisis. Always. Even if it had icky girl stuff going on.

Joan called through the door, "NooooOOOOooooo ... "

I jangled the doorknob loud enough that she should hear me. "Joan. You're going to have to let me in, or let the paramedics in. One or the other."

Ryan didn't say anything, but his body leaned toward the exit in a way that screamed *Paramedics, paramedics.*

I reached for my purse hung at the front door. There was only one upside about finding Lawrence's body: ever since, I carried a pair of gloves in my purse at all times. I slid them on, sheathing my hands in an unearthly blue latex-free barrier. I could've used two pairs of gloves. Sometimes we double-glove if there's a high-risk patient. Next time, I'd make sure I had a backup pair for myself and another two sets for Ryan. Just in case.

As I walked back to the bathroom, I thought, *You've heard of the dream team. Ryan and I are the death team.*

No. Joan was alive. I had two patients to look after now. That's what OB/gyn's say: they're the only ones who have two patients. ER docs have multiple patients, but usually not hanging out within each others' bodies.

Ryan said, "If she's in trouble, I'm calling. I don't care what she's saying." His finger punched the numbers 9-1.

The tough part about being a doctor is making the decision. Call for help too often, and you're a dumbmuffin crying wolf and wasting everyone else's time. Call for help too late, and the patient dies.

Thump.

From inside the bathroom.

Ryan and I jerked around to stare at the closed door.

It sounded like she'd fallen against a wall with her entire body weight. Never a good idea in anyone, let alone a sick, pregnant woman.

Ryan pressed the final 1 of 911, his lips tight.

We both saw the doorknob turn and the door drift a few crucial millimetres inward.

"She wants me there," I said to him.

He grabbed my shoulder.

I knew what he was thinking: 14/11. It never left my mind, either.

"I'll come with you," he said, but Joan shrieked, a noise terrible enough to make my heart stop beating for a second.

I could see the whites all the way around Ryan's eyes now, which struck me as distantly funny, even as I said, "No. I'm pretty sure that's not okay in her culture. I'll leave the door unlocked. And you talk to the paramedics. Okay, Joan?" I raised my voice, but she was sobbing now, and praying for sure, because I heard words like "Jesus, help me" and "in this hour of need."

I can't tell you how many bad memories reared up and smashed me in the brain.

I wanted to pray, too.

I'd been running away from patients. I'd run away from Montreal. Hell, you could say I'd run away from Tucker, albeit with his permission.

But God damn it all, I was going in there.

I reached for the doorknob.

CHAPTER 26

She was sitting on the toilet, naked from the waist down, her panties ringed around her ankles.

I stopped. Even for a doctor, this is not a common sight.

My first instinct was to sprint out of the room, howling, "Excuse me!"

Instead, I pressed my back against the fragile wooden door, sealing Ryan out, and tried to figure out what was going on.

She'd been crying. Her face was still contorted, but most of the tears were silent and somehow all the more terrible, like she couldn't permit herself to cry.

She stared at me, the sternocleidomastoid muscles in her neck tenting the skin as she gulped for air. Her eyes didn't look 100 percent "there," if you know what I mean.

"Joan, it's me, Hope," I said, partly so Ryan could hear me talking. "Are you having contractions?"

Her hands drew into fists.

Her dress was Michelin-manned around her waist, exposing her powerful brown thighs and bush and—what was wrong with her skin? I tried not to look, but my eyes were inexorably drawn toward the thing I shouldn't stare at.

Her skin wasn't smooth. It was marked with dark brown spots on her upper thighs.

I've had those dark spots myself, in other places. After a rash, or a burn, the skin turns darker as it heals. It's one of the side effects of having melanin. Not a big deal, but a recognizable difference from our whiter companions.

For some reason—maybe because her ABC's were clearly okay—I couldn't stop staring at that post-inflammatory pigmentation which, at closer glance, was concentrated around her vulva and upper thighs.

I was pretty sure I knew what had attacked her in the past.

Herpes.

This poor, poor woman had been infected by not one but two infectious diseases.

When you have herpes, you shouldn't deliver vaginally if you have any active lesions.

These were old scars, not new ones, but we now think that having two viruses instead of one makes you more likely to have congenital Zisa syndrome. At least in mice, Type 2 Herpes Simplex Virus amplifies production of the Zisa virus.

"Let's get you to the hospital. Ryan—"

"I'm already on it," he said, and I could hear him talking through the door.

Joan shook her head, but she was in no shape to argue. She bent forward and grunted.

What bothered me the most was her thousand-yard stare. I usually see it on people with congestive heart failure who are struggling/bubbling to breathe. All they can do, the only thing they can focus on, is getting enough air into their lungs.

I lunged forward. "Let me get you—"

Too late. Her legs flashed open, and even as I dove between them, something splashed into the toilet.

She screamed.

I screamed too. "Get. Off. Get off the toilet!"

She hunkered down instead.

I shoved her arm. I wouldn't slap her across the face, but I needed her to get the message. Now.

She sobbed, "It's too much. Lord, it's too much. I can't take—"

"Joan. Move!" I darted to her side, planted one foot, and lunged forward with the other. Using my entire body weight, I was able to dislodge her a few inches.

That surprised her enough that she started to rise, leaning her weight into her feet to stand up.

Once she did, her legs shaking, I belatedly realized that she was still attached to her baby by the umbilical cord.

I couldn't worry about the cord though, because even with the blood and urine in the water, I could see the baby floating, curled face down, in the toilet bowl, its tiny sides working as it struggled to breathe underwater.

CHAPTER 27

I dove forward, thanking God for my gloved hands, wishing for a full gown and a mask with an eye shield, but you can't have everything.

I scooped up the baby, sluicing dirty water down on either side of it, like a fish rising out of the water, except bigger and slippery-er, and oh God, it had the bulging eyes and the small forehead of microcephaly, but I couldn't think about that now, either.

"Is she alive?" Joan screamed, and Ryan banged on the door, and I said, "Yes. Your baby is alive." I hadn't checked the sex as I concentrated on A and B.

The little mite was breathing.

Or at least heaving.

I called through the door, "Ryan, tell them we've got a 28-week-old microcephalic baby, born in a toilet, who aspirated the water and is now breathing fast and getting tired."

Baby was doing that bellows breathing that means trouble. At 28 weeks, everything looks like a colossal effort, but I didn't like the look of her.

I needed her warm and dry and breathing properly after swimming in a toilet bowl. Little ones tire quickly. They may manage for a few minutes and then wear out suddenly and catastrophically, even without bacteria water having a party in their lungs.

Ryan almost never swears, but he said a few choice things about Jesus that made Joan cry out, appalled, before he told the 911 operator, "I'm sorry, ma'am. No, not you, ma'am, the mother is upset … "

My biggest problem was that I'd shoved away Joan's bum and dived between her legs, so now I held the baby between her legs and her butt, and the cord was pulled to its extreme limit.

I couldn't yank too hard on the umbilical cord because you can actually invert the uterus, as in flip it inside out. A fellow medical student did that the month before I rotated through obstetrics.

At least the ABC's were intact. I could see and feel baby's heartbeat pulsing in her chest at over 100 beats per minute. I told Joan, "Let me get her warm. I'm not going to cut the cord right away, because she needs a little more blood, but I need a towel." I pointed at the yellow hand towel on the wall-mounted bar facing the toilet.

Joan's legs trembled. Actually, her whole body was shaking. Maybe stress, maybe maternal sepsis, maybe normal variant. In any case, she was not about to grab me the towel.

I considered swaddling the baby in my shirt, but the towel was almost within my reach. I shifted the baby to my left hand and stretched out my right. One advantage of a miniature space: I managed to snag the fabric between two of my fingers.

I swaddled the baby as best I could in the cheap terry cloth. It was big enough. She was less than a double-handful, such a tiny mite.

That's what I would call her, mite. No, Might. Because she Might live. And she could end up Mighty powerful. How many babies could survive potential Zisa, herpes, and a toilet birth?

"Do you have any other towels?" I asked, nodding at the damp cloth.

Joan's legs wavered. She made as if to fall back on the toilet, which would potentially drop Might back into the water.

"No! Stand up!" I pushed her in the back and kneed the toilet handle to make it flush, so at least we wouldn't be dealing with urine water anymore.

"What's going on?" Ryan yelled.

"We're okay. Baby's still breathing. ABC's intact but laboured," I said. I tried to switch to soothing. "Joan, I know you're tired and in shock. I'll get you sitting in a minute, but I need to get your *baby* away from the *toilet*. Spread your legs, Joan."

She stepped her feet eight inches apart. Good enough.

I threaded her baby's body through her legs, bringing Might toward Joan's belly, so she could see her clearly for the first time.

After a long moment, long enough for her to recognize the microcephaly, Joan cried out, a sharp sound that could have been pleasure or grief or both.

In the ensuing silence, I paused to see if she would scoop Might up in her hands, freeing me to cut the cord. Delayed cord clamping usually doesn't mean waiting more than 180 seconds, or until the cord quits pulsating.

I pinched the cord between the fingers of my left hand. It was still pulsing faintly, so I relaxed my fingers and let the blood flow, for now.

Joan began to sob.

I flinched. Bawling sounded even worse in a teeny, enclosed space that smelled like blood and amniotic fluid and old urine. And I was sweating.

Joan's lips trembled. She looked greyish. Her forehead gleamed with perspiration. I had to get her and the baby in a safe position, fast, before she fainted or the baby stopped breathing.

The cord would have to wait. "Sit down, Joan. Please."

She plunked down on the toilet seat, hard enough that I could feel the vibration in my feet.

I brushed aside the towel folds with my left hand.

Might was gasping away. Her chest reminded me of a bullfrog inflating his throat. The most disturbing thing was that her sternum was starting to suck inward with each inhalation because her ribs were more cartilage than bone.

She was tiring out.

"Joan, it's hard for her to breathe."

Joan closed her eyes. Her torso swayed in a semicircle before pitching forward.

I shrieked and propped her up with my left hand, holding Might with the other. "Ryan, Mom's going to faint on me! Do we have an ETA?"

I heard him shouting into the phone on the other side of the door.

Joan opened her eyes and righted herself on the toilet. She said, with dignity, "I am not fainting."

"You're weak. You just had a baby. Lie down."

"I am not—uhhhh."

She slumped over Might for a second. My heart stopped, but she caught herself again. I could feel Might panting away in my hand. Not great, but not in respiratory arrest. Yet.

Joan was bleeding into the toilet. I couldn't monitor a post-partum hemorrhage when it was all going into the plumbing. It's hard to tell the difference between bloody and bloodier water, but she sure wasn't acting like someone who had all her faculties.

I glanced around the bathroom for hemorrhage supplies. I finally noticed some spare towels folded on a mini-shelf above the toilet. A cabinet under the sink might prove useful. The rest of the room was barely big enough for the toilet, a plunger, and a shower stall against the far wall.

I rubbed Joan's shoulder in circles, trying to bring her back into her body instead of spiralling away in a mental fog. My therapist had me do jumping jacks, which I wouldn't recommend in this situation.

"I want you to lie down," I said. "It's better for the baby too. She can lie on top of you. You'll be like a big, warm Mommy mattress for her."

She seemed more stable. I risked grabbing a towel off the mini-shelf to my left. "Let's keep your baby warm and dry. I don't want her to shiver." The last thing I needed was Might's glucose and maybe calcium dropping when I couldn't monitor it.

I unfolded another towel on to the cold, wet tile floor. Lying down on it wouldn't feel good for Joan, but neither would cracking her neck and squashing Might.

"It'll be like a bed. Please, Joan."

She sighed, but she began to lever herself on her back.

"They're coming. ETA 10 to 15 minutes," Ryan told us through the door.

A septic premie can die in 10 minutes. Easily.

"That's the fastest they can do it?" I hollered.

"They said it might be closer to ten, but they couldn't promise it. It's snowing, maybe freezing rain."

No. The only thing worse than a premature herpes/Zisa baby was having to keep one alive, solo, in a bathroom, with no equipment.

CHAPTER 28

"They're asking—is baby still breathing?" Ryan yelled through the door.

"Yes! But she's tachypneic. That means she's breathing fast." I stopped to count her breaths. "Like, 75 or 80. She's going to tire out."

Joan made a noise. She shifted on the ground, propping her head up on her elbows as she avoided putting her feet in the shower stall. Then she held out her hands for Might, and I cautiously handed her to her mother, adding, "But she's tough. She's done really well so far."

I had limited options on how to help the baby breathe.

1. Warm the baby up and stimulate her. Done.

2. Give mouth to mouth. But I didn't want to suck Zisa +/- herpes into my lungs, as long as she was holding her own.

3. Call for help, which Ryan had already done.

After Joan delivered the placenta, we could get her covered up and let Ryan in.

If either of their lives were in danger, I'd throw open the door, but right now, since we couldn't offer the baby much and the EMS were on their way, Ryan could stay on the phone.

Joan bent her knees, planted her feet on the ground, and groaned. Not a short grunt, but a prolonged sound.

"Are you delivering the placenta?" My sense of time was off-kilter (*complètement foqué*, as we say in Montreal), but the placenta can take 20 minutes to disengage on its own. Normally, we apply traction to encourage it to come off, but I'd been focused on Might's breathing— and not looking forward to more blood on the floor.

Joan rolled on to her right arm, toward the wall. She struggled to sit upright, heaving her hips off the tile and pressing into her feet, like a bridge pose on her side.

"Hang on. Joan?" Her bum was pumping up and down in a way that seemed all-too-familiar. "Are you—"

She twisted on to her front, still cradling Might.

"Give me the baby!"

She ignored me, crawling back toward the shower stall on to one hand and both knees. She reached for the edge of the shower door with her Might-free hand.

"Joan, wait!" I crouched over her and scooped Might into my hands. Joan didn't resist, although Might crunched up her face like she wanted to cry.

Joan sank into a squat, still holding on the shower stall door. She was taking up all the room between the toilet and the wall and the shower stall, so I backed up toward the wooden door.

"Hang on, Joan." Might was so small that I thought I could hold on to her and catch the placenta one-handed, like the "football hold" in breastfeeding. The towel made Might a bit bulkier and easier to hold on to.

Joan ignored me, sinking down so low that her buttocks nearly touched her heels.

The ululation that ripped from her throat almost made me scream back.

And then a small, smooth, glistening bit of flesh protruded between her legs.

It didn't look like placenta.

Placentas are dark. Really red-brown, kind of like liver, only round and smelly.

This one was ... holy shit.

Holy SHIT.

I dove on to the ground, one hand extended underneath her vagina. "Push," I babbled. "That's right, Manouchka, good job."

"Manouchka?" said Ryan, from outside the door, but he had to remind me of the wrong name later, because I was so busy using one hand to catch Might II.

The surprise twin.

CHAPTER 29

"Ryan, we've got a twin here. Repeat, we have a twin," I shouted, even as my eyes locked on the miniature, red body lying so still in my hand.

Might II wasn't breathing.

I couldn't see her heart beating, either.

"I'm starting CPR."

I needed to resuscitate. I needed both hands.

I placed Might I on the ground. "Joan, don't move!"

Then I tried to set Might II on the floor beside her sister, to free up my hands. Only Might II didn't reach the ground. She was still attached to Joan through her shorter umbilical cord. And for whatever reason, Joan was struggling to stand, using the shower door as a wobbly ladder.

"Joan, stop!"

I'd have to cut Might II's cord.

She needed CPR. And I couldn't do CPR in mid-air. I couldn't do both delayed cord clamping and CPR. Unless …

I got down on my left knee, like I was doing the classic wedding proposal, and balanced Might II on my right thigh. She was so weensy that she fit lengthwise with inches to spare. I could easily interlace my fingers around her torso and overlap my thumbs on her sternum, above her xiphoid process, to start compressions.

Human Remains

And 1 and 2 and 3 …

Joan swayed. I shouted, "Joan, can you squat for 30 more seconds? I need your placenta higher than your twins, but I can't have you pulling Might I off the ground!"

I had to compress fast and strong, over a hundred beats a minute, while I roared, "Ryan, I need help! I need mouth-to-mouth on this twin! And I need you to check the other one!"

The position was so awkward, I was afraid I'd drop Might II, or at least get the seal wrong, if I tried to do mouth to mouth on my own thigh. Yet she needed oxygen.

I could switch to the one-handed technique CPR to milk the umbilical cord, which held oxygenated blood, but I was already afraid Might II might topple off my thigh or that Joan would fall backwards and crush us all. I needed Ryan.

He rattled the door knob.

"No!" Joan called, gripping the metal edge of the shower door.

"Joan, unlock the door for him. Please! Pull down your skirt. I'll follow you with the twins." Her babies' need for survival trumped her modesty.

"No, no, no, NO!"

"Joan, *unlock the door!*" I bellowed, as I pumped on her second baby's chest. "He can breathe for this baby! He can check on the first baby!"

Joan tried to drag her skirt back over her thighs. But even as she did so, blood squirted out of her vagina, swiftly followed by the brown-red mass of placenta.

Which meant that she was no longer providing oxygen to this baby, but we were also no longer tied to Joan. I could let Ryan in.

I scrambled to my feet. The floor was slippery with fluid. My feet skidded, but I managed to scoop up both babies and use my quads to push myself up without squishing either twin. At least all the liquid decreased the coefficient of friction as I carefully towed the placenta across the floor by the umbilical cords.

Joan lifted Might I out of my hand. I hesitated, but I didn't fight her. I needed a hand free.

I unlocked the door, breathing through my mouth. "I need two breaths."

I wanted out of this bloody hellhole. I wanted to put Might II on a clean, flat surface, like the dining room table, instead of cupping her in both my hands, but I'd start with the breaths.

Ryan managed to press the door open two inches while I belatedly backed out of his way. His eyes widened at my Carrie-like appearance before his gaze shifted behind me.

My elbow bumped into something soft.

Joan. She'd squeezed between the sink and the door. She was no longer holding her first baby.

I started to yell before I spotted the bundle of Might I, complete with a bloody umbilical stump, in the sink. A pair of used nail scissors rested on the counter. While I goggled, Joan reached for her second twin.

"Don't!"

My hands clutched Might II, but my hindbrain realized that Joan wasn't snatching her baby away. Her deep brown hands aimed for Might II's head, tilting the chin upward while pushing the forehead down.

Joan opened her mouth over the baby's nose and mouth and exhaled once.

The baby lay nestled in my two hands as she did mouth to mouth.

She was saving her own baby's life, calmer than I'd ever seen a woman who'd just given birth, let alone given birth to premature twins, after the death of her husband. She was tough.

"Now stop. I'm going to do compressions." I moved Might II to the floor towel, which was bloody and askew but better than nothing. I encircled her teensy chest and started pumping.

"Hope." Ryan's voice. I had my back to the door, but I knew he was trying to reach us.

I heard Joan hip-check the wood. "No, Mister Ryan."

"Joan, I can't run two codes!" I yelled, while the 911 operator burbled in the background.

Ryan started to answer the operator, which gave Joan the edge to slam the door and lock it on him.

"No! I need more breaths!" Joan ignored me, bending over the baby in the sink.

I gave the breaths myself. Might II's skin was already cold. I could see her tiny chest move with my exhalation.

I could pop her lung if I wasn't careful. I was probably breathing too hard out of stress. Premies have very stiff lungs. That's why we try to delay delivery as long as possible and give them steroids before they're born.

I touched Might II's brachial artery. No pulse.

I restarted compressions.

But this baby had never taken a breath. I'd never felt her heart beat. She might have died in utero.

Might I was more crucial now.

If I had to choose, I chose Might I.

It sounds horrible, but that's triage. It's the battlefield. The first twin, the stronger twin, the one with the heartbeat and working lungs— that was the one I'd have to focus on. She had microcephaly, but at least that wasn't DEADoceaphaly.

Joan lifted Might I from the sink and held her firstborn to her chest. I couldn't see anything from down on the ground. "Is she breathing?"

Joan didn't answer me.

"Is she *BREATHING?*"

Chapter 30

No response, except that Joan bundled Might I so tightly, she might smother her.

"Joan! Let me see!"

I craned my neck, keeping up the compressions on Might II, but my attention was laser-focused on Might I.

"Ryan! *I need you.*"

The door shook, with some squeaking noises, and then it thrust open. Ryan tossed a disposable pie plate in the garbage—he'd folded it and used it to finagle the lock—while talking on the phone. "Up the stairs. The elevator's really slow. Unless you're going to have trouble with the stretcher." His voice died as he took in the full-blown scene: me doing CPR on Might II on the floor, surrounded by blood, amniotic fluid, umbilical cords, and placenta; Joan half-naked with her first twin.

Points for not fainting.

Joan screamed and tried to shield her nether regions with Might I. Her skirt covered most of her, but obviously not enough.

I called, "Ryan, please take over CPR here. I need Twin 1."

He whipped his head away from Joan, closed his eyes, and swallowed. I could see his Adam's apple bob up and down. I was asking a lot of a civilian. Most of them couldn't even stay coherent on a 911 call.

"Ryan, *please*."

He looked at me with those dark eyes, the ones that made me melt, the ones that made me scream, the ones that made me swear to be a better person. His face was wooden.

Maybe he couldn't deal. The blood alone would send most people screaming into the hallway.

Ryan set his still-squawking phone on the sink ledge and dropped to the ground on his knees, ready to do CPR on Might II.

Tears stung my eyes.

That's my man. He always comes through.

I showed him how to landmark, and he started compressions.

"After every six compressions, give two breaths." Not as good as 3:1, but better than before. "I'll be back to help."

He didn't have gloves. He'd never done CPR on a human before, let alone on a premature newborn, but I had to get to Might I.

"Joan, if she's not breathing, she needs mouth to mouth and CPR. She's the one who's more likely to—" *Live*, I almost said, and caught myself in time—"benefit."

Ryan said, after giving a breath to Might II, "Please, Mrs. Acayo. Immaculate Joan." He said her name beautifully, like music. Ryan sings in his church choir. "'The whole creation groans'"—breath, breath—"'and suffers the pains'"—breath, breath—"'of childbirth together.'"

He was quoting, probably from the Bible. Even though he was a guy who'd never seen childbirth, he emitted a calm energy.

Me, screaming and pounding on the baby's chest and calling out orders—that was technically correct, and I knew how to save a baby's life better than anyone here, but Ryan was reaching her heart.

She lowered Might I toward him. I intercepted her.

Joan's legs buckled, and Ryan lunged toward her, temporarily abandoning Might II so that he could lower Joan on the toilet.

Meanwhile, I stared at Might I.

Who was not breathing.

Her face was frozen in place.

When I pulled back the towel, her little chest wasn't moving.

"Shit," I said, and I was on my knees, laying Might I on the ground. I was giving a breath, because this was a respiratory arrest, God damn it. If we could get any air in her, her heart should start beating again.

Might I's skin was warmer than her sister's. Only by a few degrees, but I'd take it.

Baby, breeeeeeeeeeathe.

Breeeeeeeeeeathe.

When I put my fingers to her arm, I cried out. "I can feel her heart!" She had a pulse.

A slight, slow one, compared to the usual newborn pulse, but she had one.

Joan made a noise deep in her throat.

I ignored it. I had to count. If the heart rate was under 60 beats per minute, I'd start CPR.

It took me a moment to find the second hand on my watch, I was so messed up. But then I had it, faster than one per second.

Ryan got on his knees beside me, struggling to find the pulse in his twin.

I told him, "Start CPR!" I was not optimistic about his twin.

I counted the beats on Might I. Eighty beats. Not great—almost two thirds normal—but not needing chest compressions. Just breaths.

I concentrated on Might I. On lifting her head up gently. On covering her nose and mouth when I gave her two more breaths.

The 911 operator was calling out in a tinny voice from the speaker on Ryan's abandoned phone. I called, in case she could hear me, "Twin 1 has a pulse again."

I gave three more breaths, and then I thought I felt Might I move. She was with us.

Someone hammered on the door. The paramedics had arrived.

Now we could do proper neonatal resuscitation.

And then I'd go to the hospital myself. Not only to accompany the Acayo family, but to register as a patient and request two tests on me:

1. Zisa.
2. Pregnancy.

CHAPTER 31

WEDNESDAY

I tiptoed into Joan's hospital room after dawn.

She lay alone in her bed. No babies, and her roommate's bed was empty.

My throat tightened. I blinked.

Joan curled on her side, toward the dim light shining through the white horizontal slats. I was glad that she'd gotten a room with a window.

She was breathing so quietly, I couldn't hear her, but her chest rose and fell. Under her thin, white blanket, I could tell that her belly was smaller today. Vacant.

My eyes stung, and not only because I hadn't slept all night.

My mother had given me a square wicker basket full of apples and oranges. I placed it as quietly as possible on the bedside table, nudging aside a black laptop to make room. Joan might not feel like eating, but Mom had insisted that the nurses "and maybe even the doctors!" would appreciate it.

I spun toward the door. My boot heel squeaked on the tile, and Joan's sleep-roughened voice said, "Doctor Hope."

I faced her, agonized. "I'm so sorry, Joan."

She held out her arms. She enveloped me in her warm, spicy scent and kissed my forehead. "You did your best, Doctor Hope. You and Ryan, that fine man of yours. I can never thank you enough."

"But your babies—" Might I was in the NICU, and Might II …

"I know." Her eyes glimmered with tears, but she didn't allow them to fall. "My littlest girl is with God now. I'm going to call her Hope."

I started. It was an honour, and yet a creepy one. I tried to look appreciative.

"You can help me name my big girl."

Her "big girl's" eyes flared in my brain. I remembered Might I's miniature body, the skin so thin that it was transparent, showing the red tissue underneath. I remembered the feel of her learning to breathe again. The odds were never in her favour, but this girl was a fighter. Like her mother.

"Do you have to go to work now, Dr. Hope?"

She looked so lonely, I lied, "Oh, I can stay a bit." I perched on the edge of a chair at her beside. There weren't any decorations in her room, only a bed, white walls, and this padded cream vinyl chair for visitors.

"Thank you. I would normally be surrounded by family at home, but the flights are too expensive, and … " She hesitated while I nodded vigorously. I wouldn't spend money on a plane ticket as a pregnant wife of an academic with no funding. She added, "Lawrence was worried about infection."

Might II's small, still face replayed in my mind. I squeezed my eyes shut. "Of course. Everyone is worried about Zisa nowadays."

"Not only Zisa, Doctor Hope. His father told him about a truck driver from Burundi who was vomiting blood and bleeding from his mouth and nose—"

My entire body seized up. "Ebola? But that was only in Liberia and Sierra Leone, right?" I don't know much about African geography, but I do know that we managed to contain Ebola's attack on West Africa. Uganda's on the east side.

Joan clucked her tongue. "No, not Ebola. Everyone thought he had Marburg, and they were afraid of touching him. Even the ambulance drivers did not want to take him. They said they didn't have the proper protective equipment. The truck driver was trying to walk, but he was so weak, he had to stop by the side of the road because he had diarrhea as well as vomiting."

Wow. I kind of didn't want to know that. I suppose it was written across my face, so she added, "They did get him to hospital eventually. He had Rift Valley disease."

Hemorrhagic fever is so rare in Canada, all I knew was a) Ebola, and b) Marburg. I'd never heard of Rift Valley disease before Stephen Weaver's poster, but now I couldn't get away from it. I know it's a psychological coincidence that you can stumble across something obscure and end up seeing it everywhere. I even know the name for it, the Baader-Meinhof Phenomenon. Still, what were the chances that the Acayos came from a region that was attacked by the same virus Stephen Weaver was studying?

On the other hand, Zisa came from Uganda, too, and I wouldn't blame Lawrence for Zisa. Mother Africa contained a motherlode of diseases.

I tried to stick to the facts. "Doesn't Rift Valley usually affect animals and get spread through mosquitoes? Dr. Stephen Weaver has a picture on his wall, so I looked it up."

Joan closed her sunken eyes for a moment. "Yes, Rift Valley disease is mostly a disease of animals. Most people who get infected don't get very sick, but Lawrence said that one percent of them get hemorrhagic fever. They start bleeding everywhere. Not only do they have bloody vomit and stool, but blood comes out of their gums, their noses, their skin, and their injection sites."

Eesh. I couldn't recall how we'd gotten on to this cheerful topic, but it reminded me how little I knew about medicine. Rift Valley disease sounded like a weird combination of Zisa (spread by mosquitoes, and most people don't even know they have the infection because it's so mild) and Ebola (epic exsanguination that only a vampire could love).

"Lawrence's father knows three men who went blind from this disease during the last epidemic. Another little girl started seizing in church. They had to carry her out. The virus had affected her brain. She survived, but she still has trouble talking, and she walks with a limp."

"That's horrible!" A fresh surge of guilt welled up in my chest. I should be on the front lines, fighting pathogens, instead of cowering in a lab. Then I caught myself. You combat disease in a lab, too, perhaps even more effectively, because you attack it at its source. "Well, at least Stephen Weaver is working hard on Rift Valley disease."

Joan pressed her hand against her post-partum belly. The extra flesh folded in over her hand. "Yes. I am grateful for that. He spoke to me and Lawrence about it, although I explained that I'd never seen a case. You know, Doctor Hope, I didn't agree with Lawrence about staying in Canada. I wanted to see my parents and my brothers and sisters. That truck driver was in Kabale, about 200 miles from the capital city of Kampala. The farmers, the herders, and the veterinarians who handle the animals are infected before the city people. It was unlikely that I'd get the disease. Lawrence was adamant that I shouldn't take the risk. He said, 'You can't tame a mosquito. I'm waiting for the first report of Rift Valley disease from Kampala. I don't want it to be you.'"

"That's a good point." I'd always wanted to go to Africa, but I can't say this was making me book my first ticket.

She crossed her arms over her breasts, which seemed swollen under her hospital gown, although I tried not to look. First I noticed Summer's bosom, and now Joan's. Probably that wasn't what Anne of Green Gables meant when she talked about "bosom friends." Joan said, "Lawrence was very protective of me. He didn't trust the government. He said the first case was officially diagnosed on the fourth of March, and the government sent a rapid response team that included six students from the Health Club at the university. Lawrence understood why they were sending them. They would be young and eager, and we would need as many people as possible, but to send young people with almost no training into an epidemic … "

"Are they okay?" I had a mental image of six students charging into the fray, wearing lab coats and gas masks, only to be carried out in coffins.

She nodded. "Lawrence was keeping in touch with them. He even helped one of them publish a blog about his experiences on a health care network site."

"That was good of him." I smiled.

"He was a good man." She took a deep breath and covered her eyes for a moment, but when she lifted her hands away, she still didn't cry.

"My girls wanted to come meet him. That's why they came early. They didn't want to miss him. They want justice, like their mother."

Weirder and weirder. "Um, I don't know if babies or fetuses can decide—"

She kept talking over me. "One of the women from my church came to visit me. She asked if she could bring me anything, and I said yes, Lawrence's laptop." She pointed to the black case beside the fruit basket. "I didn't trust anyone else to go through it, Doctor Hope. Only you."

I swallowed. I both did and I didn't want to pry through his computer. "Why don't you do it yourself, Joan? You're his wife. You knew him the best."

She closed her eyes and shook her head. After a moment, she said, "I'm afraid."

She had never struck me as fearful. Not when she was crashing the lab meeting in the wake of her husband's death. And certainly not when she was delivering and saving two premature babies. She was one of the strongest women I'd ever met. I licked my lips. "What are you afraid of?"

"I'm afraid of what I might find. Perhaps we could do it together."

"Okay," I said. This was a lot easier than trying to resuscitate twins. "I can stay for ten more minutes. Let me text one of my colleagues." I chose Summer, for obvious reasons.

I'm at OHSC with Joan Acayo. She delivered twins last night, and one of them died. I'll be at the lab soon, but please tell Tom not to worry. I can stay late tonight.

She answered right away: *OMG! Take your time. Take the day off.*

Meanwhile, Joan had booted up the laptop.

I opened his Internet browser and clicked on History, which offered me an option for recently-closed windows. Amongst the boring scientific stuff, I found a motherlode of site listings.

free-white-girl-porn videos
big-white-girl-porn videos
blonde white woman with black man
Sexy Asian girls tits & ass
Asian female XXX sex videos
Black porn free XXX

My first instinct was to slam the laptop shut, but that would have been counter-productive, so I said, "Um."

Joan snorted. Clearly, she'd read the site names too. "He liked white women."

He liked all sorts of women, but I could see her point. So far, the white women were winning the browser battle. And in real life, how often do you see a black guy and a white, usually blonde, woman? Pretty often. Maybe as often as a black man and black woman.

Asian men end up with white women too. Sometimes they start off with an Asian woman, under familial pressure, and then they dump her and "trade up."

No one talks about this, but when non-white guys go for white women, it's like they're upgrading. Meanwhile, if white guys pick a woman from any other race, they're fetishizing us. "Jungle fever." "Yellow fever." Like you can't be lucid and like a woman from another culture.

Although, to be fair, a lot of the guys *are* fetishizing us. They don't see us as people, just another type to bang and brag about.

I don't think Tucker sees me that way, but it is weird how much he relishes other languages and cultures. Who else tries to learn Arabic and Urdu from random patients? I never asked if he dated a straight up white, Canadian, "my family's been here forever" girl, partly because it would make me crazy to find out.

In any case, I didn't feel great commenting on Lawrence's sexual proclivities. I changed the subject. "Lots of people like white women, but he chose to marry you."

The corners of her mouth turned down. "You are so innocent, Doctor Hope. Uganda is not like Canada. We are not—the men are not—" She stopped to select her words. "We recognize all sorts of marriages. Christian, Hindu, Islamic, or a customary marriage."

"What's that?"

"It is performed under African customary law and includes polygamous marriages. You may have heard of President Uhuru Kenyatta's law in Kenya."

Of course I hadn't.

Her breath escaped in a sigh. "He removed the clause that a man had to consult his first wife before marrying another wife. A man can also marry as many women as he wishes."

"Well, that's nuts," I said. "Who would want that?"

She burst into laughter. "Ah, Doctor Hope. You are so refreshing."

It made me sound like a soft drink ad. I shook my head. "No, seriously."

"Seriously, Doctor Hope, I admit that many women were not in favour of this law, but some Ugandan men spoke of moving to Kenya after it was passed. So you see the cultural differences between my country and yours."

"Yes," I said. I try to appreciate other cultures, but I couldn't see any advantage for women when guys could spread it around everywhere. Putting emotion aside, how many kids would he have? What about disease? "Does it make a difference if you were married in a church?"

"Yes, we had a white wedding."

I sat up a little straighter. Did she mean white as in a white dress, or white as in that's how white people do it? Either way, Western customs were taking over the world. Traditionally, white is the colour of mourning in China, but I had a cousin get married in a white cheongsam, or traditional Chinese garment, before she switched to a red one for the reception, and most didn't bother with a cheongsam at all.

"Lawrence was progressive in many ways," she said. "That was one of the things I loved about him."

Huh. I'd never related to the Christian cannon—among other things, I didn't respond to the idea of God sending his son down to be tortured, even if he did get resurrected—but if the alternative was a world where guys could gather wives like Pokémon, I'd go for the church.

"Are you saying … " I had to phrase it carefully. "Was he allowed to have sexual relations with other women?"

"The church discourages it," she said.

The church. But what about her, Immaculate Joan? Didn't it matter what *she* said?

She gave me a sad smile. "I wanted to keep my husband, Doctor Hope."

In the Western World, if we want to keep our men, we may offer more blow jobs than we really feel like, but we don't give them carte blanche.

Then I thought of Ryan and Tucker. I would rather rip my heart out of my own thorax than give either of them up. I was in no position to lecture anyone about monogamy.

So. "Do you know if he was having sex with other women, or just watching porn?" I know some people think there's no "just" about porn, but come on. Would you rather your husband stared at the computer screen, or got jiggy with other real, live human beings?

Joan shook her head. "We didn't talk about it. We used to talk about it, many times. I would cry, I would beg him, I would bring him to church. Nothing would change. I thought Canada might be a new start for us."

I made a sad face and nodded before I glanced at the computer. "Did you ever read his e-mail or his texts?"

She shook her head. "I don't have his passwords. He only gave me the one to unlock his laptop. After I got pregnant, he said I could check my e-mail on it instead of walking to the library."

What a saint. Even the fact that he didn't wipe his browser cache after looking at porn—blah. "Can you figure out his password?"

After about ten minutes of dreaming up different combinations, the conclusion was, no. She settled back into bed with a sigh.

"Listen. Let me see what's not password-protected, okay? And maybe I can copy some of his files on my USB."

"All right." She sighed and started pressing on her breasts, grimacing, while I clicked. Her baby needed her. But first, I pointed out the most obvious thing I'd found, a graphic that had been saved under his non-protected Pictures folder. "He made up an ad for Craigslist."

"What's Craigslist?"

"It's like classified ads, online."

Her face contorted. "You think he was meeting women?"

"Not with this ad. Craigslist is for everything. People buy and sell furniture on it." They hook up on Craigslist, too, but not through this graphic.

"He was always looking. The women he worked with, they were all single, none of them Christian. They wouldn't come to my church."

I could not imagine Dr. Hay taking up with anyone. Ducky would probably run away screaming. I thought of Summer, with her conspicuous breasts, and her blushing, and the way that everyone had a crush on her, including the security guard. I shook the thought away and pointed at the

Human Remains

screen. "Joan, he wasn't trying to date anyone with this. Look!" I blew up craigslist04.jpg to 120 percent size.

RESEARCH SUBJECTS NEEDED
Are you 19 to 35 years old?
Are you female?
We are currently looking for volunteers for a research study.

If you are interested, please call or e-mail for more information.
All queries are strictly confidential.
Compensation provided.

Joan's forehead crinkled. "What is this?"

I hadn't known that gathering research subjects on Craigslist was a thing. But when I used my phone to comb through the Craigslist volunteer section, I found quite a few ads, some of them associated with a university and/or hospitals, as well as companies promising weight loss or help with gambling addiction. The legit-sounding ones had posters of happy people and prominent contact information.

Lawrence's was a homemade blue text box.

Here was the first concrete proof that Dr. Lawrence Acayo was going rogue in recruiting research volunteers.

He didn't have funding. He didn't have a grant. He did have a position at a lab, which gave him enough legitimacy to recruit your average impoverished student into a study. He knew more than most human beings about pathologic viruses, he'd researched Zisa, and he'd monitored hemorrhagic disease outbreaks in Uganda.

What exactly had Dr. Lawrence Acayo set in motion before he died?

CHAPTER 32

I tried to sneak into the lab, since I was late, but Summer pounced on me as soon as I beeped my way through the door. "You delivered a *baby* last night?"

"Two babies," Mitch reminded her, cutting toward me from Chris's back corner.

The lab smelled a bit antiseptic. I wanted to sit down at my bench, but not with Summer and Mitch converging on me. Mitch seemed to have eaten onions, even though it was only 9:08 a.m.

I glanced at the closed door to Tom's office. I needed to get some safety modules done, pronto, in case anyone checked the time stamp. At least Chris was absent, so I only had to deal with two Scoobies at once.

I squeezed past Dr. Wen to get to the computer next to the window, which was already on. I almost hit him with my backpack, and he frowned. I made an apologetic face at him before I turned to answer the Scoobies, who'd paused in the aisle on the other side of Dr. Wen. "Yes, two babies, although only one made it. Joan did all the hard work." I swiped my card over the computer's card reader and typed my password. I still had to re-type it before the computer accepted it.

My fingers shook slightly. I hadn't slept last night. I'd laid beside Ryan with my eyes closed, my mind leaping with all the things I could have done better with Might I and II. I should have made sure the door was unlocked. She must have rigged it up so that it locked when I shut the door, but I should have checked. I should have gotten Joan to sit down on the toilet after Might II was born. Then the cord might have reached, and I could have resuscitated Might II on the ground instead of on my thigh. I could've started the 3:1 compression to breath ratio right away. And Ryan could have gotten in sooner, and and and …

The biggest thing was, why hadn't Joan told me she'd been carrying twins? But blaming her seemed like a dick move.

I shoved my backpack in the shelf under the counter, ignoring the lunch I should put in the fridge. I'd eat it in a few hours anyway.

"You delivered babies at her dinner party? I mean, who *does* that?" said Summer.

Dr. Wen raised his eyebrows and sidled away from me.

"Maybe it's more common in Uganda." That was Mitch.

"Home births are getting pretty standard," I said, trying to keep it cool. The stupid lab safety module didn't want to load, no matter how many times I clicked on it. I restarted the computer.

"Yes, but with proper training and equipment. You didn't bring anything for a home birth to a dinner party, did you?" said Summer.

Although I liked Summer, her tone raised my hackles. It sounded kind of TMZ/Perez Hilton to me, with an extra side dish of *What will these savages do next?* amazement. "Maybe I should have. Maternal stress increases the chances of premature labour by as much as 25 to 60 percent. I looked it up last night."

Summer flushed and let her hair cover her face, but Mitch didn't care. He scratched his arm and squinted at the snow on the rooftops outside, clearly visualizing the scene. "That's wild. What was it like? I've never seen a baby getting born. And this was like, in their living room or something?"

Samir clucked his tongue. He was obviously listening all the way from the fume hood at the back of the room. Hell, maybe Chris and Tom were tucked in there, too. Windows was taking forever to load on my computer.

"Bedroom. That's where I'd do it," said Summer, recovering.

"You'd probably hire someone to massage your feet while you were in labour."

"That's a great idea. Know anyone?"

"I'd do it for free."

"I bet you would, you pervert."

"Hey, I'm offering you a free massage!"

While they entertained each other, I logged into the lab safety module. Eventually, Mitch wandered to the back of the lab with Samir, but not before he threw over his shoulder, "We want the whole story at lunch."

"Yeah! And we'll take you to Petra's tonight." Summer grinned at me from behind Dr. Wen's disapproving countenance.

"Uh, I've got a lot of work to do—"

"This is more important," Mitch called from halfway across the room.

I'd managed to escape them. For now.

I buckled down on lab safety, watching the videos on 2x speed, clicking the quiz answers as fast as I could. Then, when I could hear Summer's feet tapping across the floor toward me, I cut out of the lab and into the central bathroom. There's one set of bathrooms, in the hallway between the two labs, with one regular stall and one handicapped stall, both of them barely illuminated by a flickering fluorescent light.

I took some deep breaths and avoided watching myself in the mirror as I washed my hands. It's best not to check yourself out when you're sleep-deprived and chock-full of trauma. Even though they say sex makes you glow, Ryan and I had been too shell-shocked to hook up last night.

The door pushed inward while I was drying my hands on a scrap of paper towel and dropping it into the recycling bin.

I stiffened, but it wasn't Summer reflected in the mirror.

I spun around to face Dahiyyah. Our eyes met with a shock of recognition. Of what, I couldn't say exactly, but she looked as wrung-out as I felt while the door drifted closed behind her.

We didn't speak. We gazed at each other for a long moment, listening to a tap drip behind us. The lights quivered like a poor man's dance club, making it even harder to read her expression.

I finally nodded my head in a silent hello, which broke the spell.

She licked her lips. "You delivered Lawrence's babies."

"Yes, Joan gave birth last night." The rumour mill clearly extended its reach to Dr. Hay's lab. I'd never mentioned my part in the delivery and resuscitation, but everyone already knew.

"One of them died?"

I closed my eyes and nodded, silently apologizing to Might II.

She shuddered. "That's two."

I had a dreadful feeling I knew what she was talking about. The faucet plink, plink, plinked its drops into the sink. Almost like tears.

"*Jamais deux sans trois,*" said Dahiyyah, glancing over her shoulder, even though no one else approached the bathroom door.

I cleared my throat. We have that expression in English, too: never two without three. "That's a superstition. You're a scientist."

She hiccupped a small laugh. "Am I?"

"Of course you are. You're going to grad school next year, right?"

She pressed the back of her hand to her mouth, but I could still make out her words behind it. "You need references for that."

"Dr. Hay—" I stopped right there. Dr. Hay was her supervisor. The head of the lab. If she wouldn't give Dahiyyah a sterling reference, this R.A. would never get into grad school. She might not even be able to get a job in industry. She was stuck.

Dahiyyah hunched her shoulders. She couldn't meet my eyes anymore.

No. Hell, no. I started brainstorming for her. My voice bounced off the bathroom walls. "You need another reference. That's all. Someone who'll write a good letter." Actually, she'd need at least three of them, but we'd start with one.

She closed her eyes. "Dr. Acayo said he would. If I worked hard enough for him, he would write me the best letter. And he had contacts at Stanford, and in Miami, and around the world ... "

"Ah." His death would have been a personal and professional shock. The only good news was that it dropped her down on my suspect list. "Yes, that would have been fantastic. I'm sorry to hear that. I suppose ... " I paused. It sounded heartless, but I should point out another option. "There is one more person in your lab who went to Stanford, who might give you a reference."

Her pupils seemed to dilate, although it was hard to tell in the bathroom's erratic light. "I would never ask him. I don't speak to him."

"Oh." But Stephen Weaver had mentioned her making almond cookies. She didn't have to chat with him over her cuisine, but a full stomach could predispose him to writing a strong reference letter for her. "Why not?"

Her arms tightened in an X over her chest, her hands balled in her armpits. If she'd been Catholic, she would've crossed herself. "He's—" Her thyroid cartilage bobbed in her throat. Her eyes were wide and agonized. "The last time I saw him, Dr. Acayo told me to be careful of him."

"On Sunday?" She started to nod, and I couldn't believe it. Harold hadn't mentioned her specifically on the video feed, but everyone always seemed to overlook Ducky. "You saw him when he left on Sunday?" I didn't even realize I was reaching for her arm until she snatched it away.

"No! I mean, I was working, but I didn't do anything to him! I was researching plasmids for him. He said it was important, that he'd write me a reference letter, but he kept fooling around on his phone and on his computer and eating all the cookies I'd made for the lab meeting on Monday. I was the one doing all the work, so when he said he was feeling sick and wanted to go home, I told him to just go, I'd finish up here!"

It was the most exasperated I'd ever heard her. I liked her for it. On my thoracic surgery rotation, the senior resident once told me to stop being so meek. Then he was surprised when I started speaking my mind, but he seemed to appreciate it. Apparently I, too, preferred more mouthy women.

But I needed to know more who, what, when, where, why. "When did Dr. Acayo leave the lab?"

Her lower lip stuck out. "Around six o'clock. He said he had to have supper. You'd think eating most of my cookies would've been good enough. I had to buy Oreos for the lab meeting the next day, and Dr. Weaver told me I was lazy, always taking short cuts … " Her lips trembled.

Honestly, I didn't know how they could be so nasty to her. It reminded me of a Moth podcast where a group of American soldiers had befriended a dog while they set up a base in the Middle East. When they got transferred elsewhere, they packed up camp and started driving away. The dog ran after them. He ran and ran. They'd slow down enough to let him catch up, and then they'd take off, laughing. They did that until he exhausted himself and couldn't run anymore. In the desert. With no water.

My voice hardened. "I know that's B.S. Don't listen to them."

She rearranged her head scarf, drawing it more tightly around her face. "They make fun of me. They take my equipment without asking. Even Lawrence did it. I couldn't find my round-bottomed flask or condenser all last week. Dr. Hay told me I didn't need it, but I like to keep things in order. They know it drives me crazy." Her voice rose on the last word, and she did sound off-kilter. "You should see my bench. I always keep my pipettes in the drawer. I don't like them out where other people will see them and think they can borrow them. Why do I come in this morning and find them spread all over my bench?"

"I have no idea."

"They're not even careful about it. They spill things. They mess up my papers and mix them up with theirs. I've started doing all my reading either online or keeping my papers in my bag because I don't want their nonsense. Once I found an ad for Brazilian waxing in the middle of a paper I'd printed on flaviviruses. Does that make any sense?"

I shook my head. It seemed like the sort of frat boy thing Mitch might do, to be honest.

"I'm a good girl," she said. The light overhead sizzled and darkened for a second, as if in agreement, before it lit her face again. She was young, but the dark circles under her eyes were more pronounced than Joan's. "I followed the rules. I got my degree. I do everything they tell me to. I don't have time to date the men my parents find for me. Where has that gotten me?"

"I don't know," I said, edging toward the paper towel dispenser. I knew I should stick around, but all I could think of was that I could hardly carry my own grief and fury around, let alone hers.

"They dump everything on me. Dr. Hay, Dr. Weaver, Dr. Acayo. The entire lab. On my shoulders! As if that weren't enough, last week, Summer asked if I wanted to help in Dr. Zinser's lab."

That made me pause in front of the door. "She did? Why?"

Her hands fisted, she jutted out her chin. "Ms. Graham was sick for a few days, and they couldn't keep track of everything. But instead of hiring a temporary secretary, their first thought was to dump it on me!"

It took me a second to realize that she was talking about Susan. "That's rough," I said, taking a step toward the door.

"I don't think she was that sick, anyway," said Dahiyyah. "Ms. Graham didn't show up at work on Friday, but I saw her car in the parking lot that night, and on Sunday, too."

"On Sunday?" No secretary works on a Sunday. It's a strictly Monday to Friday gig. The fact that Susan was sick made it even less likely that she would hang out without getting paid. "Are you sure?"

"I think so. She drives an old, white car, and she likes to park in the back, where people won't hit her."

No offence, but "old, white car" wasn't exactly going to make Dahiyyah a star trial witness, even though that's something I would say. "What kind of car was it?"

She shrugged.

"Did you see the license plate?"

Dahiyyah shrugged again. She chewed on her lip. "What does it matter, anyway? You don't believe me. Nobody believes me."

"I believe that you're overworked and underpaid and under a lot of stress," I said carefully. I try to avoid lying.

"That means that you don't believe me."

She was smart. And savage, in her own way. Psychiatrists often said that depression was anger turned inward. I'd never understood that, since I spent a lot of time murmuring comfortingly to patients who seemed about as tough as the tissues they shredded in their hands, but Dahiyyah? She took it personally that I didn't champion her without question.

"Look," I said, in my most soothing voice, "I want to chat, but I've got to finish up in the lab. We can talk more later."

Dahiyyah glared at me. "Right. You'll never speak to me again."

"No, I will. You seemed uncomfortable talking in front of Dr. Hay, but we can chat after hours. As long as I don't get in trouble with Tom. Maybe even after I finish up tonight, okay?"

I yanked my sleeve over my hand to cover my palm from germs as I grabbed the door handle, but I made the mistake of looking back.

Dahiyyah looked like she wanted to strangle me, tie a bag around my head, and drop me by the side of the road.

CHAPTER 33

I withdrew into Tom's office section until my heart recovered its normal rate. I was still taking deccccccp breaths when Susan gave me an odd look from behind her computer, although her fingers kept clicking away on the keyboard.

I pretended to straighten my boots on the welcome mat. If I'd thought ahead, I would've escaped the lab with my mealy tomato sandwich, but it was still sitting in my backpack near my computer. Lesson #1 from lab safety videos: never eat or drink in a lab. Sounds like common sense, but I always used to sneak my water into the ER so that I didn't get dehydrated between patients, even with the risk of C. diff and other bacteria.

My stomach growled. I glanced at the door to the lab, but I didn't want to run into the Scoobies, and especially not Dahiyyah.

Once again, I had trouble dealing with other human beings.

Susan started printing a document. The printer hummed before it spat out pages. She stood up and glanced at me from underneath her bangs.

Ten to one, she wanted to ask me about Joan's babies. I pre-empted her. "Thanks so much for helping me get my parking pass."

She walked to the printer at the corner of her desk. She was wearing an animal print tunic, black pants, and black ankle boots today. "You're welcome."

I cleared my throat, stuck my hands in my pockets, and glanced out that broad window pane. Smoke wafted from a nearby chimney, like in a Christmas postcard, except the outdoor scene was blocky brick buildings and cars shoved into parking lots. That gave me a reasonable segue. "I'm trying to figure out the best place to park. Where do you park?"

She pulled the papers off the printer and flipped through them, checking the page numbers. "In the north lot, back corner. I don't want anyone to hit me."

"Oh. Do you have a really nice car? I saw a black Mercedes this morning." My hands clenched in my pockets. So far, she hadn't contradicted Ducky's story.

"No, it's an old Camry, but it gets the job done. I don't need some idiot running into it, especially when it's icy out."

"Yeah, it was kind of snowy on Sunday. Must've been hard to come in. But at least there are lots of parking spaces on the weekend, eh?" My cheeks heated up. I don't do casual chat, which is kind of a liability for a pretend detective.

Susan stared at me without speaking for a long moment. Then she said, "I have to get back to work now, Dr. Sze. Was there anything you needed?"

"No, that was it. Thanks for the parking tip!" I beat it back into the lab, where Samir waved at me from his bench. Otherwise, the lab was unnaturally quiet. It was lunch time.

"Hi," I murmured, calculating where I should best inhale my sandwich. Not the office, because Susan already thought I was insane. Not the lab, because with my luck, I'd end up eating hydrofluoric acid, which is one of the scariest acids in the world. After Tucker had showed me the clip from Breaking Bad where they try to dissolve a corpse with HF, Tori had introduced me to Periodic Videos, where they dunked chicken drumsticks in HF, hydrochloric acid, and sulfuric acid—not what you want to think about before eating.

I couldn't even eat in the bathroom, like at a bad middle school dance, because Dahiyyah might pounce on me.

I decided to risk running down to the cafeteria. If I bumped into the Scoobies, good. I had some questions for them now.

Human Remains

Samir waved instead of joining me. I guess you don't win the Banting and Best Fellowship by taking a lunch break. I met Dr. Wen on the stairs, but the Scoobies had vanished. In fact, I managed to finish my sandwich, my water, a tangerine, and complete two more modules before they sauntered back into the lab. They must've taken a walk, because Summer was shaking out her hair after removing her hat, a cute little white cloche dotted with snow.

I cut around Dr. Wen to fake-smile at the three of them before I zoomed in on Mitch. "Did Harold catch Susan on video on Sunday?"

"Hello to you, too." Mitch unlooped the green scarf from around his neck and grinned at Chris, who removed his gloves and nodded back at me without speaking.

"Oh, sorry. Hi. How are you doing? Did you have a good lunch?"

Mitch unzipped his jacket. "No, I like women who get right to the point. Why would Susan be here on a Sunday?"

Dr. Wen glanced up from his work, listening.

I said, "I don't know. But Ducky thought she saw her car. An old, white car. Susan says she has a Camry. Does that sound right?"

Mitch frowned. "I have no idea."

Chris said, "Yes, she drives a white Toyota Camry. I waved to her in the parking lot once."

I turned to Chris. "Does she always park in the same spot?"

"Same corner of the north parking lot."

I crossed my arms and tapped my right foot. "Is there any way of verifying that? Maybe Harold could check the records of which cars were in the lot on Sunday. You scan your card to make the gate go up when you drive out, right? So we'd know what time she left. It would pop up on his monitor."

"I can't talk to him right now." Mitch compressed his lips, ripped his jacket off and slung it over his arm, nearly hitting me in the process. "Harold and the rest of the guards are under the gun because Lawrence died, even though it was off of university property. The police are interviewing them. Anyway, what am I supposed to say to him, 'I want you to go through all the records of everyone who drove into the parking lot on Sunday, including Susan Graham?'"

"That'd be nice."

The Scoobies gaped at me. Chris exhaled through his nose with what might have been irritation or laughter. Hard to tell with that guy.

I attempted to recover my dignity. "Look. I'm trying to honour Lawrence and their babies' memory by figuring out what happened to him. Ducky told me that Susan was here on Sunday, or at least her car seemed to be in the parking lot. That's weird, right? That's how I solve a lot of cases. I look for what's weird."

Summer and Mitch exchanged a glance. Chris might have bit back a smile.

I shook my head. What had these guys ever done for me, besides introduce me to Harold and take me out to a bar? "Fine. I'll do it myself."

"No!" Mitch shot forward so fast, his scarf slipped off his coat, but he managed to catch it with his right hand before it hit the floor. "I mean, you're not friends with Harold. I am. Let me do it, okay? But you've got to give me some time. The police come first. They're reviewing the security videos. I can't bust in and say, 'Hope wants to know if our secretary was here on Sunday because that was weird!'"

Summer laughed. Chris's mouth definitely twitched. Even Dr. Wen raised his eyebrows.

"Sure you can," I muttered, although I saw his point. My preference is to confront people, but most of the population prefers things like "subtlety" and "manners." "You'll do it as soon as you can, though? And you'll tell me about it when you're done?" When you're running a code, this is called "closing the communication loop." You don't yell, "Give me an amp of Epi!" You say, "Heather, give me an amp of Epi, and tell me when you're done."

"Yeah, of course," said Mitch, theoretically closing the loop. Still, the way he checked Summer and Chris's reactions, I wouldn't bet on him communicating with me.

I clenched my teeth, but decided to give him 48 hours. If he claimed he still couldn't get a hold of Harold by then, I'd head downstairs myself.

CHAPTER 34

A fume hood is a ventilation device designed to contain hazardous fumes, vapours, and dust.

Oh, is that why it's called a "fume hood?" Right on. That's pretty cool for something that looks like a stainless steel cabinet topped by deep, open shelving with a glass front.

Air flows into the hood and out of the laboratory exhaust system.

I barely made it through the description of the exhaust system, or the two different types of fume hoods at OHSC, constant air volume vs. variable air volume.

A clear sliding window, called a sash, protects the worker from splashes, fire, or minor explosions that could occur inside the hood.

My phone pinged.

Thank God. Even the thought of minor explosions barely kept me awake.

Chris had sent me a message. Subject: FYI

That could mean anything. But since Chris hardly talked, I assumed it wasn't something routine like DMSO, which I now knew was Dimethylsulfoxide. DMSO isn't that toxic in and of itself, but it dissolves a lot of substances, including nitrile gloves, so even if you think you're safe, bang! You aren't.

I clicked on the link in Chris's e-mail. While it slowly loaded on my phone, I realized that the more lab safety modules I completed, the more I wanted to flee the premises and hole up somewhere with no toxic chemicals, no kidnappers, and no one giving birth or dying, but where could I find that? It was like the time I attended Grand Rounds on Australian marine animals, and every single slide ran along the lines of, "And this is the blue-lined octopus. Its venom paralyzes your diaphragm, so your heart keeps beating, but you die of respiratory failure. It may be the most dangerous creature in the history of the world, except for the next slide … "

Chris's link brought me to a notice on the Ottawa police website.

HOMICIDE INVESTIGATION IN ALTA VISTA
FOR IMMEDIATE RELEASE

(Ottawa) The Ottawa Police Department Major Crime Unit is investigating a homicide in the Alta Vista area.

On Sunday, December 9th, Ottawa Police attended Paradise Park, at the corner of Lindsay Lane and Bullock Avenue, after receiving a 911 call at 9:47 p.m. Officers located a male on scene with life-threatening injuries. He was transported to hospital. Lawrence ACAYO, 29, of Ottawa, succumbed to his injuries at the hospital.

The Ottawa Police Department Major Crime Unit is seeking the public's assistance in identifying two persons of interest.

The persons of interest are described as follows:

#1: Caucasian male, heavy build, 5'10"-6'0"(178 cm - 183 cm), wearing a black jacket, black jeans, black shoes, black gloves, and black balaclava.

#2: Caucasian male, 5'6"-5'8"(168 cm - 173 cm), thin build, wearing a brown winter jacket with some white on the sleeves and collar, dark pants with white stripes on the sides, dark shoes, black gloves, and black balaclava

Anybody with information pertaining to this investigation is requested to call Ottawa Police Department's Major Crime Unit at 613-555-1222, ext. 8477. Anonymous tips are submitted by calling Crime Stoppers toll-free at 1-855-222-8477 (TIPS), or through the Ottawa Police app.

My mouth dropped open. I said, aloud, "The police found something! Two suspects!"

Dr. Wen sighed and continued working as best he could. I cut around him, heading for Chris's bench. Mitch was already there, muttering, "You should've told me."

It was hard to make out Chris's low, indistinct murmur. "I did tell you. Same as everyone else."

"Yeah, but you should've told me first."

"Why?" said Summer, arriving ahead of me. Her voice was higher and clearer than the guys'.

Mitch didn't answer.

I was still scrolling through my phone. The Ottawa police website was the nicest one I'd ever seen. I could share the article through Facebook, Twitter, Tumblr, Reddit, Google Plus, and Blogger. I could subscribe to their updates or print out the story.

Maybe I didn't have to do anything. The police would solve it all, and I could sit on my butt and trust them.

Mind. Blown.

I could act like a civilian.

That was what my parents wanted. Leave it to the experts. Play it safe.

But I thought of Joan, fighting so hard, giving birth on the floor of her bathroom, and I knew that wasn't an option. Whatever I could do, no matter how pathetic my offering, it was the least I could do for this brave woman and her surviving baby.

"Did any of you see these two suspects?" I asked the Scoobies. "We need to talk to Harold. If he kept a copy of his security recordings, we could figure out who they're talking about. We could even try and get camera stills and post them. Mitch, what's his number?"

Mitch shook his head. "I told you, he's busy. He said he'll call me."

Summer turned to me, her shiny, black hair falling off her shoulders. "I'll see what I can do."

I smiled at her. If anyone could motivate him, she could. Mitch didn't look thrilled about it, but who cared. In the meantime, this was the best lead we had so far. "Mitch and Chris, you were here on Sunday. Did you see these guys?"

Chris shook his head. I had to wonder if he ever looked at people, period. Mitch shrugged.

Summer said, "I wasn't here, but they sound like guys you'd run into any day of the week. I mean, they're two white guys, one heavy and one thin. I must've seen dozens of them today already. Mostly, they described their clothes. And the only weird thing about that is them wearing balaclavas. It's not that cold out."

I owned a balaclava stuffed into my parents' closet, but Summer was right. I only whipped out my full head mask when it was minus 30 or so. Otherwise, it wasn't worth messing up your hair.

On the other hand, if you were going to suffocate someone, anonymity was more important than a good hair day. So this could have been a premeditated murder.

I held up my phone. "There are few things here. They've officially called it homicide. So we can take suicide off the table."

Mitch said, "I never thought it was."

"It was a possibility, although not likely. The other thing is, I wonder how they came up with the suspects. Did they find a witness to these guys kidnapping Lawrence or dumping his body? And if so, who's their witness? It had to be someone close enough to tell that they were white, even behind their masks."

We all looked at each other.

"Mitch?" I said.

He made a face. "I didn't see any guys in balaclavas."

"They probably weren't wearing them inside the building. Do remember two white guys of this size, maybe hanging around the lab?"

"No one hangs around the lab. You can't even get in without swiping your card, and there are cameras at both entrances. It's too conspicuous. The guards would notice," said Mitch.

"I guess the guards *did* notice. Or the police, when they went through the videos. Or there's someone more observant working here." I eyeballed the Scoobies. Chris met my gaze without blinking. Summer blushed, but didn't drop her eyes. Mitch's upper lip curled slightly. I watched him until he shook his head and said, "I've got to get back to work."

No problem. I wanted to talk to the most observant person anyway. The one who worked with Lawrence and might have been scared enough to talk to the police.

Dr. Hay's lab and office doors were locked. I knocked on both of them.

Human Remains

At least one and perhaps two body shapes moved in the lab, behind the frosted glass, but no one moved toward the door, even when I waved and knocked louder.

I didn't have Dahiyyah's e-mail or phone number, but I moved back into the purple-walled waiting area and picked up the plastic-framed phone numbers. I dialed Judith Hay's assistant first.

Did she have a secretary? I'd never seen one, only Dahiyyah and Stephen. It went to Dr. Hay's voice mail, and I hung up. I tried the lab number next. It rang and rang. The shadows behind the glass never answered.

I hung up. Sooner or later, I'd see Dahiyyah again, and I definitely had more questions for her.

CHAPTER 35

Meet you downstairs? Done with our run.

Ryan texted a picture of himself and Roxy in front of the hospital. It was hard to make them out as more than shadows against the brick building. The sun had set, he was wearing black, and she was black-furred except her brow eye and muzzle markings, belly, and legs.

For a second, I thought of the two men who'd beat up and suffocated Lawrence Acayo, because they'd worn black, too, before I shoved the thought away. Ryan and Roxy were innocent. That, I knew.

When I hurried down the flights of stairs, Roxy barked at me from around the mostly-deserted bike racks, but Ryan was frowning over his phone. He crossed the sidewalk toward me and kissed me. He didn't smile, though, even when I broke away to stroke Roxy's fur to tell her she was a good dog, a very good dog, such a good dog, yes, yes, yes. In response, she kept trying to jump on me.

"Down, Roxy," said Ryan. He shortened the leash. It meant that Roxy's paws clambered in mid-air, so he covered her paws with his hands and set them on the ground. She panted and tried to lick the bit of exposed skin of my wrist, between my glove and coat sleeve. That reminded me of my dream with Lawrence's body, where snow had chilled the gap between my snow pants and my boots.

Human Remains

No. I forced myself to pat Roxy's soft, black head. She whined.

"Roxy, sit." Ryan sounded annoyed.

She sat, but her tail wagged, and as soon as I laughed, she stood up again.

Usually, Ryan's in a better mood after a run. Sweat dampened the roots of his hair, and I loved the sharp angles of his face and the muscles hidden under his jacket, but something was bugging him. "What's wrong?"

"Nothing."

I looked at him. Even though most of the light was only spillover from hospital windows and a clouded-over moon, he could tell I didn't believe him.

He ran a hand through his hair. "I guess it's the stuff online."

"Your White Birthright site?"

"I'm working on that, but it's more 14-88."

I stood still. He'd mentioned that website on the way to Joan's party.

"It's basically home base for the WH movement online. White Heritage. Alt-right. Alt-Reich. Whatever you want to call it." His mouth twisted.

"Like the Ku Klux Klan or Aryan Nation?"

Roxy sniffed Ryan's hand. He stroked her head absently.

I pulled off my gloves so I could feel her silky ears with my fingertips, even though the wind whipped around the building and cooled the rest of my hands. Roxy looked up at me and sidled closer to both of us, stepping on my right foot. The one with the sprained ankle, although it was getting better. I laughed at her.

"Funny that you should say that. 14-88 started up as part of a campaign for David Duke. He was a white supremacist who ran for the US senate. He used to be a grand wizard in the Ku Klux Klan."

"Was that a long time ago?"

"Nineteen-ninety."

If I could've whistled, I would have. "No way. But David Duke lost, right?"

Ryan nodded. "Still, 14-88 has over 300,000 registered users. It's in the top 15,000 websites on the Internet."

"But not here. Not in Canada. Not in Ottawa."

He shrugged. "There's a thread about Ottawa, started by a Slavic high school senior. I joined it."

"What?" I wanted to seize him by his jacket collar, lift him off the sidewalk, and shake some sense into him.

He stared at me, brown eyes unflinching. "Hope, if my website's going to have any credibility, I have to talk like they do. I have to establish a presence on their forum. And then I can get them to click."

"Ryan, no. This is more than you signed up for."

"It's not as dangerous as what you do every day."

"Ryan, I help—I used to help—*sick* people. So yeah, I might catch a virus. But I'm not hanging out with white supremacists. You don't have to do this, Ryan!"

He turned away from me, so I couldn't see his face, and started walking back toward Lindsay Lane.

Roxy whined, following him but craning her neck at me. I hurried after them. She lay down on the snowy grass next to the sidewalk and rolled onto her back, tucking her front paws away so I'd have maximum access to her belly.

Aww. I still wanted to haul Ryan back to safety, shutting down his Wi-Fi and zip-tying his wrists if I had to, but in the meantime, who could resist this animal who wanted love so desperately?

I crouched to rub and scratch Roxy's belly. Her head rolled side to side, and she flexed her paws even further, retracting them as much as she could. I laughed, trying not to scratch her small, pink nipples as I massaged her tummy. "Aw, Ra-Ra, you're so good. You would never chase after bad guys on your own. You're too smart. Yes, you are."

Ryan snorted.

I squinted and grinned as I looked up at him. It was starting to snow, and the street lamps illuminated the fat, wet flakes, turning them yellow before they fell on my face.

He exhaled and said, in a calmer voice, "I'm fine. It's not like I got kidnapped and held hostage with a gun to my head."

"That's true, but the difference is, it's optional. If I could've, I would've avoided the gun. You don't have to do this, Ryan. You can walk away."

"I'm not going to. These people are f—messed up. I'm not stopping now." His masseter muscles flexed in his jaw before he glanced down at Roxy. "I guess they'd hate Roxy, too. Because she's black."

We both laughed, but it caught in my throat. "Ryan. This is no good for you."

"I want to do this, Hope. I don't want you to go alone."

I stood up and tucked my hands under his jacket. His skin was toasty, but he didn't flinch. I stared directly into his eyes. "What if *I* stopped? What if I started … baking apple pies instead?"

The corner of his mouth twitched. "That's not going to happen." Roxy stood up and nudged our legs with her head, obviously looking for more attention. Since Ryan was the only one with free hands, he patted her head, and she let out a comical little groan. "We both know that. We can't go backwards. Anyway, apple pies remind me of 14-88. They have a whole thread for 14-88 'ladies.' Their tag is 'sugar and spice and everything nice.'" He played with Roxy's ear, and she shook her head, ringing her tags together and gazing at him adoringly. "Don't go on there, Hope. It'll mess with your brain."

My fingers immediately twitched in anticipation of logging on. It's like Bluebeard's chamber. We tell each other, "Don't look! Don't look!" but it made us want to rubberneck even harder.

For now, I took a deep breath and slipped my hands below Ryan's belt line. His abdominal muscles tensed in response before he grinned at me, and I kissed him.

CHAPTER 36

THURSDAY

Since it wasn't even 8:20 a.m., I decided to cut through the parking circle. I'd be stuck inside for the rest of the day. I admired the bare branches of the deciduous trees outside the circle. Even leaf-free, they were, in their own way, as beautiful as pine trees looped with Christmas lights.

I glanced downward to make sure that salty slush didn't kick up onto my pants. Damp air chilled my face. I strode past the cars nudging their way around the hospital, and then I caught my breath.

Three white cars emblazoned with the word POLICE filled the short-term parking spots.

Had they come to investigate Lawrence's homicide? But why converge on the hospital en masse four days later?

I yanked open the double doors and pressed the handicapped button so it would stay open for the old lady toiling behind me on her cane. I barely glanced at the elevator, clogged with people whispering to each other, before I rushed up two flights of stairs.

My stomach tightened as I pushed open the door to the third floor landing.

Human Remains

Yellow police tape cordoned off Dr. Hay's lab.

POLICE LINE
DO NOT CROSS

BARRAGE DE POLICE
PASSAGE INTERDIT

The air seemed to squeeze out of my lungs for a second, although the logical part of my brain noted that, yes, in Canada, we pay double for bilingual police tape. Maybe triple, because it also had the Crime Stoppers number stamped on it.

Two officers stood in front of Dr. Hay's frosted glass doors. A young, male officer with a brown crew cut held out his hand to stop me. "This area is closed."

I had to swallow to make my throat start working again. *Please don't let this be what I think it is.* "I work at the Zinser lab." I pointed at the glass doors opposite them. "That one's open, right?"

He nodded, but said, "I'm going to need your ID."

I showed him my badge. Good thing I'd remembered to bring it, and even better that it worked under the police's watchful eye. I hurried into the Zinser office, pulling the door closed to help it along. Then I bent over to take off my boots and work my feet into my shoes.

Someone bumped into my bum. I whirled around, ready to yell at Mitch, but Susan was trying to edge her plump form past me to her secretarial desk. "I'm sorry," she said. "I can't believe this. First Dr. Acayo, now Ducky."

Ducky. No, no, no, no, no.

They make fun of me.

They dump everything on me.

They spill things.

They mess up my papers.

Jamais deux sans trois.

They'd been gaslighting her, making her think she was the crazy one.

I'd thought random acts of cruelty wouldn't escalate to murder.

"You mean it's Dahiyyah?" I waited for Susan's nod. For a second, my vision telescoped. Susan looked like she was in a tunnel, far away from me, with only her head showing. Then my eyes reverted to normal. I shook my head. "And she's dead?"

"Dr. Hay found her this morning. She was—deceased."

You'll never speak to me again.

Dahiyyah had been right. I would never speak to her again. I'd tried, I'd gone back to her lab, but she hadn't answered. Had she been too afraid to answer the door? "Somebody killed her?"

"No! I mean, I don't think so. She sent out a note at 5 a.m." Susan pressed a hand to her own cheek. She reached into a pocket of her black trousers and pulled out a Kleenex so she could touch her eyes.

"What did the note say?"

"They think it's ... it's suicide. At least that's what I heard. What a terrible thing! Dr. Hay wants to reach her family, but their lab is cordoned off, so I'm going to try to—excuse me. I have to find her next of kin, if I can." She put out her hand to steady herself on someone else's desk before she made her way to her own computer.

I followed her for a second, but I was still in my stockinged feet, and I'm not great at comforting people. Mostly, I sit and listen to them. Susan was rifling through her file folders, so she didn't need a sympathetic ear.

I turned back to my shoes as the card sensor clicked from yellow to green. Mitch pushed open the door.

I jerked back, my socks slipping on the tile floor, and he nodded sympathetically. "Hell of a thing, eh? Poor Ducky."

The woman was dead, and we still couldn't give her the respect of her real name. "Her name was Dahiyyah. Dahiyyah Safar." At least my brain cells managed to dredge that up. "What happened to her?"

Mitch shrugged. "No one's talking, but my security guy said it was a mess. They found her on the ground with vomit and diarrhea, you know?"

"No, I didn't know that." But I was thinking. "Vomit and diarrhea makes me think of an anaphylactic reaction. Or a poison. Did she have a rash? How did she die? Do we know?"

He raised his eyebrows. "My security guy didn't know that part."

"Did he read the note?"

Mitch shuffled his feet. He glanced around the office. Susan was tapping on her computer, and Tom's door was closed; we were fairly

Human Remains

isolated. "Well, I did. We all got a copy. She e-mailed it to everyone in the two labs."

"She e-mailed her suicide note?" Bizarre. I'd never heard of that before.

He pulled his phone out of his back pocket and unlocked it before handing it over. The beginning was in Arabic, but the English words jumped out at me.

I love my family. I want them to know that I have been working very hard. I have the proof on my computer. If anything happens to me, the password is SWJHRVDZSA.

Some Arabic words followed.

"This is not a suicide note," I said immediately. "This is her protecting herself."

Mitch shrugged. "I don't know what it is, but she sent it to everyone at 5:13 a.m."

"Who's everyone?" I hadn't checked my e-mail, but I bet I'd been excluded.

"That's the funny thing. She didn't bother to bcc, so I can tell you exactly who. Judith, Stephen, even Lawrence, from her lab. Everyone in Tom's lab, except you, and I bet that's only because she didn't have your e-mail."

"The police have this note, right? Did you send them a copy?"

"Yeah, I downloaded the app and pasted it in. I bet they got, like, 200 copies."

"Good," I growled. "This woman did not want to die. She only needed to get away from that terrible place. Can I forward this to myself?"

Mitch shrugged, which I took as assent. While I figured out his phone and typed my e-mail address, he said, "That's a pretty dramatic way of putting it. She was a research assistant. We all know what that's like."

"She wanted to get out. She was applying to grad school. She didn't know how she was going to get there, but that was the plan." The most dangerous time for abused women is when they try to leave. But I didn't know who wanted to kill Dahiyyah. Why would Dr. Hay kill her own research assistant and right-hand woman? Wouldn't it make more sense to keep her around as a slave?

Mitch raised his eyebrows and glanced at Susan, who was sniffing but back to typing on her computer again. "I have no idea."

"Okay. Do you know if there was a handwritten paper note, too?"

He shook his head.

"An e-mail is too impersonal. And she gave everyone her computer password. What if that was her e-mail password, too?" People are pretty dumb about passwords. Ryan had told me to get two-step verification for Gmail because otherwise, anyone could hack my e-mail and reset my accounts everywhere else.

"No clue. I've got to get back to work."

While he hastened into the lab, I slipped on my black flats and followed him.

My iPhone rang. The coroner was delaying our appointment until next week "due to further complications." I agreed and hung up.

When I pushed open the lab door a minute later, Summer was huddled with Dr. Wen and Samir. Dr. Wen looked like he didn't know what to do with her, especially since she was crying and saying, "I feel so bad for her. She was only 24!"

Samir leaned in from the aisle to pat her on the back. "Yes, it is a tragedy."

"She probably blamed herself for Lawrence dying!"

"It is very difficult indeed." Samir made circles on her back. When he noticed me, he dropped his hand to his sides, but continued to hover.

Dr. Wen cleared his throat and shook his head. He nodded at Mitch, who was standing in the doorway a step ahead of me, and turned back to Summer, clearly non-plussed.

Summer spotted us. "Mitch!" she cried, throwing herself in his arms.

He caught her with an almost-inaudible oof. "Yeah, baby. Yeah, sweetie. I know, I know," he said, holding her close, and then he started whispering in her ear.

I turned my head away. It was too intimate. I didn't want to see.

Samir sighed before he returned to his lab bench. Dr. Wen, who had already donned his lab coat, strode toward the fume hood at the back of the lab.

Business as usual, except in less than four days, of the four people working in Dr. Hay's lab, half of them had died.

Chapter 37

First things first. I couldn't think with all the commotion in the lab, so I headed into the office. While Susan typed in her corner near the main entrance, I found an empty desk by the window and figured no one would care.

I downloaded the Ottawa police app and pasted Dahiyyah's suicide note into it. Mitch said he'd already done it, but better double than nothing when death is on the line.

I texted Ryan, Tucker, my family, and my friend Tori, to let them know I was okay, in case they'd heard the news and wondered who'd died. It took longer to craft a carefully-worded message to Joan that I was thinking of her and the babies. No details, only reassurance.

Ryan called me immediately. "You okay?"

"Yeah. I wasn't even there. I feel really bad for Dahiyyah and her family, though. Are you okay?"

"Didn't sleep much. I don't like this. I was going to tell you that I got some activity on my website, but now—"

"Hang on. I want to go somewhere private." I beeped open the door to the lobby, giving a tight smile to Susan and then the police officer. I thought *I'm sorry* at an invisible Dahiyyah as I sequestered myself in the bathroom, checking both stalls to make sure that I was alone with the Koala Kare change station. They still hadn't fixed the faucet, and someone had already splashed the countertop with water. I kept my voice low as I murmured to Ryan, "You mean the White Birthright website?"

"Yeah. People logged on from both labs."

"Both labs? You mean—"

"Your stem cell lab and the virology lab. Other spots in Ottawa University, too, mostly on the landing page. Someone from the virology lab clicked the 'Contact Us' page, and someone from the stem cell lab hit every page."

My mind tried to picture the browser activity as dots on a map of Ottawa University, much like the historical map of a cholera epidemic where black bars illustrated the number of cases, with maximal clustering around one contaminated pump. The stem cell lab was the contaminated pump. "What time was the hit from the virology lab?"

"Last night. Before my run." Ryan hesitated.

I knew him too well. I could see my own wide, frightened eyes in the mirror, but it didn't stop me. My voice echoed off the bathroom walls. "What are you not telling me?"

"I solicited the hits. You told me Chris had gotten spam, so I sent it directly to everyone from both labs, plus a few other places to make it less obvious that I was zeroing in on one place. Lab e-mails are on the university contact page, so it was easy."

My heart thudded. Ducky was dead. Lawrence was dead. Both of them were people of colour. Could Ryan's web page have tipped the balance for Ducky, or was it a coincidence? "Who was it?"

"The one from the virology lab was hidden. I'm not sure how they managed it, but I'll work on it when I have a chance. Someone from your lab clicked on my site, read all the pages, and posted repeatedly on 14-88. com. I'm pretty sure I know who it is. I set up an HTTP referrer header, a web bug, and super cookies, and I've got his browser fingerprint—"

I could barely understand what he was saying. I sort of know what computer cookies are, at least enough to try and block them. I seized on the one piece that made sense to me. "It's a guy?"

"Do you want to know who it is?"

"Of course." My mind shot toward Chris, who'd gotten the first spam. Why did he send me that homicide link? Was he *bragging?*

Human Remains

"The one from your lab was Mitchell Lubian."

"What, Mitch? That seems wrong." Pothead Mitch, who had a yen for half-white Summer—he was a white supremacist?

My gut said no.

Evidence said yes.

We're taught to use evidence-based medicine. Don't counsel patients because "we've used this for a thousand years, so it must be okay." Use the best studies at your disposal to guide your practice. Evidence pointed to Mitch. I breeeeeeathed and said, "This is crazy."

"Yes. I can show you what I've got—"

"I wouldn't have any idea what it meant. I'd be better off looking at Roxy." I missed that big dog. She was part of my life now.

"I know you like the guy, but it was either him or someone using his account."

I relaxed a little. My teeth shone in the mirror, reflecting the intermittent light. "Well, he's the most likely to leave his computer lying around unlocked. He let me use his phone this morning. But the other possibility is that he's the racist one. Maybe he even sent that spam to Chris, although why? None of this makes any sense. And I'm not convinced Ducky killed herself."

He sighed. "That poor woman. What happened to her?"

"I don't know. They think she committed suicide, but I don't have any details. Just her last e-mail, which I'm sending to you." I forwarded it to him and bcc'd Tucker, who was now text-bombing me. Tucker would have to wait. Snooze and lose, my friend. We talked a bit about Ducky, and then I said, "I've got to go."

"I don't like this, Hope."

"Me neither. Listen. I've got this app." I explained the whole Finding Friends thing. "You'll know where I am, and I'll know where you are."

"Where your phone is."

"I'll keep it on me. I promise. I've got to get some work done." I paused. "Thank you for doing this. It must be even worse for you, because you want to believe the best of everyone, as a Christian."

"Christianity doesn't mean you ignore sin. It means that you confront it. At least, that's the way I used to think about it, when I was a Christian."

"Wh-what? Are you not a Christian any more?" I almost dropped my phone. "I mean, obviously I knew you were more, um, open to recreational activities, but—"

I could hear the smile in his voice. "I don't know what I am any more."

Seriously, for me, Ryan's biggest flaw has always been his religiousness. I know it's a big up for some people. My grandmother has been in love with him for aeons. But I don't like the church or anyone else dictating the way I should think and behave. I want to make my own moral and immoral choices.

I knew I'd changed, especially since 14/11. I hadn't considered how Ryan was evolving in front of my eyes. He'd never had a dog, but now I could hardly see him without Roxy. He'd always put work first, until he started trapping racists for me. He'd been surrounded by loving, sane, stable friends and family until he hooked up with me and faced both death and birth head on, when the average guy couldn't handle a tampon commercial.

The one unshakeable core of Ryan had always been his Christianity—until now.

"I don't trust anyone you're working with." He paused. "I know this is a strange question, but are there any other non-white people in your lab?"

"Summer is half. I think Dr. Wen is Chinese, and Samir looks Middle Eastern."

I could almost hear him shaking his head. "I don't want to make a big deal about my website. It could be nothing."

"Could be," I agreed, but now that we knew people I worked with were actively clicking on WN websites, it seemed like something.

I had to talk to Mitch.

But first, I needed to figure out what happened to Dahiyyah.

CHAPTER 38

As soon as I re-entered the lab, Summer engulfed me in a wet hug. "Isn't it awful? You should take the day off."

I could feel her tears on my neck. I patted her dark hair awkwardly. My Zisa and pregnancy tests had both come back negative last night, but I still felt contaminated. It might take me a while to seroconvert, so I'd rather avoid all close contact, except with Ryan and Tucker. I withdrew as graciously as I could. "What happened to Ducky?"

"We don't know." She touched a tissue to her red eyes. "Mitch said she might've taken some poison."

He could have been quoting me. "Oh, yeah? Where is Mitch?" I asked, as casually as I could. Chris and Dr. Wen were back at their benches, and I'd passed Samir on his computer in the office, but Mitch was AWOL.

"He said he was going to talk to Harold." Summer blew her nose, which was puffy. "This is awful. I don't know if I can keep working like this. I can't even think."

I'd been fantasizing about busting my way back into the security booth. I came back to my body with a jerk. Summer was right in front of me, sobbing and smelling like strawberry shampoo, and I was contemplating murder and revenge. In books, people usually throw up when they find a dead body. I'd taken a shower and shagged one of my boyfriends after finding Lawrence. Another sign that I'd checked out of the human race.

Then again, I remembered Ryan's warm hands and the tears I'd shed after we left Joan and her babies, and I thought, *Maybe I'm checking back in.*

I took Summer's hands in mine. Hers were cool, and her fingers were finer than Ryan's or Tucker's. "It's going to be okay." My voice was so low and reassuring, I almost believed myself.

Summer threw herself back on me. "I hope so, Hope!"

And then we both laughed, because of my name, which seemed more ironic than ever.

"Do we know anything about Dahiyyah? What happened to her, who found her?"

Summer shook her head. "Just her e-mail. The one she sent it to everybody. Did you get a copy?"

"Do you mind sending it to me?" I was curious if hers was the same as Mitch's. I assumed so, but you never knew.

She nodded and bent over her phone to forward it, but started crying over the note. "This is so terrible! I can't believe it! She was a research assistant like me, and now … "

"Horrible," I agreed. Instead of touching Summer, I murmured soothing things.

She said, "That poor thing. I wish I'd talked to her more. We should've made her come to Petra's. Oh, one of us should call her family. Her parents. I think she had sisters and a brother, too. Oh, my God. What's going to happen next? It's so scary!"

"Yeah." I wasn't going to get any more information out of Summer. I know it sounds callous, but I call it CNN Syndrome. It's like watching the news after a tsunami. You want to know more, so you turn on the TV, but it's a bunch of people saying the same thing over and over again. I'd have to wait until the police or the rumour mill came up with more information to piece together what happened to Dahiyyah. "That's a good idea. Oh, thanks, I got the message."

I opened the e-mail on my phone. The text and the time were the same, but this time, I noticed an attachment, which I downloaded. It contained a vaguely familiar picture of a molecule with a surface covered in what looked like miniature suction cups.

Summer was still talking, but I showed her the phone. "I opened the attachment. What is that?"

She barely glanced at it. "The Rift Valley virus."

My mind tessered to Stephen Weaver's poster, leapfrogging over the dead cow fetus photo to zoom in on the virus itself. She was right. Holy kahuna. "Maybe that's a clue!"

Summer raised her eyebrows. "That's her sig file. It has been ever since she started helping Stephen Weaver on his project. When she started helping Lawrence, she added the Zisa virus. I'm kind of surprised she deleted that one, but maybe it was too upsetting a reminder after he died."

"Maybe." I thought it was strange that Dahiyyah had included Rift Valley disease in her signature file, when she couldn't bear to talk to the guy. But I searched for Rift Valley disease online, and the virus looked exactly like the sig picture.

I forwarded the message to Ryan. Maybe he could work his computer mojo on it.

Summer shook her head. "You're not supposed to forward lab e-mails. Well, I guess you can, but it's not the best idea on your first week."

My stomach plummeted. I glanced at my phone, but it had already whooshed. "Crap. You guys already sent it to the police, though, right?"

"I think Mitch did."

"That's what he told me, too. Well, I'll let the police know I've got it. If they ask for it, I'll forward it to them. If they've already got it, they won't care."

Summer sniffed, clearly leaving me to my risky e-mail habits.

I sat down at my desk and pulled out the police officers' business cards from my wallet. Cops are surprisingly analog. They have notebooks and real business cards. I messaged the woman and the man separately. They'd probably call me a kook, but that was nothing new.

Then I booted up the lab safety modules. Most people got them done in two days, so I was running late. Meanwhile, I scanned Tucker's old texts, which made me smile.

It's 8 degrees Celsius here. Not that I'm trying to make you jealous or anything. But it's a short plane ride to LA.

[After the twins]

WTF. You're kidding me.

[After I told him some details]

You're not kidding me. Holy shit.

[After Ducky]

This is Crazytown. As soon as I've got my colon back together, I'll protect you, Batwoman. In the meantime, I'll check out the WN.

That one, I had to respond to: *No. Your job is to convalesce.*

No way, Hope. This is something I can do from Cali. I'm doing it.

Me: *No. I don't want you endangering yourself.*

You think someone's going to fly down to LA to take me out? ;)

Me: *They're in LA already. They probably have Meetups.*

Maybe an earthquake will take 'em out. But in the meantime, I can check on WN. I'll read up on Lawrence and Dahiyyah. I already found this.

He sent me a bunch of PubMed article links from Dr. Hay's lab. I glanced through them while watching a video on the proper way to use the Lentihood, the fume hood for lentiviruses at the back of Tom's lab. Tip: use Virox before and after, to kill all the viruses. Since HIV is a lentivirus, Virox would be my best friend. They also suggested manipulating lentiviruses only during regular working hours. Yay, an excuse to work like a normal person.

By lunchtime, I celebrated the end of my second-last safety module by checking Lawrence's laptop files, which I'd copied from my USB to a netbook I'd borrowed from my dad. He'd insisted I take it because the Internet was too slow off my phone, and the lab used Windows computers.

Lawrence had used Word, so it was pretty straightforward to read his files. His scientific notes were so dense with jargon, I skimmed whatever I couldn't understand.

After a few minutes, I forgot all about lab safety and read in earnest.

A functioning Zisa vaccine was the current Holy Grail. We're talking billions of dollars, dozens of corporations, nations, and government agencies throwing their hat into the ring. At least 30 different groups were working on it, making it one of the most pursued vaccines in human history.

Zisa is a flavivirus, which means it's in the same family as yellow fever, dengue, West Nile virus, and all that other fun stuff.

Like Zisa, West Nile is transmitted by mosquitoes, and 80 percent of infectees don't have any symptoms. The media got a mini erection about West Nile virus, and so did researchers, who developed a vaccine for it in case it became the next big bad. But it turned out that less than 1 percent of people have any serious consequences from West Nile (meningitis or encephalitis), so the vaccine never went anywhere.

However, you can use West Nile research as the backbone for a good vaccine against Zisa.

Lawrence believed we could use plasmids to make the vaccine. Here's my simplified take on it: a bacterium carries most of its DNA in an uncoiled mass, except for some backup or complimentary DNA it carries separately in things called plasmids. It's like having most of your money in the bank, except you carry a gold nugget in one purse and a Bitcoin in another. At least one purse has a separate pocket for bear spray, because some plasmids carry genes for antibiotic resistance.

Bacteria can pass plasmids back and forth to each other, even across species. It's like lending the gold to your family or your cat. (I know, I know. What would your cat do with gold? Ask the cat millionaires.)

It's a pretty nifty system for bacteria—and for us, once a human thought of exploiting plasmids to replicate the DNA we want.

Like Zisa DNA. Not all the DNA, because you don't want to cause the epidemic you're trying to avoid. Just enough of the chromosome for the body to recognize Zisa DNA, make antibodies against it, and slaughter it whenever the real thing comes around.

This may come in two stages. First, the vaccine so that northern travellers can get a sun tan on the beach in January without worrying about their future progeny. The vaccine for endemic areas comes afterward. Right now, the money is in protecting the rich travellers.

I texted the info to Tucker.

He wrote back right away. *Yeah, I can see how plasmids would work, but it looks like NIAID is already working on it.*

I clicked on his link. Sure enough, the National Institute of Allergy and Infectious Diseases had already started human clinical trials in August. I have to say, that stunned me. I never heard of a vaccine developing that fast.

Which meant that one man, isolated in a lab in Ottawa, had almost no chance of beating the big guys with the money. No matter how brilliant or determined he was, he couldn't win against 30 different teams with billions of dollars.

On the other hand, Lawrence was the kind of guy who wouldn't give up.

I texted back, *Thanks. If you really wanted to go rogue and develop a vaccine on your own, how would you do it?*

I endured a few minutes of silence and of " … " percolating while he thought about it. *I would try to develop some sort of process and patent it so that whatever they did, they'd have to pay me to access it.*

I shook my head and typed back. *That's if you want money. But it would slow down the process, and what if your wife had Zisa?*

He shot back, *If you had Zisa, and you were pregnant, I would do anything*

My heart halted for two beats. Tucker was thinking about marrying me. Even in passing, that was a seismic moment.

Then he texted, *If you weren't pregnant, I would trust your immune system to get over it, and then I'd work with whoever had the best chance of developing a vaccine.*

I could breathe again. Relieved and disappointed, I tried to concentrate on the medical part. *Lawrence didn't join a team. He came to Ottawa, probably because of his wife. I'm trying to figure out what he was doing, and so far, I'm pretty sure he was gunning for plasmids. He didn't have any funding, though, and it would take him months to secure that, let alone do the molecular bio, the animal studies, and then jump through the hoops for human trials. He didn't have a team except one research assistant split between up to 3 people. He was probably soliciting volunteers on Craigslist, but that's illegal.*

Tucker: *So he should pull a Barry Marshall.*

A what?

You know, the H. pylori guy. He did his own gastroscopy and biopsy, infected himself with H. pylori, and then scoped and biopsied himself again before treating himself with tinidazole, to prove that HP causes ulcers.

I said out loud, "My God. What if Lawrence tested a vaccine on himself?"

Chapter 39

What if self-vaccination had gone wrong?

What if that had made Lawrence sick on Sunday (Ducky: *He said he was feeling sick and wanted to go home. I told him to just go, I'd finish up here!*), so he hadn't been able to work, had stumbled out of the lab, and … ended up suffocated in a ditch?

No, it still didn't hang together.

But I could test my theory, if I had evidence.

First of all, had he been working on the Zisa virus in his lab? I'd need to search their fridges and freezers. If he'd labeled everything ZISA, that was a no-brainer. However, if he'd mislabeled the samples or hidden them because he didn't have permission, I'd have to be a real detective to track them down.

Next, to check for self-experimentation, I'd need samples of Lawrence's blood or urine. I'd have to ask someone in lab medicine exactly what tests to run. The bigger problem was getting a hold of his bodily fluids when he was already deceased.

Lawrence's funeral was on Sunday. They might have cremated him. I hadn't asked, and I didn't know if that was culturally acceptable, but obviously, if they'd burnt his remains, it was game over.

Somehow, it seemed more likely that they'd opt for a viewing, even though that was more expensive.

I started Googling. If they'd drained Lawrence's blood and replaced it with formalin, could I access it for testing? Probably not. I bet they dumped all blood into a central repository. No chain of evidence. Even if the lab was willing to test it and found Zisa antibodies, I couldn't prove which body the blood had come from.

Work intervened. Tom sent me an e-mail detailing several projects I could start on. I could assist any of the scientists with their project during my month. He wrote, "Normally, we would have discussed this earlier, but with Susan's illness and the events of the past few days, we'll have to set a goal for you tomorrow." He'd enclosed links to everyone's bios and papers.

I'd have to skim all the research and then pick whichever project was not only compelling, but would garner a good research paper. Although I was tempted to pick Samir, because he was a prize-winning researcher eager to have a student, I should do due diligence. I clicked on the first link.

Before I could absorb the abstract, Mitch flung open the lab door from the hallway.

I leapt to my feet. This was my chance to grill him about White Birthright, and I had to nab him before he either started working or cuddling with Summer. "Mitch. Hey!"

He glanced at me before his attention lasered in on Summer, at the fume hood near the front of the lab. He boomed, "This just in. They found cyanide."

Summer nearly dropped her pipette. "What are you talking about?"

"Ducky. That's what I heard. Her test came back positive for cyanide." Mitch stood with his shoulders back, eyeballing each of us.

Dr. Wen frowned and turned off his tablet.

Samir rushed toward him from the rear of the lab. "How did you hear of this?"

"I have my connections," said Mitch.

Yes, Harold. Who else? This time, I'd bet on someone from the hospital ER.

Chris strolled toward him from his corner. Mitch edged closer to Summer, who was spraying down her fume hood, tossing her gloves, and hanging up her lab coat on a hook on the door to Tom's office. She said, "I don't believe it!"

Samir echoed, "This is a travesty."

Summer ignored him as she hustled to Mitch's side. "Tell us everything."

Mitch repeated, *à haut volume*, "Her blood tested positive for cyanide." He wasn't adding information. It was CNN Syndrome all over again.

I cut in. "Do you know what the levels were? Smokers have higher levels of cyanide in their blood."

Mitch's eyes widened before he rallied at me. "Ducky wasn't a smoker. She was Muslim."

"I understand that. But do you know what the levels were, or just that she tested positive for cyanide?"

"Just that she tested positive," he said, clearly hating me for raining logic on his parade, but both carbon monoxide and cyanide levels are elevated in smokers, because guess what? Cigarettes are lethal, baby.

Still, that was interesting. A tablespoon of potassium cyanide can kill you within hours. Inhaling cyanide works even faster. A cyanide molecule resembles oxygen to the point that the body preferentially binds to it instead of oxygen. This shuts down the Krebs cycle that you need to bring energy (ATP) to any cells of the body.

Without oxygen or energy, your brain doesn't work, so you get confused, dizzy, and light-headed. You start to seize. Your heart doesn't work, so you go into heart blocks and arrhythmias. And then you die.

I'd never seen a case of cyanide poisoning. I know it's an ancient toxin. Hitler and Eva Braun killed themselves with cyanide, although he also shot himself to seal the deal.

Cyanide is a classic emergency medicine exam question: if you see a patient who's been in a fire, you should test them for cyanide, or consider treating on spec, because when plastics burn, they can emit cyanide. If you don't remember to treat for cyanide, your theoretical patient will start to seize and die.

Ducky hadn't been in a fire. So if Mitch's source was correct, Ducky had been poisoned. Exactly as I'd said when I first heard about the vomiting and diarrhea. Even though other things can cause V&D—anaphylaxis, gastroenteritis, narcotic withdrawal, drugs like physostigmine—now the question was how someone had managed to slip her some cyanide. It could have been suicide, but I didn't believe it.

"We should do something for her family," Summer was saying. "Maybe we could send flowers, or have a memorial."

"We could," Mitch said.

"We could take donations," said Samir, and Summer bestowed a smile upon him.

I nodded my agreement. I'd donate, but the last time we talked about this, it was to raise money for Lawrence's family. Now would we split the proceeds between Joan and Dahiyyah's families, or have two different funds?

Awkward. I'd let Summer handle it.

I glanced at the USB memory stick plugged into my computer. As discreetly as possible, I ejected the memory stick and pocketed it. Dahiyyah's death was going to make it doubly hard to check if Lawrence had been testing the Zisa virus, because their lab would stay shut down and cordoned off.

The only people who'd return to the lab quickly were Dr. Hay and Stephen Weaver.

How could I get those two to test for the Zisa virus in any of his samples, when I wasn't friends with either of them, and they could've harmed Dahiyyah?

I cleared my throat. "How are Dr. Hay and Dr. Weaver taking this?"

Mitch frowned at me. I'd interrupted his treatise on how to use GoFundMe. "Stephen took the rest of the day off. Dr. Hay is at a meeting."

Attending a meeting seemed like a cold-blooded reaction to her "invaluable" research assistant's death. I know the show must go on, in research as well as in show business, but come on. Meanwhile, Stephen Weaver taking the day off meant he was either too upset to concentrate, or he was treating it like a holiday. "Were either of them present when Dahiyyah died?"

"What are you saying, Hope?" said Summer.

Mitch's voice cut across hers. "Dr. Hay found her and reported her right away. She seemed shaken up when I passed her in the hall."

"Hmm." I've heard a few truisms about crime. One is that you should always look to the spouse/partner. Another is that you should question whoever discovered the body. "What time did she find her?"

Mitch tilted his head back to look at me. Everyone else's gaze swung back and forth like this was a ping pong tournament. "I heard them say it was at 6:40 a.m. I came in around 7:30. You want to arrest me, too?"

"I'll leave that to the police." I checked my watch. It was 12:23 now. That was a fast turnaround time for cyanide, but maybe her blood gas had shown a metabolic acidosis. Combined with a high lactate level and a negative carbon monoxide and methemoglobin test, they could have assumed it was cyanide. Even so, it was awfully speedy for them to announce it, and for the news to spread to Mitch. "Who told you about the cyanide?"

"Ah. I never kiss and tell." He winked at me.

Chris raised his eyebrows.

Summer said, "Thank God you've got resources. Otherwise, we'd have no idea what was going on."

Right. Or else we still had no idea what was going on, and Mitch was trying to mislead us. I watched Mitch nudge Summer with his elbow and give Samir a high five, and I wondered, *Who is this guy, and what, exactly, does he do?*

CHAPTER 40

I kept my cool for the rest of the afternoon. Or at least, I tried to.

I shot a glance at Mitch, ensconced at his bench near the back of the lab, two over from Chris. My bench faced toward Mitch's, but he faced the Lentihood. Although I couldn't deduce much from the back of his head, my eyeballs were magnetically attracted to him. I'd pretend to check the clock, or scratch my nose, but really, I was watching Mitch.

Before Lawrence and Dahiyyah had died, I'd been swimming in a fog of fear. In medicine, it's called generalized anxiety disorder, because I was perpetually worried instead of having individual panic attacks.

Now that Mitch was a person of interest, I'd ramped up from a 6 to an 8 on the eternal anxiety scale.

Just because you're paranoid doesn't mean they're not out to get you. Denis, my therapist, had said and cackled. Then he'd apologized, because I sure as hell hadn't found it funny.

I'd assumed the Scoobies were benign. Friendly. What you see is what you get. And maybe they were. But when people around them dropped dead, it behooved me to exercise caution.

I still wasn't worried about Summer. Chris, I withheld judgment because I didn't know the guy. He didn't talk. It was early days for Dr. Wen and Samir too. I couldn't stand Stephen Weaver. I wanted to like

Dr. Hay, because she was a strong woman who headed her lab, but she seemed so cold.

My head spun in too many directions, like a bad Choose Your Own Adventure™.

I texted assurances to Ryan and Tucker and my dad. *Yes, I'm alive. I'm fine. Don't worry about me. Just another day at the killer lab.* Then I started researching Mitchell Lubian. I ignored his social media accounts, including the video of him playing guitar on YouTube, and zeroed in on his publications.

I had trouble decoding some of his more technical papers, like the use of bone marrow stromal cells to make hyaline cartilage. Luckily, he'd co-written one with Tom on human pluripotent stem cells, so I could read that and legitimately educate myself. Before I came here, Tucker and Tori had to explain to me that George W. Bush's campaign against the use of embryos for stem cells became obsolete in 2007, when Shinya Yamanaka figured out how to reprogram adult cells into stem cells, and co-won the Nobel Prize for his efforts.

Next, I checked out Dahiyyah Safar. It's an unusual name, so she should have lots of unique hits.

Nope.

She'd graduated from Ottawa University two years ago. At several different conferences, she'd presented her thesis on the neonatal rat model for the virulence of the mumps virus in humans. And that was about it.

I didn't expect her to be all over social media, like Mitch. But her online presence was weaker than my baby brother's.

My phone buzzed. Joan sent me a picture of Might I, who was sleeping. *What do you think of the name Angella?*

Inside, I recoiled at both the religiousness and the spelling, but naming a baby is the parents' prerogative. *It's a name that reminds me of angels. We usually spell it Angela here.*

Angella Acayo!!!!!! Followed by a gif of floating hearts.

I smiled and sent her a happy emoticon. She deserved whatever pleasure she could get.

I flipped to Dr. Judith Hay. She seemed to have a pretty good score on ResearchGate, a site designed to measure your influence on the research world.

Stephen Weaver's name began appearing as an author and co-author with Dr. Hay. He hadn't been working long enough to have publications with her, but they'd submitted articles together, and he'd presented in Washington last month.

Suddenly, I understood what had bothered me. Dr. Hay had insisted Ducky was so, so crucial, and yet Ducky/Dahiyyah didn't have a single article published under her name since she'd started working for Dr. Hay. I know publication schedules can drag out, so it's possible that she might have something cooking for *Science* or *Nature* or whatever the big virology journal is.

But in my limited experience, research assistants and lab techs usually get their names on an article or two. They'll be listed last. Everyone knows that first authorship is prime and that real estate worth goes down accordingly. I'd met one professor who threw out any papers where the grad school applicant hadn't made first or second author. Still, it was something for your c.v.

Dahiyyah had gotten nothing. Nothing except slaving over pipettes.

Would she really have killed herself? And with cyanide? I know labs use cyanide, so it's relatively easy to obtain, but it's not the nicest way to go. They talk about the "cyanide scream," because the victim collapses with a cry. Sure, you might be unconscious for the shortness of breath/seizing/death part, and I don't think it's as consistently horrible as strychnine, but it still seemed like a hard way to go.

I rubbed my eyes. Until we got more information on Dahiyyah's death, I was better off concentrating on Lawrence.

One of Lawrence's first hits was that Ottawa University diversity video, which I ignored in favour of his considerable papers. He was third author on an Influenza A paper with Dr. Kanade. Pretty impressive.

Joan texted me again. *Can you call me, dr. hope?*

I glanced at Mitch, whose head was tucked over his laptop. I edged into the hallway and returned to the women's bathroom before I called her back. "Hi, Joan. What is it? Are you and Angella okay?"

"She's fine, but Doctor Hope, the coroner called me. They did the autopsy. They think he was poisoned with cyanide."

CHAPTER 41

My blood congealed.

My lips felt numb.

Joan started crying, so it was hard to understand her, but she said, "Somebody beat him. He had bruises and internal injuries, and that bag on his head. They hurt him so badly, and they poisoned him, too!"

"Wait a minute." My voice reverberated through the bathroom. I tried to whisper instead. "The autopsy showed that he was beaten *and* he died from cyanide poisoning?"

"Yes, that's what they said. I had to call you, Doctor Hope. A nurse told me that another girl died from cyanide at the lab. What is going on, Doctor Hope?"

So she'd heard about Dahiyyah. "I don't know." I was still trying to process what she'd told me. He'd been assaulted. That much, I'd figured out from the police report and the broken ribs, and Joan had confirmed it. But the cyanide was new. Had his blood tested positive first, so they had a high index of suspicion for Dahiyyah?

Too many questions. So little time.

The police had pointed out two persons of interest, the white guys wearing black. Did they beat him and give him cyanide? Or cyanide first, to make him easier to beat up?

Cyanide and beating are two different ways of killing someone. Not that you can't murder someone in multiple ways, but it's overkill. If cyanide's going to do the job, why beat the guy up?

Unless two different sets of people wanted Lawrence dead?

Also, how was it possible that both Dahiyyah and Lawrence had taken cyanide?

Mental vertigo.

Joan blew her nose, pulling me back to the phone pressed against my ear. "I had to warn you, Doctor Hope. That lab is killing everyone."

"I hear you, Joan. Thanks for the warning."

"I'm scared. What's happening to us? What if they want to hurt me and Angella?"

My breath puffed out. I hadn't considered that angle. "I don't think anyone can hurt her in the NICU. A nurse is there 24 hours a day." Angella would be under guard for the next few days or weeks, as they tried to help her gain weight and develop as normally as possible. "Are you admitted to the hospital for a few days?"

"They said they would observe me for infection for at least 24 hours. They want to study us. Angella is only the second Zisa baby with microcephaly in all of Canada." Her voice trembled.

"Stay there as long as you can." I made some rapid calculations. They'd be pressed for beds before Christmas, but she was right, they'd want to study the pair of them. She and Angella would be safer in a public space than sequestered in that crummy apartment.

"We're holding a service for Lawrence and Baby Hope on Sunday at 2 p.m. Will you be able to come?"

"Of course," I said. I would make it happen, even though I winced every time I heard Might II's official name. "I'll come and visit you after I'm done at the lab. Do you have people from your church visiting you?"

"Yes, my friend Ruth is leaving now. I was doing skin-to-skin care with Angella when the police called."

"Good for you, Joan. That's exactly the right thing to do. I want you to have as many friends around you as possible. I'll see you soon, okay, Joan?" I was saying her name over and over, like a telemarketer, but it was the only way I had to reassure her.

"Yes." She didn't want to hang up, but she did.

Even if Dahiyyah had killed herself, something was very wrong with this place. Two young scientists and one fragile baby had died before their time.

I strode back into Tom's lab, ready to confront Mitch.

CHAPTER 42

Unfortunately, Mitch had slipped out in those few minutes I'd spent on the phone.

To quote *The Princess Bride*: Incon*cei*vable!

I gnashed my teeth. I didn't have his number. I wished I'd forced him to join my Finding Friends app.

Looking around, I belatedly realized that the Scoobies and even Samir had cleared out, leaving only Dr. Wen and Susan in the office. The lab itself was eerily silent, except for the hum of the shakers and the refrigerators.

Mitch couldn't have heard about Lawrence's cyanide and beating, no matter how good his contacts. The police would first notify Lawrence's next of kin, Joan, and I was pretty sure she'd called me right away. It was a coincidence that Mitch had taken off as soon as I'd left the room.

I texted Ryan to update him on the poison situation, but mostly, I was ready to fight.

Since I had no one to engage in Mortal Kombat yet, I sat down at my computer and began researching white nationalists, starting with the site Ryan warned me to avoid, 14-88.com.

Strange name, but as the website explained, a white supremacist terrorist named David Lane had made up a fourteen-word slogan: *We must secure the existence of our people and a future for white children.* Actually, he made up two of them. The second one was equally appealing/appalling: *Because the beauty of the White Aryan woman must not perish from the earth.*

Eight-eight was a significant number. The eighth letter of the alphabet was H, so 88 means HH, or Heil Hitler.

Something niggled in the back of my brain, and it wasn't the fact that eight is a lucky number in Chinese. I couldn't remember it right now, though, so I shoved that aside for the moment and dove into the website.

It was set up like any website forum, if you normally go on sites with a red slogan on the top that says, *We speak for the newly armed White minority!* One thread, Introduce Yourself, had a bunch of sticky notes saying "Read This First." An activism section highlighted its latest post, "Join the Ku Klux Klan here."

Although most of the posters were clustered under the Ideology section, there were subheadings for Science and Technology, Money and Investment, Creative Writing and Poetry, and even the Environment.

Looking for Aryan love? Check out White Singles (latest post: "I <3 redheads").

I scrolled down to the whole international section, headlined by 14-88 Europe, but also broken down by country, including Español y Portugués, Nederland & Vlaanderen, and Croatia. I was totally unsurprised to see South Africa, although how scary is that? Officially kidnapping, torturing, and murdering protesters under apartheid simply wasn't enough to satisfy them. I bypassed Australia and clicked on 14-88 Canada to survey the headlines.

We need a Trump in Canada ASAP [3 pages]
What would the White Canadian Flag look like?

This one included some pretty crude art. One of them had an inverted triangle within a triangle that reminded me of the Deathly Hallows symbol in Harry Potter, but it turned out to signify the KKK.

Another flag included a noose, referring to lynching black people.

I backpedalled out of that thread.

Stop scum like this getting into our country

Do you have an ex girlfriend or relative married to a nonWhite? [5 pages]

Meet up Regina

Toronto Police investigates Alt-Right as Hate Criminals??????

Make Canada Great Again [2 pages]

Some of them would've made me laugh, if I hadn't still been thinking about the noose:

Justin Trudeau: a Muslim? [4 pages]

Gay Canadian Zombies

I could practically hear Tucker chortling over the gay zombie apocalypse. Speaking of Tucker, I hadn't told him about the cyanide for Lawrence, so I texted him quickly.

Although this was amusing, in a sick kind of way, I already knew there were plenty of racists in Canada. I needed to zero in on the local ones. I searched for Ottawa and ended up with more hits complaining about the government; our Prime Minister's pro-Syrian refugee stance sure made him unpopular 'round these parts. I switched to Google and came up with **White salutations from Ottawa!**

I copied that link and pasted it in a Notes file. Maybe Ryan could help me figure out who the posters were, based on their IP or something.

Then I had another thought. I searched for +Zisa and found a thread titled **Immigrants and disease**.

Trojan Rebel: We can't have them come here, spreading their disease. You know where Zisa came from? Uganda. You want those monkeys spreading their contagion? We've got to stop them.

AngryWhiteMale: Yah i know man their discusting hahahaa lmk what i cn do to help hahaha

EQ326: fucking gross. we see it all the time hear.

Odin Revision: I agree. When our governments let in monkey people, they lost their bid for a fair vote.

I copied and pasted that, too. I sent the entire file to Ryan, titled HELP.

Then I called him. He said he could talk for a minute, so I whispered to him about the cyanide connection between Lawrence and Dahiyyah before I confessed, "I went on 14-88. I'm sorry."

"I saw what you sent." He sounded disappointed, but not surprised.

"I know. I suck. I just had this thought. What if there's a white nationalist connection to Zisa?"

"How could there be?"

"I don't know. I'm not paranoid. I don't think they invented a virus and planted it in the Zisa Forest for scientists to discover in 1947." Those scientists had trapped a rhesus macaque monkey in a cage and placed it on a tree platform, using it as bait in their study of yellow fever, but when rhesus #766 ran a fever of 39.7 degrees Celsius, they drew its blood and injected it into mouse brains. After the mice fell ill, they harvested their brains and discovered Zisa. "But maybe 14-88's using Zisa politically. The fact that Zisa was first isolated in Uganda doesn't mean that it originated there, but at least one person, Trojan Rebel, blames Uganda." I hesitated. "And Trojan Rebel can spell."

"Most of them can. I've seen it on a few threads. You'll have more senior members encouraging the younger ones to read, to go to school."

"It's more than that. Trojan Rebel is an educated—I'm going to guess man, although it could be a woman, and he's inciting people to hate, especially around Zisa and Uganda. Can you help me track him down?"

I could hear Ryan's frown. "Trojan Rebel could be anyone around the world, Hope. You're grasping at straws."

"I am. I could be completely wrong. But most people like leaders. They like being told what to do." I'm the opposite. I only realized it after I started residency. I don't take criticism well, not even from Ryan. "I'd like to know if that person is based in Ottawa. And then if you can tell me who it is."

"Even if it's Dr. Hay, it doesn't prove anything."

"If it's Dr. Hay, I'll give your intel to the police and let them deal with it. It would give me an excuse to avoid her, though." I pinched my nose and closed my eyes.

"Why don't you avoid her right now?"

"I'll try. It'll be easier if she's arrested for a hate crime."

He sighed. "I'll see what I can do. But Hope, be careful."

"Always."

Ryan half-snorted, half-laughed before he hung up.

CHAPTER 43

FRIDAY

By 5:20 p.m., I barely had the strength to push open the lab door. What a week.

I'd stayed up until 01:00 the night before, researching mighty whiteys and cyanide. I'd devoted today to skimming everyone's articles, but I was so tired, I'd decided on Samir to get it over with.

A bunch of faces glanced up as I dragged myself into the room. Tom, Dr. Wen, Samir, Summer, Mitch and Susan were huddled at the front of the lab, between Tom's door and Summer's lab bench.

My face burned. Were they talking about me? I opened my mouth, but Summer put up her hand, looking paler than I'd ever seen her. "They think Ducky did it," she said.

"Dahiyyah did what?" I tried to sound calm. In control.

"Killed Lawrence Acayo. They found traces of cyanide in her flasks and condenser, and in the almond cookie crumbs on Lawrence's lab bench. She'd even printed out a research article on the best way to extract cyanide from fruit pits."

Fruit pits. Something pinged in my brain, but disbelief overrode it. "You think Ducky—I mean, Dahiyyah—poisoned Lawrence Acayo?"

Summer bobbed her head up and down, looking miserable.

"That's circumstantial evidence. Didn't other people eat those almond cookies? Stephen Weaver told me they were good. He's fine, right?"

Summer turned away from me, back to the people in the circle. Even from a few feet away, I could see her hands shaking. "I can't believe we were working next to a killer all that time. I'm glad she's gone."

"It's traumatic for everyone." Samir patted Summer's shoulder, and she gave him a little smile.

"Hang on. What about the 'persons of interest' the police were looking for?" I said.

Summer clicked her tongue. "They can look for them. But I know that if I'd poisoned someone, even by accident, I might kill myself."

Mitch nodded. "I don't know if I could live with myself, if I killed someone."

Mitch. I clenched my teeth. I had to make a conscious effort to relax my jaw and fists. I'd deal with him soon enough.

I avoided looking at him so that my rage wouldn't tip him off early. "You think Dahiyyah beat him up and tied a bag on his head? She didn't seem like she could tie a bow on a birthday present, let alone overpower a guy who was what, six feet tall?" It was hard to estimate Lawrence's height on the ground, but he'd seemed like a long, rangy guy.

Tom interrupted, his eyes keen. "Who said he was beaten up? All I've heard is the cyanide found in his system, in Ducky's, and her implements."

I turned away. I couldn't let them know that Joan was giving me a direct line into everything she carved out of the police, but it was too late. "Just something I heard. I don't know what's going on." The police had set up a Crime Stoppers line about Lawrence, but if they concentrated on Dahiyyah as the perpetrator, I bet they'd locked and loaded on the wrong person.

"It could be worse," said Tom. "There was the Ph.D. who shot Dr. William Klug at UCLA."

Mitch nodded. "That man killed his wife, too. And what about Annie Le, the Ph.D. candidate at Yale? You know they found her bloody clothes stashed above a ceiling tile—"

Summer covered her ears. While the guys apologized and changed the subject, I took a deep breath and brandished my ID card at the hallway door, beeping my way out.

I didn't need CNN Syndrome.

I needed Dr. Hay's lab.

Where the cyanide had been administered. Where I'd find the answers.

No one patrolled the corridor between the labs. The police tape had been taken down. When I knocked on the door, no one answered.

I lingered at the frosted glass, trying to peer through it. I could make out a few dark, unmoving shapes, possibly furniture.

Did anyone lurk inside?

"Knock, knock motherfucker," I whispered to the glass. I wasn't scared anymore. I was angry.

Movement inside the lab caught my eye. A long shape unfolded itself into standing position.

My entire body jerked in response, but I didn't scream. Once the shape began to move, it resolved itself into a medium-built man, maybe five foot ten. Not as thin as Lawrence, and much more alive.

My fingers flexed. I planted my feet.

My mouth opened, ready to unleash a tirade at one Dr. Stephen Weaver.

The man took his time swiping his card before he pushed the door open and gazed down at me with a benign, slightly blank expression, his deep-set eyes nearly hidden behind shoulder-length, wavy, brown locks, so he looked more like Jesus than ever, if Jesus wore a lab coat, brown corduroys, and running shoes.

"Chris?" I said, confused.

"Stephen asked me to keep an eye on his experiment."

"He's not here?"

Chris glanced over his shoulder. "The police wanted to talk to him."

I took a deep breath. This was a risk. I didn't fully trust Chris. On the other hand, he had access to the Hay lab as well as the knowledge I needed. "I came to ask you a favour."

It took him a long time, but in the end, he said yes. He'd see what he could do.

CHAPTER 44

That done, I considered it safest to retire to Tom's lab, where, with any luck, they'd stopped discussing the murder of Annie Le.

They had.

Unfortunately, they'd reformed their circle to include a new visitor.

"Unnerving," said Dr. Hay, who'd donned a pair of high heels, so she was now two inches taller than Summer. Dr. Hay wore an immaculate white lab coat over a crisp navy pantsuit, and commanded every eye as her hands swept the air. "To think that I trusted such an individual for over two years of my life—to think that I, too, could have died … "

I eyed Tom and Summer, who were facing the door and standing on either side of Dr. Hay. Surely they could extrapolate her point. If Ducky had, indeed, concocted some cyanide, why would she attack a new post-grad student, instead of the woman who'd oppressed her for the past two years?

I worked my way into the circle, into a gap between Samir and Dr. Wen. I needed to distract Dr. Hay so she didn't stumble upon Chris in her lab. "This week has been insane," I agreed.

"Bone-chilling," she said, her pale, blue eyes barely registering me. She pivoted to her right to raise one well-groomed eyebrow at Tom, whom I thought was married, but Dr. Hay's intensity hinted that she wouldn't be adverse to a little R&R on the side.

Tom nodded. "It is frightening. I try to remember that crime has been decreasing in Canada, with homicide at its lowest level since 1966."

"Right, Stats Can released a report on that." Mitch grabbed his phone. My face would betray me if I looked at the guy directly, so I watched him out of the corner of my eye.

Tom's pocket buzzed. He reached for his own phone and said, "Sorry, I have to take this." He shut his office door behind him. I suppressed a smile. He'd told me that researchers often fell somewhere on the autism spectrum, and here was the proof.

Dr. Hay tossed her head. Her silver hair caught the light. I'd never paid attention to grey or white hair before, but hers was lovely. She had more time to tend to it because Dahiyyah had done all the grunt work. More importantly, her hair and the rest of her aimed for the hallway door while everyone else ambled back to their research stations.

I hung back long enough to note that her pass unlocked the door. Which meant she had access to Tom's lab. Why? And did he have access to hers?

I didn't have time to pursue that, though, as I chased her out the door. "Dr. Hay, I'm about to choose a research project for the month. I wonder if you could advise me on my decision? I know you're very busy, and this is a traumatic time, but while Dr. Zinser is tied up … "

She glanced back over her shoulder, at Tom's still-closed door. I was basically feeding her an excuse to stick around for a few more minutes. She checked her phone and allowed, "I have fourteen minutes before my next appointment."

"Wow! That's awesome." I steered her back into the lab, around Dr. Wen, and sat her down at my computer. "See, Tom sent me links to everyone's research. I was thinking of Dr. Al-Sani—"

Her lip curled.

"He won the Banting and Best Fellowship," I said, pretending not to notice.

"It would have been better suited to other students. We've made stellar advances on Rift Valley disease this year, using the MP-12 strain." She gave a shrug and a tinkly laugh. "One never knows what the committee will do, or what kind of quotas they might try to fulfill."

Her voice was loud enough that Samir could hear her from the next lab bench down. His shoulders stiffened.

Dr. Hay followed my gaze. The corners of her mouth drifted upward.

I crossed my fingers in silent apology to Samir as I said, "I was impressed by his paper on neural crest lineage as a determinant of disease heterogeneity—"

"You're so new to the system, my dear, you have no idea how politically correct universities have become. It's not only a matter of the quality of science anymore. It's who you know and what kind of affirmative action has become fashionable this year."

She used such big words, it was possible that Samir might not understand her implications that he hadn't won the Banting and Best Fellowship based on merit, but on the colour of his skin.

The heightened colour in his neck said otherwise.

The little I knew of Samir amounted to three things: 3. Summer made him swoon; 2. He seemed kind; and 1. His work was his life. His pride. His *raison d'être*.

Was it possible Dahiyyah had slipped into the same trap? Did she finally lash out at this woman, accidentally killing Lawrence in the process?

But Joan had said he was beaten. I couldn't picture Dahiyyah steamrollering him, even if he were unconscious from cyanide.

"I thought awards were based on the quality of research papers," I said, loudly enough that Samir and the rest of the lab could hear.

Dr. Hay chuckled. "Oh, Hope. How naive you are. Now, if you were in my lab, I could teach you something." Her smile revealed her perfectly even, white teeth. "Would you like to help fill in while I'm hiring a new research assistant?"

CHAPTER 45

I couldn't say yes.

I couldn't go back to the killer cyanide lab.

Still, I needed to block her from Chris's activities as long as possible. "I'm committed to Dr. Tom Zinser's lab," I said slowly.

Her nostrils flared. This was not a woman who took failure gracefully.

I have to admit that most labs—heck, most businesses around the globe—use cheap labour. It's a way of cutting costs in a competitive environment. Plus, when she was setting up her lab, she must've suffered decades of discrimination. That could warp anyone. Everyone likes Tom and other Mr. Nice Guys, but they haven't had to battle their way through sexist B.S. every hour.

"However, I'm sure he wouldn't mind if I took a look. You said that Dr. Stephen Weaver's research on Rift Valley disease is seminal?"

"It will blow your mind. Ground-breaking rather than derivative." Her powerful voice echoed throughout the room.

Mitch slammed a drawer shut.

Dr. Wen set a glass flask on the lab bench with an audible click.

I hesitated. "Your lab isn't closed off for the investigation anymore?" I knew the answer. I was buying Chris as much time as I could.

"Of course not. The police understand that we have crucial work to do, and that every moment counts. Now, come along. Bring your laptop. Chop chop."

Was that an ethnic slur? Like chop suey? Hard to tell, with her. I slid off my stool and tucked my borrowed netbook under my arm.

Summer cast me a *What are you doing?* look. I smiled at her, showing my teeth, which have never experienced braces, and only the occasional white strip, but are plenty strong. Summer might not know me well enough to understand that I had a plan. Sort of.

I let Dr. Hay beep the door again and followed her out. I belatedly realized this meant I didn't pop up on the security guys' monitoring of our badge whereabouts. They could still view me on the security cameras, but that would require either someone watching in real time, or a lot of boring hours combing through footage afterward.

I raised my badge to beep the door again, and I waved at the camera. Anything to get their attention, like a modern Hansel and Gretel. I trailed Dr. Hay by a half-step, not enough for her to object, but enough to slow her down. "I'm a little worried about the cyanide the police found."

She snorted. "They cleared all of Ducky's equipment away for testing, and the area has been thoroughly cleaned. *You* won't have anything to worry about." She poked my arm.

Her nail cut into my deltoid hard enough that I glanced at my right arm, half-checking to see if she'd managed to slice through the material of my grey tunic dress.

She smiled at me with those teeth again.

I tried not to shudder. I found her unpleasant and casually racist, but she was at least twice my age. She couldn't beat up Lawrence.

True, he might have been weakened with cyanide first, but I knew I hadn't eaten any of those almond cookies. I could take on a 60-year-old lady. No one was going to hurt me.

And yet, I had the distinct feeling I was walking to my doom. Like one of ten little Indians in the Agatha Christie book.

I lingered in the elevator area and raised my voice, in case Chris could hear me behind that frosted glass. "I heard they found cyanide in Ducky's flasks and condenser." I deliberately used the nickname, falling in with Dr. Hay's language.

"Yes. The foolish girl seemed to have followed the instructions from the article she'd left in her drawer, 'Potential Toxic Levels of Cyanide in Almonds, Apricot Kernels, and Almond Syrup.'" Dr. Hay shook her head. "It was devastatingly simple. She heated up water in one round-bottomed flask and collected the steam into a glass tube that was attached to a second round-bottomed flask holding the apricot pits. The vapours of hydrocyanic acid, released through maceration, were condensed and collected in silver nitrate."

I couldn't visualize it, but I tried to remember the name of the article so I could look it up later. "That would be easy to set up?"

"If one has access to the equipment and the time and inclination to do so." Dr. Hay blew out her breath in frustration.

Another detail nudged my brain. "How did you know she used apricot pits?"

She sighed. "That was an educated guess. Stephen and I discussed it yesterday. He bought apricots in bulk over the summer and ate them continuously. He's a fruitarian, you know."

"Yes, he mentioned that." The only other fruitarian I'd heard of had been Steve Jobs, who died of pancreatic cancer. Not a recommendation.

She clasped her hands together in front of her, as if she were lecturing in a classroom. "It would be a simple matter to collect his apricot pits and distill the cyanide. People often talk about the cyanide levels in apple seeds, but at least one study found only 3 milligrams of amygdalin—the cyanogenic glycoside—per gram of apple seeds. The average 70 kg male would have to chew up to 200 seeds in one sitting to suffer the effects. Meanwhile, apricots have 14.4 milligrams per gram. It's a matter of efficiency."

She certainly didn't seem intimidated by the process. If anything, I'd say she seemed fascinated by poison, the way people glom on to serial killers, or anacondas.

She knew an awful lot about cyanide. I'd have to look up amygdalin, and how to distill cyanide from it. "How do you think the cyanide got on Lawrence's almond cookie?"

She brushed her hand through the air like she was waving away a fly. "That man was always eating. He knew it was against the lab safety rules, but he kept bringing in his sports drinks and his coffee and eating everything in sight."

"Do you think his food might have been contaminated by accident?" That hadn't occurred to me, even though I'd been watching lab safety videos for the past few days.

Dr. Hay shrugged. "The police will tell us. It's very unfortunate, of course. His widow was devastated, and she gave birth to premature twins."

I studied her to see if she knew of my role in that birth. She looked as blank as Chris. "The police are looking for two persons of interest. Maybe Ducky had nothing to do with his death—"

She touched my shoulder, more gently this time. "It's not up to us. The police will find out, and they'll inform us in due course. All we can do is continue our work." She sounded reasonable, even likeable. Before I could figure out how I felt about Dr. Hay, she held her card up to her lab's reader. The sensor beeped. The light turned green.

I glanced at the camera above our heads, and I knew I couldn't delay anymore. If Chris was still messing around in there, we'd have to improvise.

CHAPTER 46

"Once you start working here, we'll have to update your card access. Especially in light of recent events, you'll need a badge to enter and exit the lab," said Dr. Hay, holding the door open for me and earning herself another point, even though I hadn't agreed to work for her.

"A research assistant would need easy access," I agreed. "What sort of duties would an R.A. have?"

"You don't have the technical knowledge, so you would have to start with manuscript preparation, assisting me with presentations and posters, and doing the clerical work while I interview the first candidates," she said, gesturing at the computer and inbox trays neatly laid on the table next to her office.

Aha. She wanted a scut monkey. That's what makes the hospital run smoothly, so I knew how to do crap like that, but I'd be better off doing actual research for my designated supervisor than photocopying for Dr. Hay. "I'll be busy at the Zinser lab. I'll see what I can do," I said as she steered me through the office and toward the lab.

"I expect the very best work, and I am never disappointed."

I held my breath as she opened the lab door.

I surveyed the empty room, with its banks of black lab tables, glassware, and fume hoods.

No sound. No sign of anyone in the room.

Chris had left, possibly during the short time we'd transitioned from office to lab.

I sent a prayer to whatever deity was looking over us. The netbook battery's was so hot, I could feel it through the shirt under my arm, almost like it was a living organism my dad had sent to protect me.

Dr. Hay clicked her tongue. "I wanted you to talk to Stephen about his superior work on Rift Valley disease. I can't think where he's gone."

Harold, the security guard, had said Dr. Hay and Stephen Weaver were always at the lab. Stephen Weaver seemed to be taking an awful lot of time off lately, and even Dr. Hay didn't seem to be frothing at the mouth to restart her experiments.

"Oh, does he normally work at this bench?" I pointed at the completely empty bench nearest her office door, directly in front of us. That would be Summer's bench, on Tom's side. I was pretty sure I knew who'd run that bench, but I wanted her to answer.

Her lips twitched in a mirthless smile. "That was Ducky's bench."

"This was where you ... found her body?"

Her chin dipped in acknowledgement. For a second, she didn't meet my eyes.

"She was on the floor?"

"Yes. I didn't have to approach her to know that she was ... deceased. It didn't require any medical skill," she added, out of the corner of her eyes.

Maybe she was casting aspersions on me for trying to resuscitate Lawrence. I ignored that. "She was lying on her back?"

"She was slightly curled up, with her hands next to her face and her knees bent, but yes, she was on her back. I must ask you, Dr. Sze, how you find this relevant to working for me?"

My heart thudded in my chest. I struggled to maintain an impassive face. "I liked her. I feel badly about how she died. I've heard cyanide is painful." It sure didn't sound great if she was found in a fetal position.

Dr. Hay nodded. "'When justice is done, it is a joy to the righteous but terror to evildoers.'"

It sounded like a quote, but I didn't quite understand her meaning. I raised my eyebrows.

"Proverbs 21:15, Dr. Sze," she said.

I still didn't get it.

Human Remains

"Guilt is all-consuming, Dr. Sze. She was trying to do penance. Poor, misguided girl. I hope she found some peace, in the end."

My brow furrowed. How would a confused, convulsive death in your own bodily fluids be considered a peaceful end? I switched to more concrete questions. "What time was it?"

"Before 7 a.m. She came early."

Or stayed late. "What time did you leave the lab the night before?"

Her eyebrows drew together. "Are you trying to establish an alibi for me? Really, Dr. Sze. I've told you, the police have this case well in hand. There is no need for you to meddle."

"I'm trying to piece the story together."

At last, her cool, blue eyes met mine directly. "I left around 9 p.m. Ducky had already gone for the day. Are you satisfied?"

Of course not. Ducky could have come back any time, and she obviously did. "Was Dr. Weaver working late as well?"

Now she smiled. "He always does. Now, Dr. Sze, if you're going to work here, you'll have to follow the rules and work hard instead of questioning everything. Is that within your realm of capability?"

The hallway door beeped, saving me from answering.

Dr. Stephen Weaver glared at me from the opening.

The saliva dried up in my mouth. I had to try not to bite my lip as I stared right back at him.

"Oh, Stephen." Dr. Hay sounded delighted to see him. "Dr. Sze has offered to work for us for a few days, while we establish a new research assistant and lab technologist. Would you like to show her around?"

Stephen shook his head. "I need to start on my experiment. I've been away too long."

"Well, show her what you're doing and then put her to work. There's no reason why you have to handle all the menial details. That's what Hope is here for."

I opened my mouth to object, but she was already pulling up the sleeve of her lab coat to glance at her watch before she raised her badge to beep herself out. "I've got a meeting. Farewell and Godspeed."

CHAPTER 47

Stephen glowered at me while Dr. Hay swept out of the lab. He said, "You can't do my experiment. I don't trust you. Go in the office."

The way he ordered me around made me want to punch him in the head. On the other hand, he'd given me free access to his office, under the guise of "helping" him.

"Okay," I said, trying to sound meek, like Ducky, as I grasped the silver door handle.

He cast me a suspicious look, but I was already migrating toward the four desks in the central room outside Dr. Hay's closed-off office. One desk had collected a bunch of odds and sods, including a water bottle, a Christmas card from someone named Helen Ford, and a bulky old computer, so I ignored that.

The three other desks must have belonged to Stephen Weaver, Lawrence Acayo, and Dahiyyah Safar. Which one should I attack first?

The one with the dead cow fetus. I zoomed toward Stephen Weaver's desk on the left side of the room, near the hallway door.

He was hideously neat. Nothing on his smooth, black laminate desk but a stapler and a stack of research papers, but his desktop computer was practically begging me to access it.

I hit the Esc key to wake it up. It asked for a user ID and password.

Well, damn it. I hardly knew the guy. I wasn't going to figure out his password. But I tried his names, separately and together, with upper case and lower case, then riftvalleydisease.

If Ryan were here, he might be able to pull some hacker mojo.

Ryan.

I pulled out my phone and texted him. *How do I log into a computer without knowing the User ID/password?*

My phone rang. I hit the green button and glanced over my shoulder, waiting for the Big Bad to burst out of the lab and rip my face off. "What?" I hissed at Ryan.

"Never text stuff like that. They'll pull it up from your phone history, even if we delete the messages. What are you doing?"

"I'm trying to get into Stephen Weaver's computer!"

"You have to get the password."

"How do I do that?"

"Put a keylogger on it."

"How do I do *that?*"

"Too complicated to explain. Also, illegal. Don't do it. And did you know the message from Ducky has embedded files?"

"The e-mail? Where?"

"Can you bring it up?"

"Sure." I set my netbook on Stephen Weaver's desk. Part of me enjoyed violating his blank space. I quickly typed in my password and logged into Gmail. "Got it."

"You'd better do this on a Windows computer, not your MacBook."

"Done."

"Okay. Bring up the picture in her sig. Go to the toolbar at the top, the one with File, and click List. It should be right between Edit and Favourites. Then View."

I'd never noticed List in the grey toolbar on top before. I clicked View. "Got it."

"In the drop down menu, read me what you've got."

"Okay. Print, DOS Prompt in Containing Folder, Open with Notetab, Open with Audacity, Open with jEdit, Preview, 7-Zip—"

"That's it." His voice was tense with excitement. "Click on that, and then Extract here."

The list changed. Under riftvalley.jpg, more files materialized: 2_secret_riftvalley.doc, 3_secret_SW.doc, 4_secret_JH, hidden_video.avi, private_picture.gif …

"My God," I said aloud. Ducky hadn't dispatched a suicide note. She'd been delivering evidence against SW and JH. Stephen Weaver and Judith Hay. "I've got to send these to the cops. They wouldn't have gotten this attachment through the app."

"I already forwarded it to them, but you can do it, too."

"Doing it." Good thing I already had the cops' e-mail addresses handy. I added Tucker's for good measure. While Outlook took its sweet time, I opened Lawrence's files and searched specifically for Rift Valley disease.

1997 outbreak: 90,000 infected, 500 deaths

The fatality rate wasn't too bad, but I remembered what Joan had said about hemorrhagic fever, and kept skimming.

Rift Valley disease mainly affects domestic animals, including cows, goats, sheep, and even camels. Young animals get weak with diarrhea; adult females may not look ill until they spontaneously miscarry their pregnancies. By that, I mean a 100 percent pregnancy loss rate.

It's spread by Aedes mosquitoes, including the *Aedes aegypti* mosquito.

It's like the poor cousin of Zisa virus.

And I do mean poor cousin, because it only attacks sub-Saharan Africa and Arabia in epidemics after a heavy rainfall. That's economically devastating to the people trying to survive off their livestock, but since researchers are fighting for ever-decreasing dollars, do you honestly think they're going to prioritize poor farmers on the other side of the world?

2000: 120,000 people infected, 900 deaths
2003: 187,000 people infected, 3200 deaths
2006: 225,000 people infected, 9000 deaths
2007: 275,000 people infected, 12,500 deaths
2008-09: 300,000 infected, 13,000 deaths
2010: 250,000 infected, 12,000 deaths
2012: 200,000 infected, 11,500 deaths
2016: 350,000 infected, 17,000 deaths
Vaccine safety questioned.

Holy crap. I didn't want to break out a calculator, but obviously, in 20 years, the disease had become far more prevalent, not to mention lethal by another order of magnitude.

How had we not noticed?

When the U.S. sneezed, Canada caught a cold, and sub-Saharan African and Arabia …

Joan's voice rang in my head. *They start bleeding everywhere. Not only do they have bloody vomit and stool, but blood comes out of their gums, their noses, their skin, and their injection sites.*

I started running through the papers.

How did they go from an outbreak every four years to some not even a year apart?

Ryan's voice broke into my reverie. "You're still in that guy's office?"

"Yeah. Listen, Ryan, I've got to send you these articles. WHO developed a vaccine this year, but Stephen Weaver is blocking it. There are a bunch of articles about prenatal abnormalities that are—"

The poor bovine fetus leapt into my mind.

A 100 percent pregnancy loss rate.

You can't tame a mosquito.

Stephen Weaver wasn't trying to help the people of Sub-Saharan African and Arabia.

He was creating an epidemic to kill them.

I realized aloud, "He was *combining* Rift Valley and Zisa."

"Hope. *Get out.*"

"I will." I'd worried about Joan's double infection with Zisa and herpes, but Stephen Weaver had dreamed up a new co-infection, spread by mosquito, geographically targeting the world's most vulnerable people.

I glanced behind me. The door between me and the lab remained closed. I was still alone.

When I turned back to check the e-mail status (still uploading), the light caught on a bit of graffiti scratched into the gleaming desk top's right lower corner.

I wouldn't have noticed it if I hadn't been sitting at the desk, or if I hadn't spent so many hours as a bored student, penning desk graffiti myself.

I laid my iPhone beside my netbook while I bent forward and tilted my head from side to side, trying to figure out the design.

The crabbed etching coalesced in my brain, forming an inverted triangle inside a triangle for the KKK, outlined by the barely-legible word "miscegenation."

Below it, a crude noose.

And Stephen Weaver's voice cut through the air, dangerously close to me. "What are you doing?"

CHAPTER 48

"Nothing!" I half-screamed.

Stephen Weaver loomed over me, his bulk poised precisely between myself and the office exit to the hallway.

The e-mail *still* hadn't sent.

I scooped up the open netbook and my phone.

Diagonally behind me, Dr. Hay's office was surely locked, and a dead end besides.

The windows directly behind me? Not from the third story of a building.

I jerked the phone up to my ear. "He's here! Help—"

Stephen Weaver whacked the phone out of my hand. It spiralled out of my grip and smashed on the floor.

"Fuck!" Even as the word escaped my mouth, I realized I had a split-second choice.

I could dive for my phone.

Or I could run for it.

Run.

Not toward the hallway exit, because Stephen Weaver instinctively lunged to his left.

I tossed the netbook on his desk.

While his eyes followed the arc of my dad's computer, I darted into the central aisle, *away* from the closest door.

Past two more desks.

Toward the lab.

I thrust open the door and sprinted into the lab, taking the outside aisle, the one closest to the hallway. I was going to make it—

—except my right ankle turned over.

I gasped with pain and managed to stay on my feet. It wasn't broken, still wasn't broken, just another sprain, I could limp, but Stephen Weaver cut through the central aisle, made an L-shaped zig, and blocked that door, too.

I retreated, as fast as I could, toward the no man's land around Ducky's lab bench and the fume hood.

He'd left the office lab door unguarded. I'd exit from the office, only fifteen feet away.

Stephen Weaver's eyes glinted, and I remembered that Dr. Hay required a badge to exit as well as enter her premises.

I could toggle back and forth between the lab and the office, like a rat in a maze, but I needed Stephen's badge to unlock a hallway door to the outside world.

Stephen Weaver was bigger than me.

He was faster than me.

He wore the only key card in the room.

Still, I half-ran, half-limped toward the office. Another seven feet, and I'd have a hunk of wood between me and the guy who thought he'd solved the world's overpopulation problem in utero.

Behind me, he said a few words, and I heard some beeps, which I ignored. I could almost reach the door. Another second, and—

I lunged for the silver handle.

The office door buzzed before I touched it. I flinched, but I yanked on it.

No.

No matter how I struggled, the door shifted only a millimetre before it hit an invisible lock.

No.

How had he managed that?

I was now sealed in the lab.

Human Remains

On the third floor.

With no phone.

And the man who'd masterminded a genocide.

You chose ... poorly.

"—right now. Get rid of that UFO I told you about." His voice grew louder behind me. I could hear his footsteps.

I glanced over my shoulder. He strolled up the aisle with his phone to his ear, watching me as he spoke. I was getting cornered by a guy who was so crazy, he was chatting to his buddies about UFO's before offing me.

At last, he pocketed his phone in his jeans, his eyes never leaving mine. I wanted to lunge for his key card, which stared at me from his front pocket, as unsmiling as the real, live man who'd trapped me. "What made you suspect me?"

I licked my lips. If I started talking, would I be like Scheherazade, buying time with my stories? Or would he figure, *Yep, I've learned everything I needed to know. Time to kill this bitch, too.*

Jamais deux sans trois.

Lawrence had died. Ducky had died.

I'd counted Baby Hope as the second death, but she hadn't expired directly as a result of Stephen Weaver.

Or had she? Stephen Weaver must have rejoiced when he met Joan Acayo, a black pregnant woman who already had Zisa and herpes. Why not add a third virus?

Like Zisa, Rift Valley disease was usually spread by mosquitoes, but it could also be transmitted by close contact with tissue or bodily fluids. It was not a coincidence that a butcher died from Rift Valley disease in Kabale.

Stephen Weaver could have infected Lawrence, or Joan, or both of them, plus their twins.

A 100 percent pregnancy loss rate.

I flashed back to that bathroom. Angella's too-small head and desperately gasping chest. Baby Hope never got to take a breath, never opened her eyes.

I could be spreading Rift Valley myself right now. They'd tested me for pregnancy and Zisa and herpes, but not Rift Valley disease.

"No," I said, aloud.

Stephen Weaver's mouth twisted. "No, you didn't suspect me?"

"I did suspect you. Someone was scaring Dahiyyah, stealing her condenser and her papers. Someone in her lab would have access. That person kept going after Lawrence died."

He smiled.

I began to move. I wasn't truly cornered yet. He'd left three feet of space between us, maybe because he didn't want to get too close to the gook. "Between you and Dr. Hay, she was the loudest, but you were the one with the fruitarian diet and all the apricot pits."

He snorted. He let me edge past him, probably because he didn't consider me a true threat. He was the lion who could pounce on a rat any time by stretching out a paw. "She could have misplaced her condenser."

"No, you were gaslighting her. Driving her crazy. You knew exactly how to do it." I backed down the central aisle, toward the benches at the rear of the lab. "You stole her equipment to boil cyanide, and then planted it back on her so people would think she'd killed Lawrence. You added the cyanide extraction paper. But Lawrence was beaten before he died. Dahiyyah wouldn't beat anyone up. She couldn't even beat *me* up."

The next lab bench, on my left, belonged to Stephen, judging from the name plate on the shelf. I kept backing up. Maybe I could run a big circle around him at the perimeter. My ankle twinged, but not severely, at slow speed.

I threw out a question to distract him. "Why did you put the bag over Lawrence's head?"

"I didn't," he said.

"Oh, come on. You logged on to 14-88 and drew them a new flag. I assume you put a bag on Lawrence as a reference to the lynching that you love so much. Maybe you were too much of a coward to look him in the face. Or you needed a handy way to suffocate him. How about all three? Collect 'em all!"

He nearly smiled. "I didn't kill him."

"Right. You knocked the phone out of my hand and chased me in here because you need a few more steps on your pedometer?"

"No."

A two-toned noise ding-donged through the air. I jerked my head up, trying to pinpoint the source, but Stephen Weaver ambled up the outside aisle, over to the frosted glass door, and waved his badge at the sensor.

The closest hallway lab door opened. A huge man stomped into the room, more sequoia than human, if sequoias wore black balaclava masks. Even under the mask, I detected greyish eyes and a prominent nose. The dude was white.

A smaller, skinnier guy slid around the sequoia, wearing the same black balaclava.

#1: Caucasian male, heavy build, 5'10"-6'0"(178 cm - 183 cm)

#2: Caucasian male, 5'6"-5'8"(168 cm - 173 cm)

#3: Stephen Weaver

CHAPTER 49

Stephen Weaver pointed at me. "Take care of her."

Take care of her.

Rage hummed through my veins.

He couldn't even come out and say, *Kill her.* He had to disguise it with vague language. Murder and maim at a safe distance: from a lab bench, a conference pulpit, or a United Nations consensus statement.

These three men had killed Lawrence. They'd killed Dahiyyah. But hell if I let them take me without a fight all over this lab. They'd never write me off as a suicide.

This was a case of three on one, in a single room with three locked doors, two to the hallway and one to the office. I was alone and injured, so I'd better strike fast. "Hey. You must be the ones Stevie calls in to the dirty work."

Fat Guy shook his head from the aisle next to the hallway. Like a sequoia, he didn't move fast.

Skinny made up for it. He snapped, "Shut up," as he prowled toward me.

"Me or him? The police are looking for you, you know."

Skinny was only ten feet away. Close enough that I noted the paler skin around his eye holes and the way his mouth shifted underneath his balaclava. He moved through the central aisle, like me. Stephen Weaver stalked behind him.

Okay, this is bad. But guess what, honeys? Hostage-takers *don't fuck with me. You seriously think the three of you will do it, with your bare hands?*

I retreated to the fume hood resting against the back wall of the room. Its contents were protected by the glass sash drawn most of the way down. Signs on the stainless steel doors beneath warned of acids stored on the left and the flammable components on the right.

I heard a click.

I lifted my head.

Fat Guy creeped toward me from the hallway aisle, still fifteen feet away, but he cocked his gun and aimed it at my head like he knew how to use it.

Fucking guns.

I stared down the barrel. It was like a small, black eye trained on me. I thought, *All this time, I've been running away from pregnant women and infectious diseases. But this is what I'm really scared of. Isn't it.*

The humour drained out of me. I remembered the 14/11 Medical Post article about what to do when an active shooter enters the room.

1. Run.

2. If you can't run, fight.

3. If you can't fight, hide.

Right now, with a gun aimed between my eyes, hiding was not an option. They knew exactly who I was and where I was.

Running? When I was trapped in an enclosed space, surrounded by lab benches?

Theoretically possible. Fat Guy might shoot me, but in times of stress, shooters miss up to 80 percent of the time. Often they want you alive. The gun is a prop to make you come with them quietly. And hell no, I wasn't going.

Security could have noticed the two strangers who'd entered the Lab of Death.

If I herded the bad guys close to the doors, Harold might spot me on his cameras. The cameras were pointed at the entrance, not inside the lab, but, worst case, my blood hitting the frosted glass doors should raise a domestic 911.

Or I could dash in the opposite direction, to the outdoor windows. Smash through double panes until I made a Hope-sized hole and hurtled from the third floor.

But I could die from a three-story fall. I once looked after a woman who'd jumped off a bridge. Not pretty.

I bet those windows were made of security glass, too. I might not crack through them before I got shot.

More importantly, if I jumped, they'd write me off as a suicide.

Door it is, then.

I had three advantages over Lawrence and Dahiyyah.

One, I hadn't partaken in any cyanide. This trio might force it down my mouth after I was unconscious, or smear it over my skin, but my neurons and my cardiac muscle were still firing for now.

Two, I would not go quietly. I would smear my own blood and intestines over those walls before I'd let them take me.

Three, I knew exactly who my enemies were. Cowards.

Racists want to beat people up. Skin colour is a convenient excuse. They band together, they hurl words, they paint graffiti, they torch synagogues and mosques, they jump on a poor Muslim woman trying to pick her kids up from school.

But most of them won't pull a trigger point blank. Some of them will, like that crazy guy in South Carolina who opened fire on a black Bible study.

Most of them won't.

I looked Fat Gun Guy straight in the eye and declared, "Is that a firearm I see before me?"

Fat Guy's eyes darted toward Skinny, then toward Stephen Weaver. I wasn't fighting him like Lawrence, or cowering like Dahiyyah. He didn't know what to do with me. And maybe he didn't want to pull the trigger on a little Asian woman. Hey, I'll take any advantage I can get.

"Shut up," repeated Skinny.

Me talking made Skinny uncomfortable. He obviously preferred his victims unconscious, with bags over their heads.

That meant I should talk *more.*

Fat Guy shook his gun to seize my attention. He growled, "You. Come with me."

Human Remains

"'Come live with me and be my love, and we will all the pleasures prove!'" I shouted back at him. Why poetry? Why not. My brain was unhinged. If they were going to kill me, kill me, God damn it. I wasn't going to live in fear anymore.

Fat Guy's gun hand wavered. He didn't shoot.

"She's crazy," said Stephen, lurking behind Skinny's left shoulder. "Get rid of her. Now."

"Why should they? Why don't you do it, Stevie?" I offered him an open-mouthed clown smile, a rictus of mock delight.

"That's Doctor Stephen Weaver to you, dog-muncher."

Dog-muncher? "That's *Doctor* Hope Sze to you, *loser*." I could've come up with a better insult, but at least we had the same rank. Almost. "Dr. Hope Sze, *M.D.*"

Stevie's hands curled into fists.

I would have chortled, except Fat Guy and Skinny had ringed around me, almost within arm's length. Fat Guy pointed the gun at my chest.

Tucker had been shot in the lungs and in the bowel.

He'd almost died, except the police and the medical crew had saved him.

No police lurked outside the door this time.

I swallowed, or tried to. There was almost no saliva left in my mouth.

I made eye contact with the underlings. The balaclavas made them look like low rent versions of Spiderman. "Stevie's ordering you to do it. He never gets his hands dirty. He's not going to jail for killing Dr. Lawrence Acayo. You are."

Fat Guy's mouth twitched under his mask. He was listening.

"Maybe he poisoned Dr. Acayo first, but you're the ones who beat him to death. *Doctor* Stephen Weaver gets to sit here with his Ph.D., while you guys end up in jail. It's like he's the master and you're the slave."

"Shut up, slit," said Stephen, but I thought his forehead gleamed under the fluorescent light. The guy had apocrine sweat glands after all.

"If I were you, I'd get some evidence against him. Save his texts. Figure out where he got the cyanide. That way, if he gets you arrested, he'll go down with you."

Stephen Weaver charged forward, his face so red it bordered on eggplant.

He knocked Skinny against a lab bench, who hollered "What the hell?", but Stephen's hands were already swiping for Fat Guy's gun.

Fat Guy yanked his arms up, keeping the gun out of Stephen's reach.

Meanwhile, I thrust my hands under the glass sash of the fume hood and snatched a flask from the acid side.

The stoppered flask contained some transparent liquid. Nothing too remarkable-looking, except for the HF 16/12/14 marked on the side, which inspired me to say, "Who wants some hydrofluoric acid?"

All three thugs jerked to a halt.

Fat Guy held his arms in the air.

Stephen Weaver's claws froze.

Skinny held on to the edge of his lab bench.

Wow. Bad guys knew hydrofluoric acid. I didn't learn about it 'til med school. But maybe all they heard was the word "acid." I'd have to educate them.

I advanced toward them, holding the flask above my head so that its contents caught the light. "Hydrofluoric acid. One of the most dangerous acids in the world."

"Shoot her," said Stephen.

I tsk-tsked. "Stevie, do you want hydrofluoric acid flying in your eyes? It's one of the most frightening inorganic acids known to mankind." Usually, I'd use a non-gender-specific word, this group luuuurved mankind. Parts of it, anyway.

Stephen snorted. "No one leaves HF inside a fume hood."

"They shouldn't," I agreed. "It burns through glass. If I get this in your eyes, it will blind you. If I get it in your lungs, they will fill with fluid until you stop breathing. Your skin might seem to protect you, because one little splash doesn't hurt much. But it seeps down right to the bone, leaching out the calcium, so that you go into cardiac arrhythmias."

They didn't know whether or not to believe me. I said, impatient, "You might have seen it on Breaking Bad. They tried to dissolve a drug dealer's body with it."

Whoa. That, they'd heard of. They all stiffened and looked to Stephen to boss them around.

Stevie's weakness was that he had to be top dog, but he didn't want to kill me himself.

The thugs needed someone to order them around.

Solution: disrupt that chain of command, so they had neither head nor muscle.

Cut them off like CRISPR identifying their villainous asses and dropping them to their motherfucking knees.

I said, "I'm not lying. I'm a medical doctor. He's a chemist."

"I'm a Ph.D." Stephen raised his voice.

"Yes, probably because you couldn't get into medical school."

His hands thrust into the air like he was going to strangle me. He had such big hands, he probably could've encircled my waist and squeezed my small intestines out through my mouth.

Except I held up the vial between us. "Oh, good. I have my first volunteer for hydrofluoric acid."

"That's not HF," he said, more to his buddies than to me. "We follow the lab safety rules. All dangerous chemicals have to be secured."

"You would think. But you know, Ducky was running scared after you killed Dr. Acayo. She knew what you were up to. Maybe she even told Dr. Acayo, and that's why you killed him. Or maybe he figured it out first. Either way, Ducky needed to protect herself. And one way she did it was by weaponizing her lab. She's still careful enough to label her work, though." I twisted the flask so the neatly-written HF was most prominent.

"Bullshit," said Stephen. "Shoot her."

I unstoppered the flask and launched its contents at his face.

CHAPTER 50

He screamed so loudly, I was afraid it really was hydrofluoric acid.

Which was a problem, because now he was writhing at my feet, spraying droplets of transparent liquid and howling.

I pressed myself against the fume hood, which wasn't the safest thing to do, but I didn't want to brush against him while I tried to escape.

From the look of it, the thugs didn't want to touch him, either. They backed away from him and me, their eyes wide behind their masks.

The antidote is calcium, even if it is HF, I told myself, but that was no comfort. I didn't want to go blind or get flash pulmonary edema either. Even if we were next door to a hospital, I could die before I made it to the ER. Just like Baby Hope.

I scrambled up on the deserted lab bench next to the window, knocking down pipettes and flasks as I managed to hoist my legs and feet out of immediate splash range.

The Fat Guy withdrew, putting the safety back on his gun before he holstered it at his ankle.

I breathed a little easier, even though Stephen was screaming, "Get her!" and swiping at me like a sea monster.

I climbed to the window side of the lab bench while the thugs backed toward the closest door to the hallway.

Skinny pushed the door. Nothing.

Right. They needed Stephen's swipe card to get out, and none of us wanted to touch him.

The good news was that they couldn't get away.

The bad news was that we were all trapped together, unless someone could grab Stephen's card. Even with gloves, that was a risky proposition.

"Shoot it out!" said Skinny.

"What?" Fat Guy glanced back at us. "I don't want to shoot a girl."

"Not her, the lock!"

"I could break the glass."

"I said shoot it!"

I wouldn't know where to shoot out an electronic lock, either. But I couldn't worry about it, because Stephen Weaver lurched upward to seize my right ankle with his bare hand.

Acid sizzled my skin in the bare patch between my skinny jeans and socks.

My turn to scream. I snatched an empty glass flask and smashed it over his head. The shards cascaded into his eyes.

He yowled. His hands flew toward his orbits to shield them, or to rip the fragments out of his corneas.

And then I heard barking. Powerful, do-not-fuck-with-me barking, growing louder and louder.

I shook my head. Had I gone crazy?

The fire alarm started screeching. It made me feel like screaming, too. *Over here, over here!*

The barking cut through the alarm. Short, sharp, deep, commanding barks.

Rottweiler barks.

The thugs shouted, pointing at the shadows forming on the frosted glass panels.

One form barked, placed her paws on the window, leapt off, and barked some more.

The other simply raised a foot and kicked the glass pane. Once. A solid kick. One that made the room reverberate faintly.

I screamed. I knew who this was.

He couldn't be here. He couldn't risk his life, or Roxy's life, like this.

He couldn't have gotten here this fast.

Boom.

He kicked a second time. Just as hard, or even harder.

The glass shuddered.

"NO, Ryan! They have a GUN!"

He couldn't hear me over the alarm or Roxy. I shouted anyway.

Ryan kicked a third time.

The glass cracked.

Yelling all around me. Stephen Weaver hadn't stopped.

Fat Guy bent over for his holster.

The gun.

He was going to shoot Ryan. He was going to shoot Roxy. He was going to kill everything I loved, all over again.

I sprang off the lab bench. I barely registered the impact of my feet hitting the floor, the now-familiar burst of pain in my ankle.

I'd vaulted over Stephen Weaver.

I was running at Fat Guy.

I was screeching. I was howling. I was a force of nature, leaping straight on to Fat Guy and battling him for the gun.

CHAPTER 51

Skinny tried to wrench me off.

One hand on my mouth, the other on my neck.

Jerking my head back. Instant C-spine pain, but not paralysis.

I clamped down on Fat Guy.

Skinny smothered me with the other hand. He stank.

I bit him. Hard.

Tasted blood and dirt. Spat it out.

Stomped his instep. Elbowed his ribs and missed, but jerked my head up to head butt him.

Skinny let go, swearing up a storm that I could hardly hear over the alarm.

I bolted myself onto Fat Guy, as wide as my arms could reach, screaming with my now-free mouth, "Kill me! Kill ME!"

I could hear Ryan kicking, and Roxy barking, but they hadn't broken through. Not yet. They were still safe. The bad guys were more likely to attack me, the wild thing in their midst, instead of firing on the ghosts on the opposite sides of the glass.

"Police!" someone shouted.

I shook my head. I was hallucinating. I hadn't called them. How had they—how had Ryan—

"POLICE!"

I froze.

Time slowed down. I could smell Fat Guy's sweat. I could feel his chest heaving.

He didn't want to die.

None of us wanted to die.

Roxy's barking receded as Ryan towed her backwards.

I released Fat Guy and sprang away from the glass.

I tore back into the room. Toward Ducky's lab bench. Toward the windows.

Last time, the police used a flash bomb, a grenade that blinds and deafens you.

Have to get away. Have to—

Something tackled me.

Smashed me to the floor, left hip first, then stomach.

I couldn't breathe.

Something enormous, and sweaty, and furious flattened me.

My bare skin burned—face, neck.

Bits of glass crushed into my cheek when I hit the ground in Stephen Weaver's acid bath and glass hug.

I gulped for air.

My diaphragm heaved, but *I wasn't getting air.*

He was smothering me.

He was howling.

Breathe, God damn it.

BREATHE!

My chest heaved.

Air.

A tiny breath of air.

YES!

Glass shattered.

Stephen Weaver rammed my head into the floor.

BOOM.

Bright light penetrated my closed eyelids, even head down.

After that, nothing. Like my ears had shut down.

I knew what this was.

Flash bomb.

Flash bang.

Stun grenade.

First, the flash to dazzle the retinas.

Then the bang. Over 170 decibels. Deafening.

And now the smoke.

I could feel their footsteps through the floor as they stormed into the lab.

I held my breath, closed my eyes, and waited for Stephen Weaver to suck in the smoke.

His chest heaved.

He coughed.

Bingo. I wriggled.

He tried to clench his hands around my throat, but he was too busy sucking for air.

It's terrible, not being able to breathe.

Ask Lawrence. Ask Dahiyyah. Ask Baby Hope, if she could've talked.

I surged out from under him with my hands in the air.

CHAPTER 52

After a thorough decontamination shower, calcium gel in case it really was hydrofluoric acid, a double eye wash, and more blood and urine tests than I ever wanted in my life, I sagged into my emergency department stretcher and closed my eyes.

Breathing. I couldn't get over how awesome that was.

I could hear a bit better, too. Flash bombs aren't supposed to permanently deafen you, but this was my second one.

Jamais deux sans trois.

With any luck, not for a long time.

On the upside, because my ears' hair cells had krumped out, the cardiac monitor and O2 sat's beeps and alarms didn't bother me much.

Ryan pulled up a chair. He stroked my hair for a long, silent moment. Then he said, in my ear, "I knew you were in trouble. I was already on my way over."

"But how?" It hurt to push words through my raw throat. I didn't care. I needed to know.

"I watched you on the Finding Friends app, down to the micro scale."

I almost laughed, but it hurt too much. His words made my ears ring. I squeezed my eyes shut, still listening.

Human Remains

"I saw you going into Dr. Hay's lab. Got me worried. I dropped everything and started driving. I was going to stand by, keeping tabs on you, but after you called me, and the phone went dead, I busted in."

"With Roxy."

He half-grinned. "Rachel had dropped her off in my car. I wanted to get OHSC security riled up. That was the fastest way. And hey, it's always good to have a Rottweiler on your side, isn't it?"

"Sure is." They'd taken Roxy to a vet. I was pretty sure that she'd be okay. I hadn't touched her, and she hadn't entered the lab of death, although the flash bombs would be hell on her sensitive eyes, ears and nose. "You called the police?"

"Yeah, but I think security had already called them. Between Lawrence and Dahiyyah dying, and two strange guys going in the lab ... "

I gave a mental thumbs-up to Harold. Even though the younger security guards had beat him to the scene, I bet he'd sounded the alarm.

Ryan studied my face. "Why are you smiling?"

My face and neck smarted. My ankle hurt, not only from the sprained ligaments, but from the acid burns. My throat rasped. And yet Ryan was right. I was smiling.

I shrugged. Longer explanations would have to wait until I could say more than two words. I didn't understand it myself.

I should have been paralyzed with fear when Fat Guy pointed that gun at me. I'd been in stasis since 14/11.

Instead, my gut instinct had kicked in. I had a strong feeling that they wouldn't kill me. That I could manipulate them.

For sure, I'd jumped the shark. Who quotes Shakespeare and Christopher Marlowe at armed racists who outnumber you three to one?

But I felt like myself for the first time since 14/11. I still had PTSD. That wouldn't go away any time soon, or maybe ever. And yet, for the first time, I realized that PTSD also had me. I would not quit.

I gave Ryan the OK sign, pinching my thumb and forefinger together to make the O and letting my other fingers splay into the air like a K. That reminded me of the KKK, and my breath jerked for a second.

Like I once read in Ms. Magazine, we are all carriers of the disease called racism.

Mario Balotelli, an insanely talented Italian footballer, put it like this: "You can't delete racism. It's like a cigarette. You can't stop smoking if you don't want to, and you can't stop racism if people don't want to. But I'll do everything I can to help."

Ryan folded me into his arms.

His phone rang, and we ignored it, my nose tucked into the corner between his neck and shoulder, until he gave an exasperated sigh and checked it. "Oh. Kevin wants to know if you're up."

I gave him the thumbs up and waited for my parents to rip open the curtain and for Kevin to bound onto my belly.

I felt surprisingly good.

Last month, during 14/11, I had to protect three other people: Manouchka, her baby, and (let's admit it) most of all, Tucker.

This month, only I might've died. And if I did, oh well. There were 7.5 billion people on the planet who could replace me.

It made no sense, but I wasn't as scared of dying anymore.

All that breeeathing had some effect on me after all. It made me realize that this is what we've got: right now. A bit of oxygen and a bit of earth to walk on.

Fate kept tossing me head-first at the world's menaces. I didn't know why. Mrs. Lee, the mother of one victim, had told me that I was a young soul who was trying to grow up fast, which made my life very hard.

Was that true? I had no idea.

But the earth is full of human ass maggots who want to rape, kill, and immolate.

For profit.

For fun.

As long as I'm here, I'm going to toss them into the incinerator myself.

One body at a time.

CHAPTER 53

SUNDAY

I nearly fell asleep during the service for Lawrence and Baby Hope in the hospital chapel. Not out of disrespect, but because I was so exhausted. One thing that kept me sentient was that I had to keep standing up and sitting down on hard, wooden pews as we alternated between hymns and prayers. Ryan let me nod off on his shoulder during the sermon. We sat at the back of the small, overheated room, next to the pianist who played so intensely that the bouquet of carnations balanced on the piano top jiggled with each song.

The other thing jerking me back to consciousness was them talking about the tragedy of Hope dying so young.

It was like a funeral for myself.

I thought I spied a silver hip flask on Mitch when he sat in the pew across from us. I stared at it awfully hard, but I didn't ask to borrow it. Like Ryan had pointed out, and one of the mother characters in Amy Tan's novels said, "Don't hook on, don't need stop."

Joan made a speech at the end. A short one, since she wanted to get back to baby Angella, who couldn't leave the NICU. I kept my eyes open and let her words wash over me like a musical shower until she said, "Doctor Hope. Doctor Hope!"

Ryan grasped my elbow and lifted it upward, to cue me.

Oh. I stood up while the room applauded—Mitch whooped—and I tried to smile at the battalion of eyes feasting on me.

Joan continued, "Mr. Ryan helped to find my husband, and with my babies too!"

Ryan rose to his feet, and I clapped for him, much relieved.

We retreated to an adjoining room for food. I had to grin at all the casseroles, from macaroni to zucchini lasagna.

No banana juice. Joan had been recuperating, submitting to tests, and staying in the NICU with Angella as much as possible. The media were fascinated by the first Canadian case of Zisa-herpes. If they got a whiff of the possible Rift Valley link, they'd wet themselves. In the meantime, Joan handled Jonathan Wexler better than I did.

"You should eat," said Susan, appearing at my side with a plateful of cheese and crackers. She wore a black pantsuit that reminded me of Dr. Hay, although her open-mouthed purse and plain flats were too unfashionable for the scientist.

I flinched. "I can't." They'd found cyanide in Lawrence's stomach, along with almond cookie and some rooibos tea. For now, it was safer not to eat if I couldn't inspect the food every step of the way.

However, not eating was no guarantee. Dahiyyah's blood tested positive for cyanide, but her stomach was empty. We thought she might have inhaled it or absorbed it through her skin. Summer had told me that cyanide dissolves so well in DMSO, its nickname is liquid death.

I closed my eyes in memory of Dahiyyah. Courage is not the absence of fear, but the triumph over it, as Nelson Mandela had pointed out.

Next, I mentally saluted Dr. Lawrence Acayo. He'd protected his family as best he could before he and Dahiyyah lost their lives attempting to stop a quiet massacre.

"You have to eat something." Susan swung her plate toward me. "The cheddar is very good. Or even a cracker."

My mother had made me some spring onion pancakes for breakfast. "No, really, I—"

"You're a hero, Hope. You should keep your strength up." She shook the plate, bouncing some cubes of cheese off the edge.

"Oh, no!" Cheese is expensive. I tried to catch the cubes in mid-air, which must've looked like I was trying to swipe at her with a bear paw, because she jerked backward before she remembered to hold on to her food and her purse at the same time.

Crackers and cheese scattered on the floor, along with some personal items. Susan hurried to scoop her wallet off the tile.

I was going to grab her phone, which, unlike mine, had survived with its screen intact, but a yellow pill bottle's label caught my eye.

Graham, Susan. Valcyclovir 1 g by mouth twice a day for ten days.

My hand gripped the bottle until the ridges of its white lid embedded itself into my fingertips.

"I'll take those," said Susan, who'd managed to refill her purse and scoop up the stray food while I clutched her medicine.

"You have herpes," I whispered.

"What are you talking about?" said Susan.

I twisted the bottle so the white label pointed at her. "This is the treatment for primary genital herpes. You take a shorter course for recurrent episodes."

She snatched the bottle out of my hand and dropped it in her purse.

"You had an affair with Dr. Acayo." I'd been so distracted by the Zisa and herpes comorbidity that I hadn't considered where poor, pious Immaculate Joan had contracted her case of herpes.

He loved white women. Dr. Hay wouldn't sully herself with Lawrence. There was only one other pure Aryan woman on the floor, and she was standing right in front of me. I hadn't considered her because she was old and portly, compared to Summer "Boobs" Holdt. I tried to gentle my voice. "I know primary herpes simplex 2 can be excruciating."

Susan's mouth pinched together. "I have no idea what you mean."

"He gave you herpes. Stephen Weaver found out. That's why he was writing about miscegenation." If I hadn't been in an interracial relationship myself, I might not know the old-fashioned word for it.

Susan snapped her purse shut, tossed her cheese and crackers in the garbage, and strode out the door without a word.

My nails cut into my palms. I couldn't charge her with anything. No one goes to prison for adultery. And yet, when I thought of Joan and her two tiny babies, one of them fighting for her life, the other in a miniature casket, hatred burned in my heart.

It helped slightly that Stephen Weaver was currently incarcerated with burns and corneal abrasions. Burns are painful.

Skinny and Fat Guy had confessed to dumping Lawrence's body in a panic on Sunday night when they spied the lights for the R.I.D.E. program. Reduce Impaired Driving Everywhere became Racists Inactivated, Dumped Evidence.

Yet how, exactly, had they gotten a hold of Lawrence?

I suspected that Ducky really had spotted Susan on Sunday. Susan must have offered to bring an ailing Lawrence home, but somehow delivered him to his death, under Stephen's invisible hand.

Which meant that not everyone culpable was yet behind bars.

Herpes wasn't punishment enough.

The police would have to gather evidence against Susan. Dahiyyah couldn't testify any more, but I'd do everything in my power to bring Susan to trial. In the meantime, we knew exactly who Susan Graham was, where she lived, where she worked, and what she drove.

My eyes burned as I gazed at the doorway.

Dr. Martin Luther King, Jr. had said, "The arc of the moral universe is long, but it bends towards justice."

I'd give that arc some manual readjustment.

Summer tapped toward me in matte black heels that matched her fitted dress, ahead of the other Scoobies. She silently offered me a glass of apple juice. I shook my head.

She sipped it without taking offence. "Did you say what I thought you said?"

I shrugged. I didn't want to spread gossip, but this was a lab. They'd all know within 50 seconds anyway.

Summer wrinkled her nose. "Lawrence had an affair with Susan and gave her herpes?"

"Who'd a thunk it?" said Mitch, winding his arm around Summer. His suit jacket rode up, revealing that hip flask. I averted my eyes. "Besides you," he added politely, to me.

Chris's eyebrows quirked.

Summer turned on him immediately. "*You* knew?"

Chris shrugged.

I eyeballed him. If that guy ever spoke, what stories he could tell.

Mitch rubbed Summer's shoulder in a more-than-friends way that seemed ooky for a racist. I told him, straight out, "I thought you were alt-right. You, Chris, Dr. Hay … "

Human Remains

Mitch grimaced. "That was this thing I was trying out."

"What, like a new pair of pants?" I said.

Summer took a step back, forcing Mitch's hand to fall to his side. Her lip curled.

Mitch pressed his lips together and shifted his weight from foot to foot, his cheeks red. "After Chris got that spam, I thought it would be cool to infiltrate them. You know, like a Nazi hunter. So I started researching them. Learning their lingo. I thought ... " He sighed. "I joined up. I checked out websites. I even messaged some of them. But it got too intense. I ended up compiling all the info and forwarding it to the police."

Great. The last thing we needed was for Ryan to get in trouble for his White Birthright website.

On the other hand, Dr. Hay had escaped serious scrutiny until now. If the police turned up any kind of evidence against her, based on Ryan's website, he would consider it worth the hassle.

At least Dr. Hay's lab had been destroyed. Flash-bombed, a site of acid spills, cyanide poisoning, and broken glass, with no graduate students and no research assistants. She was the only person left standing.

Ryan appeared in the doorway. My heart rate doubled. He spotted me. I loved the brightness of his dark eyes and the curve of his lips. He ambled toward me, and I couldn't not watch him walk. He was like living, breathing poetry, to me.

Ryan's arm slid around my waist. I beamed like a goon, and Summer winked at me.

"We did it," Ryan said.

My smile widened even further.

"Roxy for the win," said Mitch.

Ryan laughed. Roxy was getting a walk around the block from Rachel, who couldn't spoil the big dog enough, but we'd borrow Roxy back as soon as we could.

Tom and Dr. Wen, who'd been sampling some of the casseroles, joined our circle.

Tom sipped some water, making sure not to spill it on his charcoal suit. "This has been the most exciting week in the Zinser lab, ever." He paused to think about it. "I hope this never happens again."

Dr. Wen cleared his throat and said, "The whole episode was very unfortunate."

We all turned toward him. I said, "Did we scare you away?"

"Only if I have to hear about the Banting and Best Fellowship again."

We had a good laugh at poor Samir, who was trapped in the lab.

As Ryan walked me out of the chapel and out of the hospital itself, he held open the door for me.

The sun was shining. An anemic December sun, with a little bit of snow covering the ground, and the wind in our faces. Someone had hung gold tinsel above the door.

For some reason, the sun reminded me of a phoenix. The bird that burns to death and rises from its own ashes, completely reborn.

Maybe I, too, could remake myself after near-shattering. Maybe I wasn't a poor, little broken warrior. Maybe I could trash labels that didn't suit me any more. Maybe I could transform into something stronger.

A phoenix never dies.

Ryan and I linked hands. He said, "We made it."

I smiled at him. I don't know much about Chinese culture, but the dragon and phoenix are major symbols. There's much ado about how the dragon is usually considered male (yang) and the phoenix female (yin). The dragon and the phoenix could be me and Ryan, evolving and interweaving and making each other stronger.

I kissed him, long and deep.

Even with Ryan's lips on mine, his breath entering my lungs, I remembered Tucker. I wondered what would happen when he came home. I couldn't hang on to both of these guys indefinitely. I was going to have to break one or all of our hearts, if it hadn't happened already.

The sun glimmered on my eyelids. I remembered that the phoenix faces south, which is considered auspicious. It represents summer and drought, but also great vision.

A friend of my grandmother's, who was a doctor of traditional Chinese medicine, once told me that I was very yang. She said that when she met me, I was putting too much weight on my right foot, which is totally true. A yoga teacher pointed it out to me as well. So Ryan and I could be the dragon and the phoenix. Or I could be the dragon and the phoenix myself, the yang and the yin. I needed a bit more yin in my life. A little less dragon, a little more phoenix.

Human Remains

A little more immortality.

My shoulders straightened. To tell you the truth, I never related to my therapist telling me to breathe. It was like trying to put on a size zero pair of pants. I might be able to squirm into them, but they weren't comfortable, and I could only wear them for a short period of time.

But a dragon and a phoenix? That, I could do.

I fitted my body against Ryan's. In my heart, I could already hear Roxy barking, calling us home.

Author's Note

Hope is a function of struggle.
—Brené Brown

Hope is like a road in the country; there was never a road, but
when many people walk on it, the road comes into existence.
—Lin Yutang, Chinese writer and inventor, nominated for the
Nobel Prize in Literature in 1940 and 1950

This was the hardest Hope Sze novel I've ever written.

I don't know if it was me burning out and getting pneumonia while
promoting the previous book, or if the subject matter and research were
the toughest for me, but for some reason, I could not finish *Human Remains*.
I called it my book monster.

Fortunately, I had a lot of help along the way.

One of my mandates is talking to strangers. This time, I was chatting
on an airplane, and my seat partner, Marie-Pascale Manseau, explained

Human Remains

how she inspected laboratories. It suddenly seemed an excellent idea to have Hope do a research block to recuperate from her last trauma.

Next, I met Dr. Bill Stanford, Senior Scientist at the Sprott Centre for Stem Cell Research at the Ottawa Hospital Research Institute because Bill and I were speakers at the 2015 University of Ottawa Healthcare Symposium. He explained the world of stem cells and invited me to tour his lab.

There, he introduced me to Dr. Lisa Julian, who really did receive the Canadian Institutes of Health Research Banting Postdoctoral Fellowship for her work on Lymphangioleiomyomatosis, a tumour that destroys lung tissue and causes respiratory failure only in women.

Dr. Debra Komar, a United Nations forensic investigator turned acclaimed author, was exceedingly generous with her time. I met her through Capital Crime Writers.

Dr. Jacinthe Lampron, the trauma medical director at the Ottawa Hospital, came to Cornwall to teach us a rural trauma course. She patiently answered my questions about primary reanastomosis, fistulas, and other Tucker-related details.

Dr. Paul Irwin, who embodied the Cornwall trauma department for years, never flinches when I ask him anything. In fact, he one-upped me by asking if Tucker was gay, because (avert your eyes) apparently penetrating ostomy sex is a thing. Sorry if you didn't want to know. All I could say was, Tucker will not be engaging in that. No, not even in L.A.

RN Kathryn Brunet asked, "So? When's your next book out? I can't wait any more." Her real-life medical story got me hitting the keyboard again. Dr. Adrienne Junek helped flesh out that story, and sent me article links besides.

Richard Quarry is a brilliant writer in his own right.

Dr. Greg Smith analyzes the fatality rate of viruses and tries to keep the PTSD real.

Dr. D.P. Lyle is a cardiologist and award-winning writer who generously answers medical questions, including mine. My new friends, John Burley and Lee Goldberg, sent me his way.

Michelle Poilly challenged me about plasmids and lab medicine. For example, I added the MP-12 strain of Rift Valley disease to make it a biosafety level 2 agent. Agnes Cadieux, from the University of

Ottawa, joined me on a CanCon panel about infectious diseases and volunteered to get me a tour of the virology lab.

Kevin Cooper took me and John Burley on a tour of his lab at Caltech, when I was a repeat finalist for the Roswell Award. Violana Nesterova also introduced me to fruit flies at the Zinn lab.

James G. Wigmore, forensic alcohol toxicologist, kindly read my simplified poison description.

I can't say enough about the officers at Writers' Police Academy and the local coroner who checked my interview scene: Paul M. Smith, Mike Knetzger, Colleen Belongea, Matt Ninham, and Dr. Bob Reddoch.

In the end, though, I had to write. All errors are my own.

Previous Hope novels were set in a particular year, but after talking to Bill Stanford about the state of stem cell research even a few years ago, I realized there was no advantage in dating a novel. Henceforth, Hope novels will be set in the present.

As for the microbiology, I wrote about the Zika virus. However, because a vaccine could render my novel obsolete, I chose to call my version Zisa, which means "to lay waste" in Lugunda.

I modified Rift Valley fever to Rift Valley disease, but many details, including the epidemic years and the bovine fetus, are real.

I offer my gratitude to my new writer-sister S, who is the best proofreader I've yet encountered, and Erik Buchanan, who edits like no other.

Merci, meticulous D, Mark Leslie, PF, Ian, Caroline, and my KamikaSze advance readers. Please sign up for my mailing list at www.melissayuaninnes.com. It's always party time for the KamikaSzes!

Thank you, librarians, booksellers and distributors, CBC Radio, the Review, the Standard Freeholder, the Glengarry News, CTV's Regional Contact, Rogers TV, and Cogeco.

And most of all, thank you, my readers. I couldn't do this without you. If you could leave a positive review, it makes all the difference to a new author.

'She read books as one would breathe air, to fill up and live.'
—Annie Dillard

Human Remains

CPSIA information can be obtained
at www.ICGtesting.com
Printed in the USA
LVOW07s0620051217
558693LV00002B/361/P